*STRANGE CHILDREN*

# STRANGE CHILDREN

*a novel*

## Sadie Hoagland

Red Hen Press | *Pasadena, CA*

Book design by Mark E. Cull

Library of Congress Cataloging-in-Publication Data

Names: Hoagland, Sadie, author.
Title: Strange children : a novel / Sadie Hoagland.
Description: First edition. | Pasadena, CA : Red Hen Press, [2021]
Identifiers: LCCN 2020043143 (print) | LCCN 2020043144 (ebook) | ISBN
    9781597091169 (trade paperback) | ISBN 9781597098731 (epub)
Classification: LCC PS3608.O157 S77 2021 (print) | LCC PS3608.O157
    (ebook) | DDC 813/.6—dc23
LC record available at https://lccn.loc.gov/2020043143
LC ebook record available at https://lccn.loc.gov/2020043144

Publication of this book has been made possible in part through the financial support of Ann Beman.

The National Endowment for the Arts, the Los Angeles County Arts Commission, the Ahmanson Foundation, the Dwight Stuart Youth Fund, the Max Factor Family Foundation, the Pasadena Tournament of Roses Foundation, the Pasadena Arts & Culture Commission and the City of Pasadena Cultural Affairs Division, the City of Los Angeles Department of Cultural Affairs, the Audrey & Sydney Irmas Charitable Foundation, the Kinder Morgan Foundation, the Meta & George Rosenberg Foundation, the Albert and Elaine Borchard Foundation, the Adams Family Foundation, the Riordan Foundation, Amazon Literary Partnership, the Sam Francis Foundation, and the Mara W. Breech Foundation partially support Red Hen Press.

First Edition
Published by Red Hen Press
www.redhen.org

*for marc*

*STRANGE CHILDREN*

The flames sawed in the wind and the embers paled and deepened and paled and deepened like the bloodbeat of some living thing eviscerate upon the ground before them and they watched the fire which does contain within it something of men themselves inasmuch as they are less without and divided from their origins and their exiles. For each fire is all fire, the first fire and the last ever to be.
—Cormac McCarthy, *Blood Meridian*


Send thine hand from above; rid me, and deliver me out of great waters, from the hand of strange children.
—Psalm 144. The Holy Bible

# Redfield Family Trees

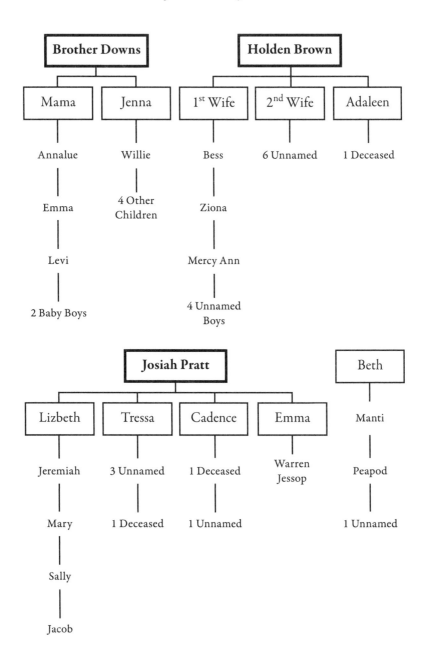

# Prologue

*Listen. Out of the desert silence the sound of dogs. Panting. Yelping. A distant barking in tempo. They came here that very week, after the fire burned the Prophet's house. Smoke curled up then bloomed above the pink mesas. Ashes fell like snow on the red earth and the temple and the houses of the faithful. Air burned to breathe. For days after, even, the smoke seemed to sink, to hang about and brown the quiet air and out of this fog the dogs came.*

*They came with tongues hanging out and dust frosting their fur; they came wagging their tails and strutting through the remains like victors.*

*The children took to them right away, sneaking them bits of pigfat and whispering them names like Chickpea and Bone.*

*Listen. Sometimes things are over before they begin. So remember this moment. Picture it: A burned town. A missing Prophet. A people wandering in the desert.*

*And when it is over, I'll be right back here, to the end, listening to the dogs freckling the pale hush that lay over Redfield.*

*But first, the children.*

*Listen. These strange children spoke the beginning and the after and they burned the ends together deep in the marrow of our hearts.*

*They cleared a place for us.*

*A place to feel for in the dark.*

I

# *Emma*

M y Mama always said that death has a sweet tooth. That's how come he took my baby brother and also how come he took aunt Emma and so for a long time I figured it must be why he took Jeremiah, who was my soul's eternal love, from me, though Mama never said this. And even though I know better now as to his fate and mine, and our story has been full up with things even so sinful as murder and arson, it's best to start at the beginning because given what God had planned for me and my destiny, people will be wanting to know the whole account.

We live in God's red desert country and we are his children but not all the people that live here in the land of Zion are God's children, some are his not-children and some are even the children of Satan. You know Satan's children by the way they stare at you if you go to Pine Mesa, hating you for dressing like we do, in our long dresses and dusty boots and wanting to tug our neat long braids and saying things about how we don't go to school. When I was still young and worked in the front pens with the other children, where my lips were always salty, the Devil children would come sometimes in a car and say these things over the fence and sometimes take pictures while we were trying hard to do God's work and to hold dominion over the beasts and feed the pigs and chickens. We always ignored them, my siblings—in all I have nine, four of them by my same mother—and myself didn't pay them no mind because they were just using the Devil's tongue to try to get us to quit our being of God's children. My older sister Annalue sometimes talked back to the Devil's children, waving hello even and once when she was mad she even said to me that she might just run away and go to live with them and even ride in their cars with them and it turns out now that she was truthing. But back then I thought Annalue was just saying this because she had found out she was not like to be married, owing to the limp she had been born with, but still it was hard on me at this time as I did not think I would be like to stand it if Annalue, who is fifteen and three years older than me, fell to the Devil or worse yet got sent away or put out to battle the Devil herself, because once you leave you can't come back. I was worried and even though I knew that Annalue was not all the time truthing sometimes I feared greatly that she really did mean what she said. "Devil ain't got no children," Annalue would even sometimes say, and our brother Levi would pinch her when she said this and tell her that in fact he did, and she was like to be one of them because of her limp and I would shake my head at how wrong she was, but that's before I found the One I'm meant to share my eternity with in the Celestial Kingdom, and learned more about how life really is, and then learned what He really had in mind for me.

I always thought Jeremiah was handsome but I never put much thought on him really because I was promised to his father, Josiah, ever since I was ten. They was supposed to wait until I was fourteen until the hitching happened, but on account of Jeremiah, it happened two some years early.

It started when I got charged in the teaching of Jeremiah's little sister Mary how to read better because even though she was nigh nine years old she still could not get through the scriptures without all her awful stuttering. So in the mornings I would go to get Mary at her family's place down the road, and we would take the Book outside and sit under some tree and I would listen to her trip over all of God's words meant to be said smooth and fine. It was hot in the morning, even in the tree shade, and bugs clicked their wings and it was hard to stay awake while I listened and corrected her and tried to make her repeat what I'd say, so it was a welcome thing when Jeremiah began to sneak away from his work on the new fence to come and visit us. Jeremiah and I always got on fine growing up and he used to tug on my braid and tease me but in a nice way, the way I liked, not like when Levi did it and really hurt me or like the other boys who would do something like let a sow out of a pen so I'd have to chase her down. But now we were working grown-up jobs, relieved of the holding of dominion and of the feedings, and I was working mainly in the house and he was off working with the men on whatever needed working and so I hadn't seen him most all summer so it was like I hadn't seen him since we'd quit our being of children.

The first time he just came and stood and watched us for a minute, like he had something to say, and I looked up at him and Mary kept reading, only louder and then he went away and I watched him disappear into the dry grasses and I think that's when I first felt I might be in trouble because it was the first time I noticed that Jeremiah had grown since he turned sixteen and his chest was wide and his hair, which was blond, was longer than God likes but still it looked good with his farm skin.

I know I was only twelve at the time which meant by the Word of the Prophet that I had two more years before I was of an age to be feeling for a man, but when Jeremiah came to the tree the second time and sat with us, chewing on a piece of grass and slapping flies away from all of us I knew I had the feelings a woman would have and I knew that God was trying to tell me something by putting this light in me.

So the next time we went to practice reading and every time after that Mary and I started going to the same tree, a big cottonwood farther from the house than the others, the one at the edge of the field, so to make it easy for Jeremiah to find us. Really this was my idea about it, and Mary never seemed to say anything if she noticed. From there we could see out from the shade and we could see the way the sun hit everything else all the same. The red rock bowl in which we lived was a ruddy brown in summer and a floating snake of dust showed where the road led from the white stone of the temple on one side of town and then right to the Prophet's old house on the far end. The Prophet's was an older home, with a porch and shutters and it was large, too, by far the biggest in town, but from where I sat under that tree I could squint and fit the house between my thumb and forefinger—no bigger than a cottonwood leaf from here. Our ranch was halfway between these two, and the second biggest after Josiah's, Jeremiah's father. The earth was dry, and besides a few cottonwoods to every house, only sage brush grew, and the small patches of growing green God somehow let us eke out of this desert valley. Under that tree, I could also imagine how small the ranch houses might look if one were even farther away and while I waited for Jeremiah I thought about how the wood ranches would look only like a flat log laid out against the red valley if you was much gone past that tree. And Jeremiah would find us there every day, and just come sit in the shade with us and he'd look at me as we sat in the afternoon heat listening to Mary's fits and starts and watch the fluffy white tufts of cottonwood seeds floating down through the air. Though he never said much of anything, the longer he sat, the longer Mary and I would practice because I never wanted to quit being so near to him and Mary read better anyway when he was around.

Nobody knew about this at least that we could tell and once Mary looked up from the passage she was reading about the Lamanites and asked Jeremiah why he come here all the time and shouldn't he be doing something with those idle hands. Then Jeremiah told Mary to hush to him and hush to everyone about it because he'd kick her if she said a word. I was surprised to hear him say this, like it was this covenant, but I understood because even though we hadn't ever done anything wrong yet, none of the fathers would have liked it because there are rules in God's country and those rules, if you obey them, keep you from burning in the flames of hell.

So as the crick narrowed with the summer drought and each day became more unbearable and Jeremiah still came to see me and I still liked it, I didn't even tell Annalue. Though I wanted to. I did.

And then one day it was hot, hot outside and Jeremiah came to where we sat under the cottonwood and right away sent Mary away. When he said for her to go she looked up from her scriptures and looked real hard at me to see if I wanted her to go away too, like she was trying to save me from myself and I thought to myself that while that child could barely read, she wasn't blind to sin. But I told her to go off anyways, so happy was I to be alone with Jeremiah. She picked up her book and brushed off her dress and sighed and left off to go see about something else to do. And when she was gone it was quiet and I looked at Jeremiah. We sat there, and a raven landed in the tree and looked his black onyx eyes down at us and then screamed that way that those birds do. We both looked up and then down to each other and then he moved closer and reached into my lap and closed the old cover of the Book and I still remember the soft slap sound of the Book closing and I do not believe I'll ever forget it. We sat there then and there were so many things I wanted to say to Jeremiah, things to ask him, private thoughts I had that I felt I could trust in him with, but it was hot, the kind of hot when it's hard to find much in your head but the buzzing of the flies and the way that sage gets to smelling in the heat, that too gets into your head so before I could really think what I was wanting to say he was saying I was the prettiest of all the birds around and that he thought about me always even in his bed at night and I started to tell him that it was the same for me with him but then he reached his fingers which were thick from work and brushed them on the back of my neck, taking my dust-red braid in his hand and lifting it off my back so that I stopped talking. I watched him take my hair in his hands and lift it towards his face and then he stuck the end of the braid, the tail below the blue ribbon, into his mouth and he started sucking on it like it was rock candy. He watched me while he did it and his eyes which were blue seemed so new to me, even though most everyone around here has those same eyes, including Annalue whose might be bluest of all. But these ones had a new look in them and I knew right then since I was so good this couldn't be bad so it must be that the light in me was God's love, and I was supposed to share it with Jeremiah and I knew this meant that he was my soul's husband and the one I should be wed to for eternity and that the Prophet thinking it was Josiah and not his son that was my eternal husband must have been a misreading of the signs of God because I knew both that it was Jeremiah and that I would let him do what he pleased with me and that I would not stop him. My certainty at the time was a testament to how strong the power of temptation can be, and how twisting of one's youth-tainted mind.

Which is not to say that things happened right away, no, it took all July for him to start reaching his hand up my dress and I never did kiss him until August.

# Annalue

I t's hard to say when things started to go bad for the whole brethren. No plague came down like in the Book. There was no locusts, no blood on the doors. No, it just eventually became clear that things had gone all rotten and even as we thought it, the orchards all turned sour and the sick sweet smell of softening and bruising apples hung about everywhere. But even with this smell no one could name any one thing that was unholy and in a land of God's people and with only His words no one knew how to say that things were going bad until they had already gone that way.

But it's not hard to say when things got bad for me. That's easy to say. It was the day that someone came to tell me that the Prophet wanted to see me after all.

I was born with a limp and this is an inconvenience in most ways. It was like my right leg had gone straight from the womb to the grave, so stiff and straight and dead is it. Even the skin is cold to touch. But I learned to walk just the same as any other child learns, only with a limp on account of having to use my leg like it was wood instead of flesh and so it's not always been easy and it's not always made me feel believing about the light of God and the general state of fairness in the world.

One thing about a limp in a congregation like ours is that it keeps you from being married off at fourteen, or even twelve after the Prophet went to loosing the standards of God, which now I suppose is a good thing. But when I was fourteen it just made me feel unwanted and unusable. Like I couldn't ever get to helping in the numerating of God's people. Though I always did like that it kept me round to keep after Emma and Mama, and I suppose it was true that it was good, though I used to dream of being somewhere else where work was not life but instead we had things like television, which I used to dream about in the dark. And I did think that if we had a box of light, like the ones I'd seen pulsing in the windows of town, and if we could see the whole world in it, things might be different. Maybe better. And even though my Pa said television wasn't magic, I couldn't see how a picture of people in one place going up into space and bouncing back down somewhere else at almost the same time, could be anything else, really, and I imagined if I had a television I could see in it a picture of a girl with a limp like mine, going about her day like me but somewhere else, and I could watch her and know I was not alone. And everyone else would know I was not alone, neither, in my gait.

And even though now I know there is no such other girl, back then I thought she would have made my limp mean something better than it did in a place where there is a history of limps, and it is not a pretty thing to tell. Other children had been born with limps and in harder times they just died outright by some way or some hand owing to the logic that when a cow or horse is born with a limp, they are just slitted straight off, as soon as they take their first stupid steps and let it be known what they got. But now for want or gain of mercy, and I've never been quite sure which, children born in that state are left to live and limp their whole life through. This reprieve is partly owing to Alice Parley Smith who, like me, was also born with a limp, and who was convinced her leg was dead because the Devil himself lived in the flesh and at times, was able to take over the rest of her body and drive her to some terrible doings. People around Redfield became afraid of Alice Parley Smith and the Devil within her so I guess they never thought about holding another limping child's head in the trough again which is what Levi told me they used to do. So I suppose I should thank Alice. But she managed to kill her own nephew and that child's kitten all in one day just before she died and so I do not thank her because now people look at my leg, and the crooked tread I leave and I swear the hair of their own necks stands up for fear of the Devil they saw in Alice and the Devil they think they see in my own stone flesh. Because Alice did blame that leg for her taking her paring knife to the child's throat when he was stupid enough to ask his aunt to please sew a button on his pants for him so his mother wouldn't find out he'd lost it and whip him. They say the boy held the kitten as he asked, a calico barn thing with fleas and big eyes like they all have and Alice first looked up from her slicing of peaches for pie making and asked to see the kitten. They say it was quick, the way she moved, with the dead flesh of her leg and the Devil in it rising up to her face and even her eyes turned the cold gray of gone-life as she stabbed that kitten through its tiny ribs and into its walnut-sized heart and bits of peach still on the knife were then stuck to the kitten's fur so that the fatal wound was so irresistible to lick by the other barn cats that the kitten's body had to be burned right off before the boy—whose turn was next and equally as quick as he dropped the button and bent over the just cooling kitten bleeding onto the table covered in flour and fruit and things for pie—was even in the ground. And when he was in the grave and everyone looked at Alice, she just looked at her leg and smiled this sad little smile and so was deemed unfit to die atoned and so was left alone to be punished by God in His time, though children never did ask her for anything ever again. And while I am glad not to have been drowned at birth I do not thank her because the children never ask me for anything either, like I was her, and I wish they would. Also I do not thank her because not two months after Alice finally died, when I was only eleven, I was out working in the pen, feeding the pigs and the chickens and doing my work as I always did when Levi, my older brother by one year, pushed me down from behind so that I was on my stomach in mud and he put his foot on my back and I saw the shadows of some of the other boys who were getting big but who were not yet men and Levi pushed down on my back and another boy, Daniel, put his palm on my head and pressed until my face sank into the mud, and the mud began to cover my mouth and nose. I could not breathe almost at all. Levi pressed down harder and then I really couldn't breathe with all his weight on me and my face in the mud and he said Don't you ever, ever try anything like Alice Parley Smith, Annalue, because if you do, if you *ever* try to kill any of us like that we will burn you and the Devil that lives in your leg will go back to hell. And then just before I lost all breath and light, he let up and they walked away and left me. So I do not thank her.

This was all hanging around my life, all these things, like a harvest smoke, when things started to go bad, and I was trying my best to hold down our side, my Mama's side, of the family. Emma was in all kinds of redheaded trouble with Jeremiah, the son of her betrothed, and was sneaking around thinking I did not know. And I had blonde hair and blue eyes and so was my mother's angel she said, but still Mama was worried about her daughters and sons and wanted to keep us close; we were hardly allowed off the yard alone unless we were with someone for some fear of hers that I did not understand. It was true that boys had been disappearing like they had been ghost children that do not die, nor live on either when they are grown. They just left and no one asked about it. Generally, it was said that the Prophet would tell the father to tell the son to leave, on account of the fact that with the girls all being the fourth and fifth wives of the older men, it would be a while before it swung back around to firsts for any of those boys. But this was not the usual way, and there was a dissettlement about it around, buzzing, in the air, and my leg began to ache, to stir a little in its fleshy grave, like some big storm was coming though I knew August to be hot and dry.

And then one day it did rain. A hot, quick storm came in from the desert to the West. My Mama and Emma and I all stood in the barn for shelter and watched it come down like some brief and passionate gesture of God's hand. Emma wanted to dance in the rain but my Mama looked at her once and said she'd like to get a fever and die for that kind of acting. It began to lit up when Daniel, the Prophet's son who had since holding my face into the mud grown up to fifteen same as me, appeared.

He came through the West field, the afternoon sun coming out behind him and shadowing his fence-post figure as we watched him come closer. Who is that? Emma asked and I said I thought it was Daniel by the way he walked, heavy on his heels, and we stood under the barn and waited for our visitor even though the rain was right near gone. Daniel was soaked and cold but trying to act like he was neither when he came to us and looked straight at me.

Prophet wants to see you, Annalue, you come now? Your Pa's already talked to him. Daniel swung his jaw like he was chewing grass but there was nothing but these words in his mouth. I looked at my Mama to see if what he said about Pa was true or if she knew about it but she did not look back at me and looked down instead. That's when my mouth felt like it was full of flour and I nodded but as I went to follow him best I could with that way I walked, I thought of Alice Parley Smith and wondered if the Prophet had decided with the help of God to kill me now before the Devil rose out of my leg and into my body, or to maybe send me off like the missing boys, into the desert, and so with these thoughts I turned and looked at Mama and Emma and saw that they too had fear in their eyes and Emma ran out into the wet sunshine then like she was going to stop me. But Daniel turned back around and looked at her and she stopped and looked at the footprints in the mud between us. We'll be watching the road for you, which is what we women always said to each other when one was going out, but this time Emma said it to Daniel instead of me, and said it fierce, but he just snorted and kept walking so that I started again to follow in my way.

The Prophet lives always in the big house at the end of town and all roads lead to it because right next to it is the gathering house and temple. The Prophet always lives in this house until he dies, and then the next Prophet moves in but this last time the new Prophet was the old prophet's son, so he had already moved in to take care of his sick father. The new Prophet is not supposed to be the old Prophet's son, but the new Prophet had insisted on this, and so much did he proclaim it as the Word of his father and God that there was a fear in choosing another Prophet, so he moved in and took his father's seat next to the throne of God and started changing rules right off. I thought about this as we walked, because watching Daniel's back from behind, which was hunched over from having grown tall too fast, I remember I wondered if he would do what his father had done and I hoped he wouldn't because now looking back, nigh two years later, I think that when a son followed a father into that seat next to God, I think that's when the trouble really started.

When we got to the Prophet's house Daniel made me stand on the porch while he told his father I was there and I waited for what seemed like a while and watched the whole world shine and dry in the sun while the clouds unmade themselves from the sky. There were sparrows making a to-do about drying their feathers and chirping like something grand had just happened in that summer storm. I watched them and felt things might be alright but then the screen door swung open and Daniel nodded that it was time to go in, and he held the door for me and pointed to the back parlor room where I limped slowly as the screen door shut and I saw that Daniel had stayed outside on the porch. I had never been in this house, as it was a place where the men communed and I was surprised how dark it was and also by the smell of cedar on everything. In the back parlor, the Prophet, our youngest one ever but still an older man, a little older than my father, was standing by the window his arms folded and gazing out like the word of God might come at any time from the sky or those noisy sparrows.

Annalue, he turned and said, I have had a revelation.

His voice was as human as they come, that's one thing to be noted about Prophets.

I have decided it would be best for you, as pretty a girl as you have turned out.

And he walked toward me then and motioned for me to come into the room farther so that I had to swing my dead leg over the edge of a rug and drag it into the center of the room,

It would be better,

and the Prophet touched my blonde rope of hair then,

if you were wed into God's house after all and so I will wed you and you will be among my wives, and you will be raised up by this union and thus spared a life without an opportunity to please God and do his duty,

and his hand fell onto my breast and I saw how old his hands were and I stood staring at the Prophet and ate my lip a little and did not say anything. He smiled at me then and I wondered what it was about this man that made me care so little about God and my duty.

And now this is when God's own Prophet must have read this in my eyes and so this is when things went bad for me. This all happened fast, and I warn you that I want to tell it even faster because of the way things like this like to stay unsaid unless spit out the mouth like a loosed tooth. The Prophet had his hands on my shoulders then as if to show me what he had just told me about me becoming his wife and I was afraid then partly because of his words but mainly because of his hands and the inevitable truth they were telling as he moved them to my hips, and that was a truth that I had escaped for three years but would no longer.

The Prophet looked at me with his black eyes like he did not see me, and he put his hands around my back and put his mouth over mine and he tasted like old milk and smelt like cedar just like the house, and I wanted to laugh at how surprised I was, but not a happy laugh, rather just a sound of helplessness in the moment. Then he pulled me toward him and what happened then was that I lost my balance.

I fell then into my crippled fate because my leg was stuck behind me at an angle I could not stand on and so that in falling, I went right into the arms of the Prophet just as I wanted to push away. It is the Word of God, he said and he lay me down on an old dusty couch and I heard the sparrows outside, all hallelujah still and so closed my eyes.

I was back in the mud then, but on my back this time, laid there by the Prophet of God himself and it was him pressing his weight down on my body, and pulling up my dress and pulling off my underthings, the garments sticking on my straight leg that would not free them and my face not in the mud but still I could not breathe as I felt his fingers dry as paper on my face and my eyes still squooze shut and the sparrows still singing yellow as he did what he felt to do because I would be his wife, and when he was finished he got up off me and smiled. I did not want to look at him, but did not want to look away like some kicked dog either, so I saw when his eyes fell on my leg. What I saw is something like scorn come into his face, or maybe even disgust, as he looked at my poor stiffened leg, blue as it is for lack of blood and I saw this look on the face of the Prophet of God and for the first time ever not only did I understand Alice Parley Smith, but I also felt the Devil inside that leg, keeping me from some shame, wanting everything to burn, and for the first time ever I let it rise up toward my heart and let it give me the strength to push myself up from the couch, shake the white underthings off that poor leg, straighten myself and walk out of the Prophet's house and past Daniel and back down the road where Emma would be watching for me, all with nothing but air under my dress while those white underthings lay still on the floor of the Prophet's house, left by the Devil and waiting to be picked up by the hand of God.

*Listen. I am the ghost of the dead girl. I have come to Redfield to watch the end come as the beginning. Backwards to get forwards. To die to be reborn to bear witness and then testimony and try my hand at being the one who whispers prophecies. The one who asks you if you believe a whole world can disappear.*

*I saw Redfield, half-finished houses and old ranchettes. Skinny horses, nubby grass, sage brush and cliffs that went from red to white like puckered lips as they wrinkled down to the mouth of the town.*

*I saw them all. The children, the women. The sisters, blonde Annalue and redheaded Emma. Their brother Levi who was overripe and you could tell had gone from too sweet to half-rotten as he grew.*

*His sister Mary, his mother Lizbeth. His half mothers shrewd Tressa and towheaded Cadence with skin as white as snow.*

*I saw the changeling boy. Manti. I saw him and his mother Beth in her pain, in his pain, in the littlest one's pain. I wanted to turn away.*

*I saw the Prophet and knew I'd be back for him.*

*First I needed to talk to her. To Emma. Across our worlds, like speaking through wool, I tried to tell her what he'd done to me. Before it was too late.*

*Who he really was.*

*I see her tender ear a cave in the night. I can waft in there, past her thick red hair. I can make my body sound, my bones syllables. Once I am in, I whisper*

Murderer.

*I come out in time to watch her start awake. To touch her throat, to catch her breath and shiver in the bleached light of the moon.*

*Emma*

Some things are like gathering waters, they get heavier and faster until no one can stop them. That's how it was with Jeremiah and me and that was how one day, when it was too hot for anyone to be paying attention to where each and all of their brethren be at, the trickle that had already been there, running down the side of Jeremiah's temple all summer, started gathering and gathering.

Even though there'd been time after that afternoon when Jeremiah sucked my hair until it was a wet rope for me to get back into His Prophet's good graces and to get a clear thought in my head and quit what I was doing and stop that trickle from gathering, I didn't for two reasons. The first reason is God's light in you telling you what you are supposed to do which is powerful and strangelike and makes you do things you usually would not do, almost as if the Devil was in you in this way but I knew it must be God because I thought then my soul to be impervious against the Devil and his sins. The second reason is that even though I knew Jeremiah as my soul's eternal husband, the Word of the Prophet cannot be undone so I knew I was going to be with Jeremiah's father as his bride and wife, and so would do always what he said, and what his son said, and it seemed like in this one case desire and obedience were mighty aligned.

So with this thinking, which seemed sound enough to be like something of God, Jeremiah kept coming to the tree, and we kept sending

Mary away almost every day so that I began to fear that poor child might forget the sound of every word I taught her and I began to take her out earlier so that we might work more time before Jeremiah came. In that time out there together after Mary left, we would lie under the cotton-wood tree our bodies so close that I could almost taste the salt of him and his hands would run over my dress so much that I would tremble at the way it made me feel so good and I began to wonder even if one of God's hands was on my body, too (though I do know now that if it were any immortal I felt, it was that fiendish Other).

It kept on in all purity like this and progressed so slow in a way that made it seem like our souls were already knowing each other plenty to be married and so it seemed like we were wed even when we really were not and did not have the Blessing, but it felt like we did and it's in this way that our relations, in all truth, began to go to the side of the Devil without me really seeing it until they were already gone and while it shouldn't a been a surprise it was one day when Jeremiah came earlier, and his face was red and he sent Mary away with a voice that put tears in her eyes and then he pulled the Book out of my hands and looked from me to the words for a half a minute and then he leaned down to my face close and he said real quiet, You, you, do you know this Book to be true, really? And I didn't understand what he was about then and why he was looking like he was about to cry, but before I could answer he let the Book drop to the ground and then he pulled me down into the dust and the grass we had been sitting on all these days. I was not scared when he reached up my skirt and pulled down my underthings and began kissing my legs and everywhere up there, up my blue dress in a way that made it feel like the ground had fallen below and I could not stop his mouth and all I could do then was look up at the cottonwood leaves and pray to those leaves to forgive me for what I was not strong enough to stop and that was my soul's love and need for the man that was then bringing his head up to my chest and my neck and tugging at my dress until he could get at more of me and I was pulling at him until finally he was inside of me and he had tears in his eyes so that I bit his lip to stop him from crying and also because by then it hurt me in a way I had not been hurt before.

It was not long until he stopped and stayed on me and we were pinned there and the cottonwood leaves were a trembling with our sin and the light was laughing at us too and while he was like that on top of me I looked at him and told him I truly felt our souls to be of one, and that I wanted to marry him and not his father and that I felt that God also wanted this for us.

Jeremiah nodded and didn't speak, and he didn't have to because I knew he knew the terrible part of our fix. And right then I felt myself to be knowing what he was thinking but now I know I didn't. But then I knew he must have felt for my soul what I felt for his to come all these days and I thought that he was quiet because he was trying to fix a way for us to be together and not in the way that I would be his father's wife and mother to his sisters. He pulled up his trousers and never did say a word before he left with his hat low over his eyes so busy was he thinking. That's what I thought then, anyhow. Now I know I did not know what his mind held.

I tried to clean up my dress as best as I could but when I came into the backdoor my Mama was standing there looking like murder, so bloody was she, and I remembered then that in the morning she had told me to come and help herself and Annalue kill and bleed and gut a sow and that's when I saw Mary was standing there, behind my bloody Mama, looking like she had forgotten how to speak and they both looked at me and my Mama looked at my dress which was still stuck with pieces of grass and dirt on the back and she turned and she said, The flames of hell are hungry, and I see you plan on feeding them Emma Downs, then she slapped my face so that I could feel the burn of hell already on my cheek. Before I could even look at her she said for me to get out to the meat shanty, and she pushed me out the door and I tripped on the steps and I heard Mary let out a little noise like a goat when she saw my Mama grab my braid and pull me like I was a horse and my hair was a lead. I tried hard not to cry because I thought then it was true I was a bad, bad girl, and an even worse woman, and on top of all of this I was in the depths of the love that God makes between a man and a woman and it's a bad fix to be in when one's just getting to be a woman. And I did keep in my tears even though I think now I would a cried if I knew how good I really am and if I knew in that moment what was far ahead in days or even just ahead in minutes because when we got to the meat shanty, Annalue had the sow dead on the draining table cut from throat to belly and it was bleeding good but smelt for want of gutting. My Mama pushed past Annalue who looked at me with a fear a God she don't usually wear but she said nothing and my Mama pulled me right over to the sow and it wasn't right but just then I thought how I remembered when this sow was born because it was one of that first farrow I helped birth and then I didn't think about anything because my Mama grabbed the back of my neck and she took my head and she shoved my face into that sow's open and bleeding belly.

I couldn't breathe none at all and it was dark and wet and warm and I didn't dare gasp even though I wanted air for fear of it all getting in my mouth and she just kept pushing me farther inside of the pig until I could feel the ribs against my own skull and the insides all making their way for me and so I thought for sure that my Mama had decided to send me to the Devil right then and there after all.

When she let go I fell backwards and coughed on the blood that got into my mouth and my nose and couldn't see or breathe for all the hot iron rot it smelt like and my Mama said something but I didn't hear because I had already set to throwing up and the next thing that was clear to me was Annalue throwing a bucket a water over me so that I could see her and the mess on me and it was strange because right then I felt the soreness of where Jeremiah had been inside me and it made it better even though I was sullied so to look like one just born and not yet washed.

Annalue looked down on me then, she was standing crooked in the sunlight from the meat shanty door and the flies were starting around me and around the sow. She laughed then but it did not make me mad because then right away after she said let's get you cleaned up good so that Pa don't find out and kill you and she pulled me up by my hands and took me to the washbasin and I sat there and she washed my face and my hair and she sang a song with no words that I didn't know and even now don't know where she learned it but I was grateful for her and felt that even though I'd been through all that I would keep going because I had the same faith that I have now in God only then I was praying he would find a way for me to be with my soul's eternal love.

Sow's blood or not.

# *Annalue*

No one ever did say anything about that August day, not right after when I limped slowly, finally down the drive, knowing that my leg that had never seemed to be part of myself really, had now revealed itself to be not only attached at my hip but to be in fact the whole of my body and my life, and not that night when I asked my Mama to be excused from dinner and she said No, best not to lick our wounds, by which I knew she knew something had happened, had guessed it, and that meant my Pa knew, too, which made me feel the shame of the Prophet's gaze on my leg all over again. And though my Mama did allow me some kindnesses in the days that followed, and excused me from temple in the service of babysitting, my Pa looked me even harder in the eye while I could not meet his and though that first night he tried to wrap his arms around me before bed and squeezed harder than usual which now, looking back, I can see as a gesture of his own helplessness against the Prophet, at that time it did not seem so. When he touched me, I felt only the stiffness of my leg spread into my pelvis and torso and neck like a small death.

No one ever did say anything but that did not stop Emma, whose red hair forever foretold her own rebellious temperament, from writing notes to me and leaving them in the hollow in the log leg of my head-board, where a small peg had been once but had fallen out, a place that as a child I liked to rub with my finger in falling asleep—a thing she had often watched me do while she fell asleep in her own bed. These notes were investigatory at first, some with just three question marks, and I did not respond, not wanting to write what no one would speak even, and not wanting to tell her how my whole body was now what my leg had always been. I did not respond to her inquiries about what Prophets say and do and when I did not, her correspondence turned threatening until a few days after the day I went to the Prophet's, she wrote that if I didn't tell her I warn't her best sister no more and she took to working alongside me silent and cold in our boiling and filling and boiling again of jars for canning and stayed this way for a few days until finally one day she was smiling to herself as she pulled at the pump handle to wash her hands, coming in for lunch, and she saw I was watching her and that night I found the last note on this particular subject. A thin piece of paper was rolled tightly around a crushed red flower, an Indian Paintbrush, and it said only that it was all right and she had forgiven me and that I was still her best friend and favorite sister and my greatest ally against our brother Levi who tormented us always. Now I know that she had likely only forgiven my secret because she was growing her own, but at the time I felt what must have been disappointment—a weighty notion that if she could give up on knowing my own fate so quickly, then she too had decided to become complicit in it which meant I alone was left to contemplate the lonely threat of my deformation and the solitude ahead and what it might lead me to do, to be. I was certainly no Alice Parley Smith, but I alone knew this, same as I knew that I was no wife neither which meant I was no scapegoat but also no lot for the Lord, and so could not write my life so easily as one fully formed. And even now these two years later, now that I know the way the world can expand beyond the edges of our vision, I still sometimes feel that disappointment again, and I wonder if I had written a note back to her, told her what had happened, what he had done and who he was to me, then maybe now things would not be as they are.

*Listen. I see things I can't help but see.*

*I wanted to turn away. But when I first saw the strange little Manti, back in the circle of time, he was standing on a three-legged stool that wobbled with one short leg. He was pulling down a cloth sack of sugar from a high kitchen shelf and a tiny figure with messy, curly hair, dark like her brother's, and big blue eyes stood watching him with her little hands clasped.*

*A mother, or a shape of a mother, lay on a bed with eyes open but unseeing. She was alive, I could see, but more than her body I could see that she was enveloped in an ethereal moss. Like time was for her a slow, heavy growth.*

*I heard him say to the little hands—three fistfuls, that's all you git Peapod. That's all you git 'cause we don't want the bitch to know. He said this last part so soft it was like he meant a word other than "bitch." Something more tired and tender. I watched as he took only half a fistful for himself. Carefully palming the sugar into his mouth before licking his fingers clean.*

*I saw they were hungry. I had not been hungry like this. I wanted to touch their sticky small hands together with mine.*

*I reached out.*

*But they were there and I was here.*

*Still, I said, I whispered: Let him say his mean words but let us try to hear the softness in them. Let us hear the sound of this image:*

*He puts the sugar bag back and softly tucks the stool under a table. He picks up the girl and kisses her cheek and tells her he loves her before he takes her outside to show her a flower, a small sego lily growing next to the foundation in the back of the house. A flower he found just for her, he says.*

*Can she pick it? She can.*

*Manti.*

*Levi*

The boys was droppin like flies which is somethin my grandmother said but only 'cause she warn't born here, of us, but came from outside. Ran way from Phoenix, Arizona which I know 'nuf about 'cause she told me and that's where I will go first thing if the Prophet comes back and says it's time. Or maybe he'll send his son Daniel like he did for my sister Annalue, but for now I can stay and everyone can stay though for a while boys was droppin like flies and there was hardly anyone left to pick up trash, as that is the lot of unmarried brothers young and old, but I was pious and kept at my rounds to the dump and was as good as ever for the longest time. In fact I have only done one thing in my life to be shame of, and I know I got plenty of time to make it up to God before it's my turn to get my own heaven in the Celestial Kingdom, 'cause it's easy to see that even though I done this one thing, I am not right for the lowly Terrestrial Kingdom 'cause as my Mama says, I was born on high. Sunday morning baby I was.

But 'cause I am honest and I absolve myself most every day I will tell you the first thing I did wrong that led to no other things like it really and even though I disobeyed in other ways, this is the one thing that I still have great shame now, but also you should know it warn't my doin, my thinkin, it was somethin done to me under the yoke of the Devil.

It was one night at the end of a work day and it was two falls ago and so already almost dark and there I was in the animal-smellin, checkin and scrapin the hooves of Blackie who is a horse that was almost mine, or was to be mine when I got my own barn, 'cause my Pa said I is better with Blackie than anyone, even him I guess.

So it was why I was bent over, the fetlock in my hand, cleaning it with the other, picking out dried shit and mud from the bad shoe done in there by the only smith here who we have to make do with.

When I stood up to clean the last hoof, the back right, I saw that Manti, who is a cousin in some way not close and who was four years younger than me and so eleven at this time was standing in the barn door, leanin and watchin me, arms crossed. He was a scraggly kid, with stick arms and freckles and black hair that was woods-messy, so in the doorway so suddenly he looked like some sprite from another world.

What'd you want? I said right away because Manti was not straight in the head, don't know why or what it was but it was somethin, some-thin in the way he was always tellin jokes that made no sense, or were just about somethin gross and then he'd laugh like a dog with barn cough and couldn't stop.

But right then Manti was standin there and sayin Levi, Levi, like it was a song and I was a cat he was looking for and I said What. He said Levi Levi I got somethin to show you and out of his pocket I saw him pull white so I let Blackie's hoof down and patted his rear and go over.

Know what these are? he said, and he danced a little with his feet and got some face I didn't like on him. The light in the barn was just one moon and just one bulb and so in his face I saw dark and light both and his eyes were changin all the time like a candle.

I shook my head and crossed my arms because I was bigger than him and said Nope. He waved the white so close in front of my eyes I couldn't see.

These be, the un-Der-Gar-ment of your be-lov-ed, he said then and waved the white underwear away from my face. Dancin back and pullin them wide between his hands so that I saw.

And THEY ARE DIRTY, he said before he started his wild coughin laugh. I snatched them white panties way and asked truth.

Ellen Mai's?

And the little dog laughed again.

Ellen Mai is who I want to marry though she will marry the Prophet when she turns fourteen in two months. It is her hair I like, which is black like Blackie's tail.

First thing I did I shouldn't a done is I put the white fabric to my face and I smelled it and I couldn't believe how sour so I did it 'gain.

Manti was watching me and I could hear Blackie stompin behind me like he wanted smell too.

Where you get these? I said and sneak 'nother smell.

I was over saying hello just when the washing started and they was right there on the basket and I said um um, I know who like to see these, Manti covered his mouth and snorted into his hand to quiet his laugh but his shoulders were shakin up and down anyways.

You like it, you like it, he said then quiet and I looked at him, the under in front of my face and so I dropped my hand and didn't answer. I didn't give them back.

I know, I know Levi, Manti said in whisper, all flappin his hands, and he told me then one way to make Ellen love me like a husband or get an idea how to is to put the unders 'gainst my own dick and somethin in me must have wanted this otherwise I would known it to be crazy.

Come on, Levi, Come on, it's a man thing to do. Manti said then and he rubbed his little hands together. I smelt the things 'gain and now I was wantin to touch them to me down there and I was thinking maybe Manti needed me to do it to know how much bigger I is.

But first I said, Nah, and I looked at Blackie like to go back to my working him.

And so I turned a little away from Manti and I unbuttoned and I stuck the panties down 'gainst my own which was blooded full then and they were soft 'gainst me so that I couldn't help but rub some.

A barn owl who-whos then and it scart me some so that I opened my eyes I did not know I closed and saw Manti there with his lips a licking, looking down at my dick and then what happened is what I got to be explainin careful like so understanding is His forgiveness.

I wanted to keep smellin and keep rubbin though I knew it was wrong it was not so bad 'cause I do want to marry Ellen Mai plus I hated the other smell, of hay and manure, right then I did. Manti said then he wanted to hold the panties and so he put his hand down there and grabbed them and then he put them up to my face, coverin my mouth and then before I knew it he was kneeling like he tripped, down me and then I felt the end of my own in something warm and wet and when I looked down over the unders pressed on my mouth, I saw the back of his head and then he did it to me, he did it to me and I know he was being evil but I could hardly do nothin, so yoked was I, my thing in his mouth and all. I didn't want him to bite.

Blackie snorted while I let him do what he did and the wind swung the barn door back and forth four times and I was expectin someone to walk in and stop this and then the owl spoke 'gain and it was done, the bulb buzzin a little and the moon hidden by the barn wall.

Manti wiped his mouth and stood up then he did somethin that made me all a fire 'cause I wanted to look away, I wanted him to leave but then he grinned at me so wide his lips still wet his face in dark and light so that it was all I knew to do; I punched him cross the mouth and he fell backwards out the barn door which swung back and hit the barn and made a loud noise but Manti made none, he lay there holdin his face like it was worth havin still.

The owl was scart and flew out too at this same time, big wings shakin air, and I put the unders in my pocket and did my pants and went back to Blackie's right rear, patting his tail-head, my face feeling like iron.

Manti took his hand way then from his mouth and he was laughin, standin then leavin, skippin out way from the barn, me thinkin how it didn't mean anything in this barn place of animals and their big hair-gone sexes, that God didn't care if I was practicin to numerate his people and he know I like Ellen Mai anyway and want her as a wife and my eternal partner for the Celestial, so I went back to scrapin the shoe out, hard this time, the owl flown, my head finally clear 'nuf to pray.

# Emma

Jeremiah didn't come the day after we were together like that, he didn't come when Mary was reading to me and I understood that he was being careful and I was also relieved because I knew my Mama had her watch on me and also I will tell you I was still hurt down there beneath my underthings. So I sat there and heard Mary's voice but not the words and I knew from the sound that she was reading bad, and that she was nervous and though I did not blame her for all that had happened, I only wanted to close my eyes and lean against the tree and feel its bark through the back of my dress until the next day when Jeremiah might come back. But he didn't come the next day or even the next and I still couldn't even bring myself to listen to Mary stutter over the words so busy was I thinking and waiting for him. It pained me to know how I was suffering with missing him so he too must be suffering and I began to imagine God coming unto the Prophet and commanding that Jeremiah and I be together or perhaps even coming unto me and telling me where to lead Jeremiah, out into the desert, where we could start having a family in our own Zion and now when I think of those days I can only see the ways the world was preparing me and my imagination to receive the wisdom of God directly.

A week after my Mama took me out to the meat shanty, Jeremiah came and Mary didn't even have to be told, she just got up and left us beneath our tree and Jeremiah sat right up next to me and I told him all that had happened. About Mary and the slap and the sow but also how it was okay because my Mama punished me herself and did not even tell my Pa and that night he had even supped in our house, and not in the house of any other wife, and had even asked why the women were so quiet and she had just told him it was on account of being tired from all the slaughtering. Jeremiah listened and he fingered a piece of long dry grass and I wished then he'd finger my hair instead but when I was done telling he looked at me and he looked so sad and also far away, like he knew everything that was to be but couldn't see it.

Then he said, It's strange, and I said What's strange and he said, The all of it, and I knew then that he didn't think there was a way it would work for us to be together but also I was just so sure then that there was a way and more importantly I knew then that I really could trust to him all the secret thoughts I had.

I told him, it will be all right, and then he leaned to me and we started to kiss and we kept kissing and you can guess what happened but I want to tell you that this second time it was all slower. He kissed me on the mouth and put both my lips in his mouth and he was careful with my blue dress, lifting it up over my almost hips and kissing me on the forehead and shoulders. The whole thing was something pretty, like the song Annalue had been singing when she was washing my hair, and right then I remember thinking before he was done that while we were laying like that together, the leaves had turned to yellow and the air had begun to smell all red like fall, all while he was inside me. And now I know the shift was not seasonal but cosmic, and that God must a been adjusting his weight in his seat for the events about to unfold. But right then so caught were we in the way we were loving each other right then that we didn't see my Pa standing at the edge of the field watching until we were fixing our clothing. Mary must have stuttered bad when she told him where we were but not so badly that he didn't understand and I'll never forget the fear I felt then, not knowing how long he'd been standing there. Jeremiah just brushed off his hands together and looked at me like I had just asked him a question he didn't know the answer to.

But then, brave as he was, he walked slow like to my Pa, still fixing buttons on his red shirt and he did not even flinch until my father knocked him straight to the ground. I couldn't tell my legs to run until he'd already kicked Jeremiah twice and not even looked at me once because this was hardly about me but a thing between men, when one has taken something from the other.

I ran back to the house then, snuck in away from my Mama, cleaned up, and waited to be told what would happen next. I felt sick with the idea that I would not be able to be with Jeremiah and I wandered about the room I shared with Annalue and I touched everything we had like I was checking for dust, wondering if I should run away and find Jeremiah, or maybe look for my Pa and try to explain, or to wait.

It turned out neither would have done much good because my father came home and said that I would marry Josiah on Friday, even though it was already Wednesday night and that I should thank the Lord that he was even still taking me for a wife, soiled as I was and at such a young age I'd like to die in childbirth. I knew this last thing he said was just meant to scare me as a punishment since girls my age carry through all the time with their babies when the Prophet deems a younger marriage, so I wasn't scared and anyway my heart was sunk down way too low to jump.

I went to bed that night and the moon was bright in our room and some crickets had started up and I thought of how things had gone all wrong, but that it was okay because there would be lots to do before I left my Mama's house for good and for always and at least I would see Jeremiah even more because I would be a part of his house and maybe we could sneak away and be with each other still sometimes. Yes I was naïve and I fell asleep happy with this idea I had of how it would be, how God would keep our souls together in spite of the false prophecy that had me marrying Josiah and I was happy even though I could hear Annalue sighing in her bed, creaking her mattress with her turning, missing me already.

But it turns out God had a plan that wasn't my plan then, because Jeremiah disappeared the night before I married Josiah, who did not look unlike his son but was not him. My Pa told me Jeremiah was gone as he was driving me to Josiah's house where the Prophet waited to give the Blessing and where he would leave me as a wife and I didn't know why he was driving me in the old skylark when it's close enough for me to walk and I had never been driven to anyone's house before this. But then the way he said this about Jeremiah and didn't look at me when he talked, I knew that Jeremiah must have been run out a town by the priested and mainly the Prophet because the Prophet didn't want any more trouble from Jeremiah or from any other unbetrothed boy and I understood why we were in the car instead of walking the short road to my future home.

Other boys had been run out of town and usually we never heard anything from them again but I had hope because Josiah's third wife Cadence and her ash white hair said that these boys sometimes get all the way to the city and are called Lost Boys by the Devil's children and I did not know if she was truthing, or just trying to console my empty heart. But then three weeks later Josiah came into my bed for the first time, in the morning, and his face was twisted with something and I thought he was angry because he did what he had come to do with me, to make me his wife really, and he did it so it hurt with his hand pushed up against my jaw, but then when he was getting dressed again he turned to me and looked at me straight and said: The Prophet has told me that Jeremiah lies dead in the desert.

And I could see his hands were shaking with the buttons on his shirt and my own chin began to tremble.

I began to cry. Josiah also hung his head and was silent but I could see through my tears that his face was twisted up again and I knew he was not lying to me about Jeremiah.

I also knew then the ground to be falling out from under me.

My Pa came over the next week while I was working in the kitchen kneading dough and thinking of Jeremiah's face left red for the birds, and he talked to me and he said that the heat and then the dogs must have got to Jeremiah but even then, before we knew what had really happened, I was sure I knew better. I was sure I knew because he was my soul's husband, and he wouldn't have given up that easy. I thought: No dogs would have kept him from me and anyway he had God's light and love for my soul in his soul so no, Jeremiah wouldn't let no sun keep him from saving me, and I was sure he was done away with by the Prophet's men who are the rough servants of God as some act of merciful atonement, but I didn't think then that that gave them the right to take one's soul's love away. I was so sure of this and thought that either way I would be with him in spirit someday since at that time I thought he must be with God and not even his father could take that eternal-after away from me no matter how he hard he tried to be my real husband.

But even though I was sure like this, I know now it was not Love nor God that so lit my heart, but when I thought it was both I would sometimes get to feeling sorry for myself and when I did I had two comforts. The first being was I thought that Jeremiah and I were still God's children because I knew God would see how we acted on his true light that we felt inside of us so I was sure he would understand about the things we did under the cottonwood tree and so I would see Jeremiah in the Celestial kingdom of God, I knew, and our souls would finally be wed for eternity together. The second comfort was that I missed my bloods and so knew there was something growing inside me and I thought it to be the child of my soul's eternal love and I thought that this child would remind God of how Jeremiah and I, denied of our time together on earth, belonged together in His Kingdom and even though now I have quite revised my knowledge of that child's paternity and I am more certain than ever of God's real plan for me and the Prophet and His people, at that time this belief and that small appleseed inside of me were of great comfort and so I knew—even when Annalue said that it had to be Josiah's because of the time and that anyway she should tell Levi to kick me in the belly with boots on just to save me from my own fool self—I knew what I needed to believe and sometimes that is different than the truth.

*Listen, Emma. Oh Emma. I tried to warn you.*

*Now you will be lonely and it will grow on your face like a layer of moon-blue skin. You will be sad and I am going to tell you about it but for you to hear me I have to be dead and you have to come here to this quiet place, to be almost dead. So lie still in your new house, breathe hardly at all and if at all—slowly, imperceptibly. Listen.*

*Listen. I am the ghost of a dead girl. I see things I can't help but see. Listen. My name is Haley.*

*You are sad because you think that the only boy you'll ever love has been killed out in the desert by either the dogs or your fathers and you lie awake wondering if it matters, if he was shot or eaten, if he was beaten to death by hands or teeth, or if his thirst killed him from the inside out.*

*You are sad and this is only your beginning.*

*Do you hear that? Your beginning.*

*You can't hear me, yet.*

*But you will.*

# *Mary*

I have a wish that is burning a fire in my heart and that is that I wish to be the youngest wife of the Prophet who is the most pious man and God's own voice for us. There was another Prophet when I was younger, just born, but this Prophet is his son and knows more 'bout the sins of even our hearts not just our bodies, mortal as fruit. This Prophet has gone now into the desert and there are those who say he won't dare show his face again but I just know He is wandering, wandering and he will return for me and smite those among us who be less faithful.

This Prophet knows to forbid the things that other kids play but I never did, not because they didn't ask me to, but because I must have known, even before the Prophet said that basketball was unholy, that it was unholy. And also the Easter celebration too. He died for us, the Prophet says, Let us Not Forget, and I don't forget and my heart flutters and buzzes like a fly in a jar but in my ribs when I hear his deep voice and his dark eyes glowing with the Spirit and I always want to say: I Would Die For You Prophet.

But of course I do not say this partly because of my stutter but I keep on wishing that he will take me for his youngest and last wife soon as I turn twelve.

I am only ten now, but I brush my golden hair everyday six times and even if it is vanity, I just want it to stay pretty for when I am the wife of almost God himself. I try to read the Book everyday even when the words swim around my eyes and smite me. I try and I like it especially when someone read it to me, like when my brother Jeremiah used to, he did the voices of Nephi but also of his sinning brother Laman and the Lamanites and I like it when someone is smited or smoted because they done bad against the true believers and very first prophets who lived in the time of Christ and then went to sleep till the Prophet Joseph Smith was born. And I don't like when the believers are in the wilderness and their souls haveth sorrow.

I, I want no sorrow.

If I am the Prophet's youngest wife I will help him serve God, and take off his socks when he is tired because that is what wives do. I have seen my Ma do it to my Pa though my mother not good 'nough for the Prophet, that is clear because if he liked her he would take her as a wife. He can have anyone because he is not like other men whose ears are deaf and dumb to the voice of God.

And then I would wash those socks better than I ever washed any of the socks in our house now and I would rinse them in sage-soaked water so they smell like fresh night air all the time and make feet feel cool as they walk the righteous path that the Prophet lead.

There is a reason I wish all this and it is not just because I am the most holy girl my age in the whole town. It is because when I was just a child a few years ago the Prophet came by our house one spring day and I was out hanging clothes and saw him and my Pa talking in the road and being curious I went to my Pa and hid behind his leg, hoping, hoping he might pull on my blonde braid like he do sometimes so that the Prophet would see me.

My Pa didn't pull my hair, so I peered my face out round his leg and leaned my ear into his thigh so that I could hear my Pa's voice stuffed down through his own body, and then I dared look up at the Prophet who I had never seen so close.

Now who is this? The Prophet said then and I will never forget that first time he look at me. Long, clean face turned down on me like a winter sun.

Pa cleared his throat and said I was his oldest girl, he said it quiet like he was ashamed, like he didn't want the Prophet of God to be noticing me.

Pretty little thing, isn't she? The Prophet said to me then and I smiled big because no one had ever said that to me before. Then my Pa did something I will never forgive him for even in the Celestial Kingdom when we get there. He said:

Yes, but dumb as stone, that one, can't read at all and can't talk straight either. And then he unstuck me from his leg and gave me a push and said back to work without even saying my name for the Prophet to hear. And so my face went burning and I ran so fast away to the back corner of the pantry under the house where it is dark and I cried so hard I thought to break the jars and jars of big floating peaches and apricots that sat in their own syrup like big orange moons in water and I thought how I am not dumb and prayed to God to tell the Prophet that I am smart and to tell my Pa too that I am smart. And I cried till I thought more and more 'bout the Prophet thinking me pretty, and hearing him say that again and again in his wise voice and I fell asleep in the cool pantry dirt smelling the fruit in the jars above me and thinking of an older day when I would be the wife of the Prophet himself and the best Ma on earth and when that day comes I will not speak at all to my Pa or my Ma, Ma who smited me for my talking more than once in this rotting life and Pa whose own mouth I have heard profane the name of the Prophet, and even the Lord, so that it's no wonder He gave him a child with a slow tongue.

## *Annalue*

In all times, and not just the end times, we're a people, as my Pa says and my Mama repeats, who take pride in helping one another and that's all well and good for God's country but it's just we couldn't help one another with what really mattered.

Like when Holden Brown's third wife, Adaleen—who would leave us and start all kinds a mess that ended with Holden in jail somewhere— showed up at House with a black eye and an arm tied up to her chest with a sling made out of an old bridle. It was not hard for anyone who knew Holden Brown and his foul temper to guess how that had come to pass, it was not. But in our world of God's words there was no language for which to help her and to still praise God and his men at once. Just like there was no way for my Mama to save me from my own cruel fate, and no way to stop a man from taking what he wants if he takes it the right way, through the word of God or rather his Prophet who speaks in a voice that everyone can hear. Plain as day.

No one can stop it unless you are the Prophet, or one of the men who hold power around here, and then if you are you can make someone disappear. Like Jeremiah, get him killed in the desert. And you can take Manti's father—a rogue man who always was wild they say, and drove a truck for money not of the Prophet, and who they say saw fit to borrow one of the Prophet's young wives—and you can make sure he is atoned for his sin, even if that leaves his wife Beth, who they say is crazy as a mad cow, alone with two small children she can't take care of as anyone can see. The Prophet could do that. Not anyone else.

But there are things we could do, us womenfolk. So every other Saturday is my day to take over a pot of casserole to Beth's house so that the children don't go hungry. And even though I didn't want to leave the house after that August day, and my Mama let me be all of September, come October she said it's the right thing to do, and doing right was what made things right. As if a crooked walk to the far edge of town and that dirty little house half falling apart would undo a day on the parlor floor of the Prophet's house. If it did believe me I'd be limping there every day.

I mostly felt sorry for those two children and having a limp as I do for me to say I feel sorry for someone is no small thing. There is nothing quite right about any one of them, and it's not just the dirt, or the broken chairs in the corner, or the dishes all everywhere so that sometimes you just had to look around and try to find the dish you brought the last time, or another one, or three, and leave with them to soak for three days. Though even though I did feel sorry for them that was not to say I liked going there, for I did not. Like Alice Parley Smith, I did not want people to think I was different in their way too, did not want anyone to see me going to and from their house and think I was like them, part of my body already dead for all to see. And Sister Beth was the most not quite right, and she often just nodded and opened the door and went back to the couch to sleep. Most of the time she wasn't dressed but in a blue nightgown, with her black storm of hair, and would mumble to herself or yell across the room as if she saw someone there though only the sunlight was there, rays filled with the dust of the house like snow. If Manti was out, the little girl would sit on her mother's feet and suck her thumb as though all was right as rain.

And if Manti was there when someone came, wild dark hair in his eyes, he usually hid the little girl in a kitchen cupboard afraid someone would try to take her and raise her up right, as we had when she was a younger baby, before we learned how much the other two would fight for her. Once, the Jens family did manage to take her home, but she howled all night like a wolf until suddenly she stopped and they went to check on her and she was gone, window open, Manti running across the back field with her in his arms, Beth waiting in the moonlight. So after that he would hide her and glare at you and you could hear the little girl muffled singing a little hymn to herself, once in a while calling Manti's name. Once when she was in there and crying softly and I was putting the casserole down where I could find a bare spot on the table, she went quiet and Manti turned the color of the river clay.

I said, Manti, let her out.

He glared again.

I said softer then, Manti let her out, what if she can't breathe. Or she scart. And he glared more. I ain't going to touch her Manti, I promise. I can't take her from you, and I limped forward to remind him I couldn't take anything from him even if I wanted. And he bit his lip but then bent down and opened the cupboard and pulled her out. She had fallen asleep and rubbed her eyes as he held her. Her almost half his size.

I watched them for a minute. The way she burrowed her head beneath his collarbone like that was safety and thought of Levi pushing me into the mud and so before I'd really thought it out I said You're a good brother, and left the casserole for them to eat. After that, he didn't put her in the cupboard when I came, but left her to play at his feet.

Still I'd rather not gone anywhere after the Prophet's house right then but because my Mama believed doing right was a cure for other injustices, I limped into the little house right at the start of October, not long after Emma married, and Manti let me in. This day the house smelled like wet plants, an early fetid rot, and the girl was hiding on her own under the table sucking her thumb and as I limped to the table, Manti started pacing and pacing and I felt a little chill run up my body, like you would with a dog who was growling at you from across the room though I never did see a dog since our last Prophet died. I put down the stoneware casserole dish with chicken and noodles and cream o' mushroom and said goodbye so soft and was about to back out of the room when Manti turned to me.

He walked right up to my face then, he was about a head shorter than me but still he looked right into me and grabbed my shoulders and I did try not to recoil, thinking that as with the dog it was better not to show any fear, any weakness other than the one written all over me, but he did not in the end want to hurt me but rather tell me something and so he said quietly,

He's afraid of you, you know.

His breath was hot on me and smelled like crick mud, and the girl froze under the table, not even sucking her thumb but rather pausing with it pushed against her upper lip. I met his eyes but did not say a word back even though it's not then that I was afraid as much as I was careful and if I am honest a little curious.

Manti looked around, at the door and windows, before he whispered to me. The Prophet. He don't know what to do with you, so he's afraid.

Manti paused and then broke into a wider grin, a face I'd never seen on him before. His grip tightened around my shoulders. And he should be, right Annalue?

I couldn't help but shiver then, but it was for no other reason than that my name in his mouth felt like cold water in my ear as if it had come from someplace deeper than the limited fathoms of his child body.

## Manti

Bounce bounce bounce I hear it and I like it, the bounce is clear but there are a million sounds in it, too, like the rubber comes alive when it hits, and it's something metal or shaking like when your mother hit you on the head and your brain shakes a little inside it, like that. Layered, vibrating, fruckin amazing shit and I love love love it.

But just as I love it He musta hated it, He musta been sitting up there on his fruckin sky chair going crazy with all the basketballs down here, smiting man, venging himself, saying smite them, smite this, hate hate hating how beautiful the sound of something he didn't make really was and maybe hating too that he couldn't even make the sound because maybe they don't have that game up there.

He musta hated it because He told the Prophet to fruckin knock it off, and the Prophet told us that the game was unholy, idle, sinful, errant, immoral, aberrant, corrupt and that the ball itself was the shape of His eye on us so how dare we play with it.

How dare we play. Bounce.

I'm fruckin sick of this shit.

I swear, I swear, I don't care.

Jesus gotta love me no matter what 'cause I just like him, with a fruckin father I can't see. 'Cause the man is dead, living in heaven, just like ole Jesus's dad and the rest of them from the Book that lived in the days of then. Though Jesus, his dad was never alive, never dead, just God, and my Daddy was alive, and he drove a truck all over this country and came home and taught me to say shit, hell, damn and f-r-u-c-kay. But now my Daddy is gone, shot straight out in the mouth by somebody nobody knows, or nobody talks about and nobody knows why or if they do they sure as heck ain't saying.

But dammit I got an idea or two, I know that the fruckin Indians shot him because my daddy used to tell me stories about them. They're mad maybe because we're here sharing their desert with them and they have all sorts of animal gods who get crazy ideas and love fire and they just rode into town one day and saw how good my Daddy's face would look dead and how good his hair might hang on their horses and they shot him. Then they left before anyone could see.

Because no one saw any Indians that day.

Bounce.

I ask my bitch mother who is mean and awful and has hair the color of coal like a witch and who does bad things and beats me but not my sister because if she touches her she knows I'll kill her with a kitchen knife because she hit the little Peapod once and I got the knife and held it to her throat from behind. I had to climb on a table 'cause I wasn't so fruckin tall as now, and jump on her back and hold the knife to her and she felt the blade and she was screaming and then she got the fruckin point 'cause now she doesn't touch Peapod and barely even me now that I am growing big so as to be like to fight back.

Though I'd never really hurt her.

But I do ask her what happened that day, who kilt him and what meat or bone was the fight over and she just look away most the time but once she start to tell the story of the day and said it was October, and the outside smelt like harvest smoke and she knew that morning that if the moon rose it would be orange and she was feeding my baby sister from her teat and things were alright and the man she loved had come home for a few weeks from the big rig road and had a cloud in his face but didn't he always and she was thinking bout making corn biscuits when she heard the shot and wondered what animal went sick now and sighed with the trouble it would be to bury something so big as livestock and so she began to get ready for the sick smell of burning horse and thought for sure she'd make the biscuits and shut up the house so as to only smell baking and not the funereal stink.

She never make it past this part of the story and so the only dang information I get is that she probably didn't fruckin kill my father, mean a bitch she is, and that she know how to make something besides pie which is all she makes now and also that maybe she wasn't such a bitch when Daddy was alive with a face still there.

Bounce.

And if it weren't Indians, it coulda been some mouth of God acting out some Blood Atonement, a word I know since I'm fixing to be a man, coulda been my dad was a sinned soul and someone trying to save his ass by killing it. He could a adulterated or killed or been smited and his body still walking around coulda been jeopardizing his soul so one of ours done him a sweet favor and killed him so that the praying for redemption could really get going without the body and the brain in the way.

They might do well to save my soul from my body and fruckin smart brain and my horse groins and if they do I'll probably forgive them once I get fruckin saved and am up there with the rest of them sly dead dogs who all know what we all waiting to find out.

What's up there, besides no fruckin basketball?

And we'll find out, sure as heck, but in the meantime we still got to figure out down here. We still got to figure out why everybody fruckin mean and why we can't hear the bounce no more.

'Cause with no bounce the court is quiet. Far end of town, the only pavement around is now quiet, quiet, quiet and it makes one think blank-like. The bounce was prayer, but the silence is a crack for me to think of the things to shoot besides the ball, his eye, and all the things to mess and mess with and the ways in which this world ain't fair and

God himself must be one mean daddy up there in his sky chair where he couldn't do nothing but stop us from having fun so we can get back to the atonement, with or without blood, and I think the silence is a crack, a long crack like the ball always in the air between bounces, a pause for me to get to wondering who pulled that fruckin trigger and made her mean and made me as bastarded as Jesus and made Peapod the only thing I got to work around.

And even if I never know, I'm gonna roll that ball all quiet around that court, softly and hush-ly and so infant-like that the Good Lord will never know and I'm going to think about where we can all go now in this time without basketball, and without fathers, and without half a sky 'cause winter's coming.

And I'm going to think of something because, shit, who can abide under this new rule?

# *Cadence*

When that first baby died inside me and I had to give birth to its rabbit corpse anyhow, I tell you it warn't the only thing that died inside me. And I don't mean I got bloated with some grief. I mean I felt relieved. Same as I felt that day I first left home, running off the porch with no shoes on, my thighs smarting with wind, my stepfather yelling behind me to get my ass back there. He spoke like that, 'cause he was vulgar and ungodly. And I would talk like that too now probably, but I met Josiah Pratt, and fell in love with him and come to God. And then I became his third wife.

No use saying all that happened between when I left that run-down mobile home in Cedar City, and when I found myself here among all these sisterwives and milk-fed children who know more about God than I do still I think, but here's to say it warn't pretty: there were nights in cow barns and there were nights in sweaty sheets and nights I don't remember. And then there was the sixty-seven days that I was married to one of the most rotten men on earth whose very soul smelled of death long before he's below ground 'cause when I left him he'd just beaten me until I could hardly walk, and all I remember thinking was that man smells like molding cantaloupe. Later, when I first heard the Prophet speak in House, I thought about that smell and decided it was the smell of a soul damned to rot in its own body, getting itself ready for the sulfur-colored fires of hell that the Prophet talked 'bout.

And when I met Josiah he smelt like cinnamon and soap. He stepped out of the Hurry-Up Market in Broadview and was chewing a little on the wood end of a match. I was just sitting there, runaway, watching cars come and go and thinking what the hell am I going do now. Well, the way I figure it, God must a sent Josiah in there just so he could walk out and see me, getting dusty as I was, still a little beat up and bruised, some of my skin looking like chewed meat, and wanting a cigarette or something else so bad the bottoms of my feet were itching. He stopped and looked down at me and moved his jaw sideways and back for a while until I looked up and met his eye mean-like. I didn't want no more trouble from men and even though this one was a looker, blonde hair and blue eyes like gems, I sure as heck didn't trust myself to know the difference between which ones you marry for sixty-seven days, and which ones look to last longer. But he didn't look away and we stared at each other until I turned away and looked up the road like I didn't care. Which was when Josiah said. Listen Now, you okay? And I had to look back to make sure he was talking to me.

I nodded, and then shrugged, and then felt suddenly like crying, 'cause I was not at all okay. I had no place to go where someone or myself wouldn't hurt me in one way or other. And he pointed to an old Ford, and he says, Come on, you come back and eat with my wife and me tonight, and get a good night sleep. And I've always wondered which wife he meant that day when he said my wife, whether he met Lizbeth his first wife or Tressa his second. And if he said it now to some other sad woman, if he might mean me. 'Cause you don't go around saying the word "wives" all over the place when you live a life like ours. It just ain't safe.

I've also always wanted to know why I went, and I think it was maybe God. But also I think I was too tired to care if he killed me or beat me or took me home to his wife and loved me. So I got in the Ford and the blue seat was hot with sun but I was so hungry that even the burn felt good against my white legs. And we drove out for two hours on dirt roads. And I thought of all the ways this man might murder me, but I couldn't see nothing in the car with which he might do it. I even checked the glove box and there was nothing but an old wrench which

I thought would be quick and painless. Josiah saw me fidgeting and told me Don't worry I ain't a bad man, I'm one of God's people and I'm taking you to meet the rest of them. So I had a pretty good idea as to where we were going then. And when we pulled into Redfield, I knew right then for sure where we were because the women had those long dresses on from pioneer times and that braided hair that floats up in front. Josiah told me you best wait here a second while I tell the women folk you'll be staying here until you see fit to go. And I sat in the car and watched a little girl washing shirts against a board like it was a hundred years ago. She staring at me with some hard blue eyes in the meantime.

That first night I spent here, the children weren't allowed to talk to me and Tressa made it clear she could talk to me but wouldn't. Josiah told her to behave herself and we ate biscuits and canned fruit and boiled chicken at a table with more people than are in my own family times four. Lizbeth was the only one beside Josiah that was kind, and I saw already the way they were taking me in. The way they wanted to show me something about God and fatten me up, too. Lizbeth gave me three servings and even though I knew it was rude to eat so much, I did. And Tressa spoke finally to let me know that there were in fact seven children to feed, and three of them were her own, and she wasn't about to let them go hungry for some stray.

I stayed there for two weeks, helping Lizbeth's little Mary with her washing and trying to figure out what the heck she was saying to me most of the time. I slept in a makeshift bed in the barn, but it warn't like other times I slept in barns because I had blankets and I warn't afraid. I would sit up and listen to the horses below me snorting, and sometimes a pig would grunt from right outside and their noises seemed so peaceful to me 'cause they were animals that got fed and did not really get beat much. Then I started thinking I can't stay here forever. 'Cause Tressa had been reminding me of that very fact more than once every day. And 'cause I knew they weren't having me do enough work for all I was eating, but mostly because there was no forever for me, not like for them. Their forever was something that seemed like the fairytales my grandmother would tell me. And I didn't know if this was 'cause in my bones I was a faithless sinner, or if because I knew that in Broadview people talked about Redfield as something to destroy, and talked about when the State would "put a stop to it all." Though at the time it did feel more and more every day like their forever might be worth looking into. Not something I could have, but real. But not something for me. So that made me think it was time for me to leave even though I was too tired to think about what I might do next. But then one night, when the moon was low and the barn was quiet save one merciless cricket trapped in the hay somewhere, I figured I would ask Josiah the next day to drive me back into town so I could start something.

About that time Josiah came in the barn and said my name in a soft voice. Cadence he said. And I think of that night a lot now, the sound of his voice, me thinking right away that he wanted me to leave right then but instead him climbing the ladder to the loft where I slept. Sitting next to me and clearing my hair from my face and kissing me. I kissed him back but was confused and thinking of Lizbeth. So I asked him and he was saying, they know they know, as he touched me. I warn't thinking I wanted it, but certainly warn't thinking I didn't. Also somewhere in the back of my head was my mother's husky voice sayin' ain't nuttin in this world for free Cadence, and ain't no one nice for no reason. And so I thought I be owing something, and this was something I had given before for worse reasons and given it without wanting to give it to bad men like my stepfather. So I let him touch me and hold me and I felt how gentle he was and I even wondered if there was some way I might enjoy this if I was not so surprised.

When it was done we lay there half-naked and the moon was coming up higher. And he said, Cadence, I've had a revelation and the Prophet has confirmed it. I'd like you to stay here and become acquainted with God, and when you do that, I'd like you to become my third wife and help me to fulfill our duty to God by giving him a multiplicity of children.

Now this was such a mouthful I couldn't help but giggle but I could almost hear the way Josiah's handsome face was falling when I did. And so I asked him if he meant what he said.

And he said yes, and told me I would have my own room and maybe someday my own house, and I'd have to work but I'd always have food and a family and so I told him: Josiah I been a bad woman. Drugs, sex, you name it, and for some reason I tell him a story about when I was twelve years old and I stole a pack of cigarettes and some Big League Chew. Josiah asked me What is Big League Chew, and I said Bubble gum. He laughed then and told me that he and God and his other wives would forgive me my past if only I could forgive myself. And let God and his Prophet into my heart.

And then I cried and said yes I could. And I knew this was the nicest thing that had happened in my life. And I wouldn't have no trouble for-giving myself 'cause really everything I'd done was things that happened to me, not things I wanted to happen, but things I didn't have a say about. But this I had a say about, even though much later down the road would be the first time I would ask myself what Josiah would have done had I said No that night, and how much a say was really a say. But for the time, I was all giddy and light and wanted to make love again to Josiah as his fiancée but he said he had to go and talk to Lizbeth right away. But first he took out of his pocket a black arrowhead on a lanyard. He told me he found it tilling the western field the day before he found me, so he had made it for me. And he put it around my neck and kissed my head and then he left. So I spent the rest of the night alone in the barn, fingering the smooth edges of the obsidian and listening to that single cricket and thinking how my life would be easier. And that I would be better than I ever had before because now I had a husband who was upstanding and sober and also his God I had to answer to.

And it was better in most ways, though Tressa liked to make my life hard, and even Lizbeth got tired of teaching me how to do everything.

And I did hear her tell Josiah that this is why we don't marry outsiders because for goodness sakes I could not even sew, let alone kill and pluck a chicken. And I hoped they'd see how hard I was trying, but the thing was, I couldn't try as hard as I wanted to because the first month there I didn't get my period and was slow moving like I'd been drunk for three days. But I warn't, I was stone cold sober.

And when I finally figured oh heck I must be pregnant, I had not the heart to tell Josiah there was a chance it was the child of my husband of sixty-seven days that I had not told him about at all, and also that this husband was not all white. And so I carried this secret for four months and smiled all the while, trying to keep so quiet about it until I couldn't.

Then I felt the pain of what turned out to be the baby dying. And then I buried that secret with a small shovel out back behind the barn with no crickets to sing and felt lighter in my womb and in my heart. But still I cried over that small shriveled child and its black fuzz for hair so unlike my own white blonde and even though I left it unnamed and moved on into today, where I can make rows and rows of mostly clean stitches, still I go sometimes and talk to that dark patch of crumbled earth underneath which lay my first child turning slowly into the ash of everything I was before.

*Listen I couldn't turn away when she buried that child in its half-born state behind the barn and it stayed there, under the earth, in her mind. She would visit the spot and pet the dark earth there but knew not that the ground beneath was empty, freshly turned, but empty save for the worms that had begun to gather in hopes of helping ferry a body towards nothingness.*

*It was empty because Josiah saw a coyote digging there and chased it away but the next night the bitch was back, pawing, leering, so Josiah chased it out again but this time fetched his shovel and begun to dig and when he felt his shovel hit something giving, not hard, he wondered which one of his children was soft as to bury one of the cats, but when he saw the white pillowcase acting as swaddling for the small thing and unwrapped it to see a small half life distorted by its early birth as much as by its early death, he held it to him not out of love or sadness but so as to avoid retching upon it when he leaned over and left his own bile in the hole where the child had been.*

*He knew what the child was, and who it belonged to, he did, but could not do anything for how sad he felt. Although he was the type of man whose anger would allow him to bring that dead thing into the kitchen and drop it in the flour in front of Cadence as she stood making, he was too defeated by the sight of something so small and so the child in fact had the same effect its mother had had that day in Broadview when he saw her: he wanted to care for it.*

*So he took it back to the edge of the field, under a big pinion and dug a hole deep enough, as a man digs a grave. For one needs to bury not only the thing but its smell, too.*

*And then he took the thing and swaddled it tightly in its cloth. Then he laid the small bundle gently into the bottom of the hole, crouching down to do so.*

*And even I, who could see all this, did not hear the words Josiah whispered then over that tiny carcass. But he did. Say words. He did.*

# *Manti*

Then one fall Sunday come that's different 'cause of this new rule and no basketball and maybe He'll change his holy mind so we got to go check. Go to House just to see. And it's not that it's easy to get Peapod out of bed, Up Up Up, I have to say and it's November cold as shit come morning and light the color of fruckin mush but I get her up and say DAMMIT Peapod, and she moans and I help her pull her one good dress on that still ain't no good and is a yesterday blue and torn on the back part but the bitch don't do anything bout it, and Jesus don't do anything bout it, so neither can I. I get warm water for her mouth and my mouth and comb her hair at least on top the bottom too knotted and we are quiet 'cause we don't want to wake bitch mother and we hope the sun is already fruckin open over the eastern table top by the time we are walking to House otherwise our arms will be cold as shit and we'll have to smite the Lord and his damn cold breath.

We sit in the back like always and I fruckin listen like always but now I give god damn mean looks up ahead since the word came down that there's no basketball and no other sin nor nothing to replace it. Peapod sleeps, her head on my shoulder and we hear that the Lord drinks our Obedience and it doth Nourish Him, and He doth with his renewal set to making our Heavens Celestial and preparing the Way for our eternal life with riches beyond any earthly capacity.

Fruckin blah, blah, blah, no good stories this day like the one I like most that Old Prophet told and my mother told but this Prophet too stupid to, but that old story I tell Peapod later, bout the men lit out across the cracked earth and walked walked walked, until they came to this place and stopped. And then they made women and horses, don't ask me fruckin how I tell Peapod, and worked the land with their hands and women braided their hair and when they did this the world was made in this place, a place God himself hollowed from red stone just to keep us in his pocket.

I ain't in no one's fruckin pocket, but it's a story that's right in other ways.

No new rules to not abide by just blah blah blah Amen and then it is over and the whole god damn place and even the bloody colored windows sigh, and we all get let out the doors in one big breath and outside people whisper and walk and watch us as we wander way into the day. Then we walk home and I'm fruckin sick of this part because of the dang families and they're loud loud loud, millions of sisters and brothers all pushing at each other and pulling at braids and laughing and shouting and getting scolded and I hate hate hate them in all my heart and in my heart too I got Peapod and she holds my hand and asks me do I like flowers?

I do, Peapod, I do.

And I love Peapod.

And then Peapod has a nap after House like always and bitch is still sleeping, her hair wild and not never fruckin braided and always in that blue nightgown and nothing else like she is furniture not mother. Not like the clean damn mothers at House with braids that shine like pony coats and I can't fruckin stand it and get out always after House. I always go to play the game and bounce bounce bounce the ball but the game has been forbid so this day I do not go, so I am home and I see everything that happens when I am down the road because today I am not down the road.

I am home and I see Him come, fruckin Prophet, to give my mother private sermon to give her nothing, to give her something and I hear her crying and his soft voice in her bedroom with door not even all the way closed and then I hear the thump thump thump. Shit, and I am not so stupid and know enough to know what he is doing Shit and I see my stupid mother's sadness crack open like her door for all to see it and I sit on the porch and whisper Whore. Like Daddy would say.

F.r.u.c.k whore.

I am there on that porch with a piece of snake grass, pulling it apart each of its parts. Fresh green hollow a whistle in each one. I slit one longways underneath with my thumb nail and am bout to blow it when he comes out, wiping his mouth with a white cloth like he a fruckin God. He folds it and put it in his pocket. Stops at the top stair and looks down at me like I shouldn't be there, at my own goddamn house.

Fruckin whore.

He don't say nothing and steps down three steps and I want to trip the old stupid man and at the bottom of the steps, he turns to me and puts his foot up on my step and leans down and we are eyes same and straight.
Man to man.
And I can smell that old man old juice smell and look into his fruckin long face, his black eyes, square hand on his knee and I fruckin see all a him. Never mind before but now my jaw twitches I'm so mad and I fruckin hate him and I make my face say this. Smiting, venging look.

He flicks his lip and makes a bitter laugh, dog coughing. He says, Boy. I look away. He says Boy and I look to him and I am bout to say F You Old Man but he musta listened in on my brain 'cause then he smacks me upside the head hard and fast so that I nearly fall off all the stairs. My fruckin brain is screaming a million things but none of them words.
He makes his dog laugh again. Boy. Your father gave us quite a bit a trouble. He had to die for his bodily sins, by my hand, by God's hand.

Prophet touches his long smooth face now. Like he love it.

But You, he laughed again, I won't let you even get that far.

He looks at the door behind us.

Your father wasn't worthy, spreading his seed to others' homes and you are his son, and if you get to even thinking trouble, and he lean down toward me, I'll get to you before you doing trouble because the Lord sees all and he tells all to my ear and I see, I hear all evil.

He looks at me and I don't a say nothin 'cause I am not fruckin stupid.

He dog laughs one more time and nods like he knew it all along and then he leans forward and grasps my shoulders and squeezes them like he trying to close me like I was a fruckin open book and then he fruckin leans forward and his breath smells like Peapod's sweaty feet.

Then he fruckin puts face to mine and lips to my forehead and kisses it like I a basketball and he shootin from center court.

In my head for God to see I spit in his face as he pulls away. I can see on his face that he did not see me spit in his face in my head, or that God not told him yet and he doesn't know, so at peace is he as he backs down off the steps that I have to fruckin grin, and when he sees this then his peace sure as heck leaves his face and he pauses like he might hit me again but then this God's man turns away and I watch him walk, Prophet he is, with one foot in front of the other, and with each step new blood blooms in my head,

*and I do like flowers Peapod,*

new ways to make his body bleed, until my mouth is wet and salty and I get up from my step to go spoon Peapod until she wakes up, so my mother won't touch her with her filth and as I do I think for the first time:

It warn't no fruckin Indians after all and also that I would fruckin atone my father, my father who I see now eye to eye. My daddy, a man with a beard and a big laugh who took me on his knee and taught me to say fruck, *like a man* he said and winked his eye. *A man who wants a little trouble,* he said, *but not too much.*

Daddy, I whisper. Daddy. We got trouble. *Too much.*

My daddy who sees everything inside my head now, but tells no one. I'm going to think of something, Daddy, I am.

*Annalue*

The next sign that ill times were upon us was when the first government car came to town since they took Holden Brown, and then his family and even my friend Mercy Ann. It moved in one afternoon, driving back and forth through town. Big and black and slow, like some earthbound storm, and it left a dust so thick and unwelcome that it took half the day to settle. The warning bell at the top of the Prophet's tall house rang and all the diminutive ones ran inside, and I was cutting Levi's hair but quit cutting it to look out the window before he hollered that I best continue or he like to have half a cut when Kingdom come, as it was fixing to do any minute, he said, with that fevered bell ringing the high notes of trouble.

So I wet my comb again and pulled his hair tight between my fingers like a loom and cut the edges up and down like he likes. The wet brown blades were sticking to my fingers and my dress and falling at my feet and one of the littlest came crawling in it, sticking bits in his mouth and I just watched as the fur stuck to his lips and gums not thinking to stop him, thinking only about the sound of the bell and the way it would sound, echoed in our minds, when it stopped. That kind of after silence when you can still almost hear what you just heard, though this time it's coming from you, not from out there.

The day was desert cool, a breeze from the west blowing other air our way, and it was a coolness that feels gluttonous at first winter and so there was a moment, when I pulled a smooth lock through my fingers again if I didn't wonder whether they in the car had come to fetch their own temperate climate escaped to us, wanderers in a forsaken land.

Emma appeared behind me and put her hand on the back of my dress, hanging there like we were small again. What are you doing she said, cutting hair at a time like this? And so I told her Levi wanted me to finish and he scoffed and went to turn his head so that I had to screw it back straight and tell him to Be Still.

Emma began biting her nails and I told her stop now, stop, and asked her why she wasn't helping Lizbeth or resting her new belly and I told her she best go get with her own and she gave me a look to fry an egg when I said that before she stomped off and I knew what she was thinking but did not know how to have been of help because I did not know.

I did not know at the time if this meant news of Jeremiah, whose body we still had not seen to bury though the Prophet had dreamspoke his desert death clear as day, or if this meant that they would take one of the men, like they did Mercy Ann's Pa, Holden Brown, and while I hoped it meant nothing it seemed little likely that the breeze and the car and the season's rotten apples were not connected to form some inevitable conclusion of a change coming.

The day they took Holden, the air was still, even the Mormon crickets were quiet. But it was a week later, when we all had just begun to breathe again that there was a breeze, and two large vans, and a news camera came and stopped in front of the houses of Holden's wives and they loaded up Holden's two remaining wives, the third, Adaleen, already gone and a party to this, and we watched as they went to the houses and took each child and my Pa later said they asked each one their name, their parentage and then had to take fingerprints and check teeth and give the children letters for names because the children would not speak.

We lay on our stomachs in Josiah's barn loft and watched through a small long crack in the planks while the children were lined up in front of the vans. The people in suits sweated and walked around them like they were playing Duck Duck Goose, and wrote things on pads and talked into radios. We watched Mercy Ann, who was sweet on Levi and always over at our house so that it was hard not to think of her as one of our father's, and she sat staring at the wheels on the van, sitting in the dirt with one of the babies of that brethren on her lap, sucking at her fingers and I wanted to go to her, and I knew we all did, want to go to them, knowing different children in different ways, but we were too afraid that if we left the cool dark barn the sunlight of such a day as that would paint us the color of Holden's children and we would be taken, too, with no one believing us that our father was a different man, still free, and standing at the fence, watching. Chewing grass, unafraid, our Pa and Josiah watched it all, and I admired the ground they held, for they were between those people and their homes, our homes and our land, and they did not move.

That night, after the vans were gone and the houses of the Brown compound empty nobody spoke except to gather in prayer before a supper no one could eat. Emma crawled into my bed that night and was shaking, and so I noticed I was shaking too, and I told her that it would be alright, that as not-of-God as those people were, I knew they would feed the children, and give everyone a bed, and when Emma asked if they had a prison for children I told her no, though this was a thing I could not be certain of then.

So when Emma came then with her child tug on my dress I knew she wanted me to say that it would be all right, but I could not. Could not, perhaps, because Levi's hair in my hands. Strange Manti told me once that when we die our hair still grows, even though our soul is long gone, and I don't know if that is true or how he learned it but with an immortal thing such as hair slipping between my mortal fingers that would surely rot off their own bones, I could not say something false or even something that would make her feel better because I felt a hollowness in me then akin to the sound on the other side of the ringing bell.

And when I was done with the hair, the bell's after ring finally out of my ears, I picked my mother's youngest child at my feet up out of it and brushed the strands off his face and hands and told Levi to get a broom and then went upstairs to put that child to nap and sit on my bed because I wanted to go outside but was afraid to.

I wanted to go sit in the cool by the creek and put my feet in the water. I wanted some unwalled place to think. But instead I sat on my cedared quilt and thought of Mercy Ann and wondered where she was and if she still had a braid, or if she was taller, or if she watched TV and went to school and if she liked any of it. I wondered if it was me who had been loaded into that van that day if I would be okay now, or still sad, and also if anybody out there where she was also had a limp. I wondered what letter they named her, and thought that I might like to be named Z.

I fingered a lock of hair stuck still to my dress and I rolled it between my fingers until the ends bloomed like a dandelion and then I opened my fingers and blew like as to make a wish. Though I did not.

I thought about how there would be a House meeting, that there would maybe be news, someone gone, maybe, but nobody arrived, because once gone they never came back, and I knew this and we all knew this, but no one better than Emma.

I wanted to find her then, to tell her that *it would be all right*, to say what I hadn't said and to speak and sow and forest her head with the idea that our world would persist beyond a doubt, that we could sleep sound, and that she could be unafraid of her own child, and that the sky and the trees and the field and the creek and the barns and the houses and the fruit we bit would bear all our burdens, even time, and the ovarian sun would come and go above us and over us until we died. But perhaps it was really myself that wanted those assuring words closed like dirt over my head, a finality I think I already knew was not the one coming.

*Oh Emma. You are sad and you miss your sister and your Mama and to you it feels like the world is a barn rotting around you, eaten wood dark with the fur of time.*

*And you think of the time when he was here, when he was alive for you to deposit your hope into, and you were going to be happy together, and not be afraid together, and even maybe live forever together.*

*But I am here to tell you about your sadness and I am here to tell you where you are wrong about it. And I will dream about you and not know you. And you will dream of me someday. Nothing will ever happen now, you think, no true love. But something will happen. No love, no, but re-demption, maybe. And it will make you forget whether or not he is dead by eating, or dead by bullet.*

*And if you want to be sad, try leaving your own body.*

II

# *Jeremiah*

It was almost morning. Though he had been in bed for a while, an hour at least, Jeremiah was still awake. It was hot. This house had a way of staying hot at night. So did the city, even though it should have been cooler by now, late fall. The desert could scald your bones in the day but at night it always let you breathe. He missed it. He was hot and lay on top of the thin covers of his twin bed and could hear the other boys talking and his brain kept listening and so he didn't sleep. He heard them tell their stories. Abuse, asshole stepfathers, mothers that were too drunk to do any mothering. It was like this a lot in the Home and he wanted to go tell them to shut up. They weren't all any longer in the times, in the places, they were talking about, so who cared? They were instead in this modular home, with cheap thin walls and sticky floors and rooms for boys with nowhere else to go. Jimmy's Home. Jimmy loved all the boys, he took care of them. He bought big boxes of pasta and bags of cereal and bulk wrapped T-shirts and boxers and brought them over and held meetings. Jimmy had let Jeremiah stay here and maybe he should be grateful but just then, as the night became a shade lighter, he wanted to burn the whole place down. Jeremiah didn't talk anymore about where he came from. It was not bad. It was not bad at all.

It was red and beautiful.

The boys stayed up late like this when Jimmy brought over beer. Jeremiah sometimes stayed up too, but never said much. He went to bed before Jimmy disappeared with anyone, into another room, but he knew it happened. If Jimmy ever tried that with him, he told himself, he would kill him. He had imagined it so perfectly, how he would say sure Jimmy, and follow him into some room and wait until Jimmy, a thin man in his late forties with graying hair and ruddy skin, turned around and smiled, maybe unbuttoning his nice collared shirt, or sliding out the tongue of his belt and then Jeremiah would reach into his pocket where he kept his folding knife he'd found on the bus, and flick it open, thrusting the curved blade right below Jimmy's heart before he even knew. Then, out the window.

Jeremiah turned over again on his sheetless bed. But what if Jimmy surprised him in the hallway? Could he run or would the other boys catch him? How loyal were they?

And if he did get away where would he go? It didn't matter. It would be like when he came here. He was trying to sleep on a metal bench at the downtown bus station when Flynn walked by. Flynn, maybe two years younger than him. Skinny with jeans sitting just above his "junk," as Duke called it. A noticeable kid. Big green eyes. Dark hair cut short and spiked on top, he walked by again. Then he stopped and stood over Jeremiah.

Yo man? You sleeping here? His words were soft on the edges and he talked like his tongue was swollen but it wasn't until another night that Jeremiah noticed his hearing aid and asked what it was. Right then, all he thought was this kid wasn't so bad, so two hours later he was sitting at the wobbly kitchen table of this place, eating a microwaved hot dog, telling Jimmy his story. The lights in the kitchen were bright fluorescent. The other boys listened at a distance, like wolves waiting for Jeremiah to finish eating. They wanted to ask questions. About the wives. About the sisters. About the rules. But Jimmy told them no, showed him a bed, told him to sleep.

It took a few weeks before it became clear that nothing was free in this world, just like Cadence, his father's third wife, said. But Jeremiah hadn't paid; he'd quit drinking with Jimmy. He quit talking to the other boys. He wondered what Flynn had been doing at the bus station that late anyway, instead of being here, with the boys, ordering late night pizza. He stayed in this room he shared with another boy, Duke, most of the time.

It wouldn't last long.

Even earlier that night, right after he went to bed, he had heard the boys talking about him. How he must have been fucked up. How he *was* fucked up. So fucked up even *those cultish fucked up freaks* won't have him. Maybe he did something worse than he says, something worse than that girl he fucked, Flynn's felted voice chimed in. Maybe it was a boy. Or an animal. Or something so super fucked up we can't even imagine it. Then they had started talking about some movie and Jeremiah had turned his thoughts to the red earth of home, the pale green sheath around the crick, the sounds of morning there. Birds. Roosters. Water in a bucket.

Jeremiah heard Duke open the door. The crack of light in his eyes. Duke flipped on the overhead.

Fucking turn it off, dumbshit. He could talk like them, now. Did talk like them, and his words were a new skin he'd grown around himself.

Duke flipped it off. Burped.

Sorry, forgot you were in here. He swayed. Forgot you even fucking lived here. Duke was drunk and breathed through his mouth. Jeremiah could see his outline approach and stand over his bed. He could feel Duke sway toward him and he sat up.

Are you a fucking fag?

Jeremiah didn't hesitate. His mind had been running itself wild around nothing, and now this was something. He jumped up and grabbed Duke by the throat. Duke was a year older, a half a foot shorter and had a mostly shaved head. Jeremiah squeezed his hand and picked him up by his throat. He heard Duke try to speak and choke. He waited a minute, feeling Duke's apple and pipe under the thin skin of his throat. He could smell the inside of his mouth. Like bad pear juice.

*No, not now.*

He dropped him. Duke gasped and stumbled backwards. He turned to go to the door. Jeremiah got there first.

Go the fuck to bed. He didn't want the other boys hearing this now. He didn't want to leave tonight. It was dark out. He wanted to sleep first. At least a little.

Fucking... He pushed Duke lightly on the chest. Go to bed. Duke slunk back and curled up on his bed.

Psycho.

Jeremiah rubbed his eyes with his thumb and index finger, and went back to his own bed. He lay down on top of the thin quilt and waited for his heart to beat slower but it just kept right on. Part of him felt like he could do it all again, that if Duke said one more word, he'd be on him. And it was a feeling that made him feel strange in his body. Like a flu.

He hadn't ever hurt anyone back home. Not really. He'd never been a fighter like Levi. But now, it was different. Now he had it inside him all the time, a badness. The wickedness of this world he now lived in, maybe. It was inside him. But maybe it was home, too, that had done this.

*Pa did not stand up for me.*

His mother had not cried after him, either. But even first wife as she was, he didn't expect her to. She was still like a finger puppet worn over his father's thumb. She never spoke against her husband, not even for her son. The worst belt whipping his father ever gave him was for something he hadn't done. The old Ford had been left in drive and rolled into the side of the pasture fence, splintering it apart. His mother knew the little ones had been playing in it earlier, well after Jeremiah drove it over to the mercantile to get flour for her. They had been playing, four of them, crawling from front to back seat and turning the wheel like they were driving. One of them must have kicked the gearstick. They had jumped out and landed in a pile when the car started its slow roll down the hill to the fence. His father thought *he'd* forgot to put it in park.

He got four extra lashes for being a liar.

Later on his pillow he found a package wrapped in a clean dishtowel and tied with poultry string. He lifted it and could feel the warm moisture through the cloth. He knew the smell, too. Gingersnaps. His favorite.

He didn't open the package but set it on the floor and pressed his boot heel into it. Grinding it down so that grease marked up the towel and when he picked it up the shit-colored crumbs spilled out. He cupped it and carried it to his mother's room.

She stood up when he opened the door, her hands wringing for forgiveness. He undid the towel and let the crumbs fall on her floor. Then he dropped the towel and string and looked at her in the eyes. He silently mouthed, *Bitch,* and walked back to his room before she could say anything.

So why did he expect her to protest when Pa repeated the Prophet's order that he was banished? Why did he expect her to scream and beg him to let me stay?

Duke began to snore. Something he only did when he drank. Jeremiah thought about throwing a shoe at him but didn't.

His father had said, It's time, and his mother had just stood there with her mouth open, not moving. Not even coming to him for one final hug. Just watching her son go from her and he looked at her and she looked away. His father held his arm tight all the way to the car. Like he'd try to run.

He wondered where they thought he was now. He'd been gone almost two months. He wondered if they could imagine him in the city. If the Prophet could see him, somehow, fighting the wickedness all the time.

He wondered if Duke would tell the other boys in the morning, and what they would do. Maybe Duke wouldn't even remember. He'd noticed that about Duke, if you talked to him about something real late, he'd never say anything about it, and if you made a reference to a conversation that happened when he was drunk, he seemed not to get it.

His father had pulled over not even on the outskirts of Pine Mesa, but in the middle of nowhere. He'd asked what was wrong. Get out, his father had said, and Jeremiah had protested. At least drive me to town, Pa. Get out, his father said again, his hands on the wheel and his gaze so straight ahead Jeremiah thought he wouldn't look at him in the eye either. But then he turned, and looked at him straight, and said, Time to get out now. And so Jeremiah did, and could hear those last words of his Pa's all the way to Pine Mesa.

Even if Duke remembered, and told the other boys and they kicked him out, it didn't matter. He'd be gone soon anyway. After he left there he'd go somewhere else. Jimmy's wasn't the only place, it wasn't any place. He'd left the only place. He left, was made to leave, and now he'd burn in hell for eternity. So it didn't matter.

None of it did.

# Mercy Ann

My life is a before and after picture. The before picture a black and white memory of Redfield that's ugly to everyone else, and the after my shiny new life now that's supposed to be better but doesn't look like me. Now, after they took me and my mama and my sisters and all the rest of the Brown clan away from Redfield and split us all up into different homes. Mama with the youngest. The rest of us pulled off her like petals. Now, it's like this: There's me in the kitchen heating up TV dinners. There's "Grandma" in her den watching old TV like Remington Steele, saying how she's sweating over Pierce Brosnan but really she's too old to sweat. There's a green shag carpet 'neath us both and the smell of her little Boston Terrier Rosie that hangs round even though the little yapper's been dead six months. Smells more even than all the barn cats from home ever did and they are still maybe alive. Alive and being chased by Levi, while Emma and Annalue leave out empty pie tins of cold milk for the one that just had kittens though now her kittens are like to be grown enough to be chased by Levi.

There's Stan asleep in the other room and Stan is Grandma's husband who says I should just call him Stan and not Grandpa. I like this about Stan. In fact, I think I like Stan over Estelle, which is Grandma's real name and what I'd want to call her, since she is not really my Grandma at all.

Estelle also likes to watch *The Golden Girls* but for different reasons. She likes it so she can go on about how the actors are much younger than the women they are supposed to be playing. Sofia, she says, now she's supposed to be about ninety, but that actress, seventy, tops. Hell, I looked better at seventy, she says to me as she peels the plastic off the top of the Chicken Alfredo-Lite box like it was layer of dead skin on a sunburn. She asks me why I am not eating and I shrug and edge into the big recliner chair that'll only be mine until Stan wakes up from the front room couch, fixes himself a drink, comes in and says Okay, kiddo. Which is when I know to get back down to the shag. Now that I've almost a year though, Grandma says, It's about time we got this young lady a chair of her own, Stan. You know, for TV time? And Stan nods like he agrees, squints his eyes under his wire gray brows and takes a drink. That's right Estelle, he says, when he lowers the glass. Then he flicks his lip out with his tongue like he's checking for the front of his teeth, like he wants to know for certain they're all there.

There's the three of us, sitting in the glow of the television well after the eating is done, watching show after show until one of them makes a small rustling with the head or hand, some swatting flick to the direction of the kitchen. Sometimes we sit there until nine. Sometimes until midnight.

It's this time of the day, in front of the shows and the commercials, that I think about home and I watch the light from the TV on the green shag and try to see my Mama somewhere in it. I used to watch eyes glued because I liked seeing into the living rooms of the TV families, but then Estelle told me that they were sets, not real rooms like I thought and her telling me this made them seem somehow different, like it was more of a show than I even thought, so now I only part-time watch and listen or don't listen. Estelle nor Stan ever tell me to do anything else, not any sewing or laundry or my homework or anything so I just sit there and do not ask them about anything. I just think of my Mama and the things I will tell her when I see her. The first thing being is that these people watch TV, a Devil's tool according to my Mama, and that they have lived to a ripe old age. Not either one of them has been struck down by any mighty hand. This is just one of the things, though.

When one of them gets to rustling I know now how to stand, how to take the TV dinner cartons to the trash compressor, to fold the stand-up dinner trays made of plastic that looks like wood. To nudge whoever is asleep, to help them both out of their chairs. If Estelle's been asleep sometimes she'll mumble for me to be sure and let Rosie out and then I have to say Rosie's gone, Grandma, Rosie's gone, and watch her eyes get big and awake until she realizes it's me and it's true and then I watch her paw over the shag on two slow feet and I turn off the TV and stand for a minute in the dark afterglow and think of the way the light stays in the screen like it couldn't really be changed that quick from on to off.

This is how it all is and I am not complaining. It's fine. Sometimes it's even good. Like when it was Valentine's Day and Stan brought home a dozen red roses for Estelle and a dozen pink roses for me. That was really nice; it was my first Valentine's Day and I'd been feeling really nervous because of the ads in the drug store windows about Being Someone's or someone being Yours and I didn't really know any of the kids at my new school at all, and they all knew who I was and also what I was so I knew I couldn't really count on any of them and then Stan came through and Estelle said she was happy to share her Valentine with me. Though I will say that when she said this, I felt unsure about whether Valentines are normally shared and then I felt nervous again, like I was missing something.

I feel that way a lot. Maybe most of the time. There is a lot of this kind of secret talk at school, and I feel I am coming about sixteen years too late for it all. And the other kids, I know they think I'm strange too, because I've never been to a dance and because I don't know how to play any of the sports in PE and have to learn all the time about myself what they already know about themselves, like that I hate dodgeball, but I like capture the flag. And I know this now, but there's always other new games and even though I try there's still always something else to learn. But some of the kids are nice, and explain things like the earthquake drills and other kids try to talk to me, like they ask me is it true that I was married. And do I have any kids. And is it true I have nine moms. And I answer them as best as I can but they always get these looks on their faces like the answer was not what they meant by the question at all. And then I feel sick, like I'll never be hungry again, and I go to the girl's bathroom and sit with the pink tile and I think how this shade of hard cold pink like a dead tongue did not even exist to me before the FBI came and took my father away and put us children in homes that were not our homes, but they told us they would be at least for a while.

Stan and Estelle do not ever ask me about my real life like the kids at school. I think this might make them good people so I guess I don't mind when I hear Estelle talking on the phone or to the mailman at the door and she says something so quiet I can't help but listen, like She's a polygamy survivor, you know, one of the Holden clan they brought down last summer in Redfield. Very tragic.

There was last summer. There was the orchard where it had always been, smelling and buzzing, there was the big cottonwood in the south field, and the sow pen and the smaller children working until mud was up past their boots. There was heat and my Mama and my sisters Ziona and Bess. All close-by. There was a day when three men and one woman all in suits came up the road and looked at me and asked me where my father was.

There was the day I pointed at the horse barn and the woman in the suit leaned over and fingered a bit of my hair like she was checking to see if I was real.

I watched the four dark-suited figures walk away down the road, getting smaller, and thought maybe they were people that were going to make us go to school in Pine Mesa again, which had happened one year and I had gone for three weeks and I had cried everyday but now I am glad because I can talk a little more like the other kids because I had that time been marked on the board every time I said a word from the Book or "ain't." And also I had found Nancy Drew books in that school library, which are unholy but not so bad, and even Josiah's third wife, Cadence—who has skin and hair as light as snow and is not from Redfield—read them as a girl. So did Estelle, it turns out.

Stan sometimes gets home early when Estelle is out shopping or at bridge club or at the beauty salon. He walks in and says Hey kiddo and I think for a minute, like I always do when these people come in from being out, that he is really not that old. Stan doesn't ask me to do anything like play cards or read books to him or look at old photos or talk about what I am feeling like Estelle does. Stan just looks at me and raises his eyebrows a lot and I think maybe this is because something Estelle told me once which is that Stan has a daughter who he never really got to know because she lives in Tucson. Estelle was worried it might be hard on him having me here, reminding him of it all, but I don't think he minds because a lot of the time I think he thinks I'm older, or more of a boy because sometimes he asks me about sports, or who I would vote for for senate, and I never know what to say so we just sit there until I think he forgets he asked the question. And these days when he comes home early Stan just says Hey kiddo, and then he goes to the little bar in the corner of the den, by the kitchen, and even though Estelle says no drinking before five o'clock he says, Get me some ice will you? And then I know to bring the ice tray in and to bend it back so the cubes pop out of their seams and then to use the nail on my pointer finger to pick a few cubes out for him and drop them in his glass and then he pours over them while I lick my finger and put the tray back and then go to see about some way to get out of his way and never mention it to Estelle because when I was told they had found a home for me and I had to go, my Mama held my arm like she did her dough, with two hands, and told me this:

Walk on eggshells, Mercy Ann, walk on eggshells.

This is how I did and this is how it was anyway for the first eleven months and then yesterday Stan asked me if I didn't want a drink myself. This is how it was: He asked, Hell have you ever even tried this stuff? You can try a little if you want. Lord knows at your age, I . . . and he trailed off and I didn't know what to say because drink was always a tool of the Devil, but the world that it had been that tool in had since been burnt to the ground like someone had turned off the TV:

I hadn't gotten even one letter from my Mama, or my sister Bess, or even Emma.

So I thought about it as Why not? And then the thing that really got me in truth was the way that I had been watching him these months pour the gold water over the ice I had just put there. My nails hadn't changed the ice at all in touching them, but that drink softened the edges of those cubes quick and I found it sort of holy to watch because it reminded me of the way a thing like an aster would wilt when one of my sisters picked it and put it behind her ear. At first it seemed fresh and sharp and then the next time I looked up from work there it would be, curled and soft.

So I heard myself clear when I said Yeah, okay Stan. And he told me to go get the ice tray again and he got a little giddy as he got out a glass and he called to me in the kitchen, You know Estelle used to have a drink every night with me but now she says it makes her too sleepy. I was standing in the kitchen almost smiling when I heard Stan sounding happy, I think it was the first time I did something he liked and all I had to do was just break one of Estelle's rules with him and I wasn't sure if we were two friends that were old or two friends that were young but either way I brought the tray in and did like I did for him except for this time it was for me so I counted the ice cubes aloud in my head. One Two Three. He nodded and I watched him pour my first drink ever before I went to put the ice tray back. I stood in front of the freezer and felt the cold, and in that air I thought that if Bess could see me now she would finally believe what I whispered to her in the dark of our bedroom. How I thought I was not afraid of the Book we had been raised on like it was milk. Then I closed the freezer door and heard it slurp shut with the kind of general certainty of the way things were and had been for the past eleven months.

I came back to the bar and Stan handed me my glass, which was wet on the outside, and he said Let's go out back. Out back was a small walled-in area that penned in their out back from the out back of other condos. It had a dirty glass table and some plastic chairs so Stan and I sat down and both began to look at the brown brick wall in front of us, and the blue sky up ahead.

We sat like that for a while and I took a sip. It tasted hot, and I knew my Mama would say it was the heat of hell. I had thought it would be sweet, like honey. That was because of the color I guess. But it burned even going down and I thought, oh this really is like hell, but after a few minutes I felt warm and kind of soft like I really was an aster behind an ear already.

I thought about what I might look like from far away.

There was the time when the woman from the news asked me if I could read. I told her yes. She asked me what. I told her Nancy Drew. And then she looked away and her hand made a pretend cut across her own throat like she was telling someone to kill a sow, and that's how I saw that she had makeup on down to her collar, but that there was a white line of skin just where the lip of her blouse met her neck.

Now that I watch TV, I wonder if I was on it, and I think a lot about being on TV when I am doing normal things, like going to the bathroom or trying to sleep.

Right then I was wondering what kind of show would have Stan and I out back with drinks like we were best friends or even father and daughter or something, even though Estelle says she won't let the TV people anywhere near me ever again. But I still think about it a lot and was thinking about it even as I was having a time like my first drink.

That's when Stan asked Do you miss it? And I looked at him for a time and he was squinting his eyes again but in some way I felt like it was okay to tell him. Yes. And he nodded, like he had known it always. We sat for another time and I heard crickets, and they sounded the same as they did last year.

Fall's a coming, Stan said, and I nodded. He squinted his eyes at me then he turned down to the glass in his hand and started to talk:

Estelle says that when they found you, you were living with your mother and father and his two other wives and twelve siblings. And that you were just about to be married off to a fifty-year-old man that was a, you know, a relation of yours of some sort. And she says this and I know it's probably true.

Stan took a drink and then set it on the glass table and looked at me, and I took my third or fourth sip and thought how it was not so hot now. Stan fingered his chin, But I look at you and I think you're all right. I mean your biggest problem is that you don't know up from down since they took you away from your family. And. Stan finished his drink and nodded at me to keep it up before he started talking again. And, well I've been thinking a lot about it and I was thinking, well, really. He took another drink and sucked his lips in, I was thinking your father probably never had an affair. Probably never went cheating on anybody, you know?

There is my father, who I think about at night. I think about him in jail. There is my Pa who I picture surrounded by concrete that's been painted thick with black. There are no bars when I think of him but I know he can't get out.

Stan was staring into his drink and I waited to see if he was done, to see if I was supposed to answer the question or if it was the kind you're just supposed to listen to.

I looked up at him, and waited.

The last memory I have of my Pa is not the day when I pointed toward the horse barn. I saw him that day, I know I did, but I cannot remember what he looked like that morning or even what he looked like being taken in a black car. The last memory I have of him is from last winter, when I walked into my Mama's room in the afternoon looking for a needle and a thread and there was my Mama, lying on the bed, her dress up over her hips, her legs blushing, her dark-haired parts showing, her head turned from me. She did not look when I came in so I turned to leave and get a needle from another mother's house when I saw my Pa by the window groaning and kneeling and praying like he was in pain.

As soon as I found a needle I went behind the barn and pricked my finger with it and watched the drop of blood swell up until finally it dripped onto the dirt.

Stan did not look up at me when I looked up at him. A plane flew overhead and it sounded like a seashell Estelle had given me my first week here. There was a dull roar when she held it to my ear but it was nothing like the roar in everything else right then.

Stan cleared his throat, I just think that you seem like such a good kid, I just think maybe your father might not have been that bad. I don't know. I just think he really probably did never do anything dishonest. Stan's voice started to sound like its parts were breaking away from each other and he took a big drink and looked away and said Lord, there was a time, what I'm trying to say is, Estelle and I.

Stan dropped his head. We weren't always happy and I.

Stan stopped and held his hand to his eyes like he was shading them from something. I did not know what. He breathed in and it sounded un-whole like his voice and I did not know if he was thinking about his daughter off somewhere in Tucson.

I waited and I waited and I thought of my father, all broken-looking by the window, staring up at an empty blue sky. What I would never say to Stan was: my father could be mean. I looked down at my pointer finger, red and wet from the glass.

Stan finished his drink but still had his glass in his hand shaking the little ice cubes at the bottom like they might get bigger. I did not know what to do. I did not know the answer to his question, if it was a question to answer. I did not know my father's life even as well as I knew Nancy Drew's life, who is a teen detective with a boyfriend named Ned, or Blanche's life on *The Golden Girls*, and maybe even Stan's now that we were having this talk together. I did not know.

But it seemed like it wouldn't matter much to say even this to Stan, or anyone for that matter. So I nodded at him and noticed his eyes were wetting and so I looked down, like we were on TV, and I took a last big drink. Like Pierce Brosnan. Like someone with something to hide. I almost gagged.

There were the two of us sitting there with empty glasses between us when Estelle walked out and leaned on the door frame for support, pushing the sliding glass door open farther with her other hand so that a rush of house smell came out and she looked at the two of us and our empty glasses and she looked back at me like she did when I told her I'd found Rosie in this same out back, lying dead under the glass table. She'd followed me outside that day shaking her head, like it must be another thing she was going to have to explain to me, like Martin Luther King Jr. Day, and then she saw the poor dead little yapper and she looked at me and said, What Happened? and so I thought Estelle thought that I had killed Rosie and I couldn't answer that I didn't know, I just opened and closed my mouth with no words for the little dead dog. And now Estelle had that same look on her face now, like she was confused, like she didn't know whether she should be angry.

Good god Stan, She's not old enough to drink, is what she said and I thought I might be in trouble but then she sighed and sat down and said that she had just learned at bridge club that one of her closest friends, and best bridge partner, was dying. She looked tired, like something was over.

Which I guess is why she said Mercy Ann, fix me a drink, and Stan said Me too, and so I went in and fixed three drinks, one for me too which Estelle would take from me, but at least I learned how to do another thing in this place.

I came out carrying their drinks and then I went back in for the one that was mine. I watched the ice clanking on the glass as I walked outside and I looked at how it never even seemed like it would break, I mean even if I dropped the glass and the glass broke, the ice still wouldn't.

When I came out with this glass in hand Estelle raised an eyebrow and then looked at Stan and Stan said two things while I pulled over a new chair since Estelle was sitting in mine.

Stan told Estelle that he was sorry about her friend, and also that she hadn't won in bridge. Then he said, as I sat down on the cold plastic, We've been talking about Mercy Ann's father.

Estelle looked at him hard then and nodded, then she bit her lip and looked at me. She reached her hand out over to the thin arm of my chair and took a sip of her drink so I saw that she was about to cry.

What I know from today that I did not know yesterday is that my Pa was tried yesterday, and that Estelle called Stan from the club where she plays bridge to tell him to tell me that my father would be where he was for a long time. That my mother would not sign a paper saying she would not go back to polygamy, and thus gave up her rights to us. But I didn't know this yesterday and so I thought that Estelle's friend must have been a good bridge player and also that there was something I didn't understand but knew enough to know there was some kind of under-sadness in it, like two summers ago when Adaleen, who was sixteen, lost her first baby before it even got to the world.

Estelle had that kind of look on her face.

Oh hell, Estelle said then and she laughed a little, shaking her head. She took off her glasses, rubbed her eyes and they both looked at me. That was when Estelle raised her glass and said to Stan, Tomorrow let's go get that chair, and I knew that I didn't really need one because I never did mind the green shag but I said, Thanks Grandma, anyway and she took a drink and nodded at my own glass and said, Well you might as well call me Estelle.

That was still yesterday which is different than today. Yesterday, when the ghost of the little yapper was under the table, keeping our feet warm as the part of sky above us got cooler. When the three of us sat out back, talking about people we loved but didn't know where they were, about times and how they change, about the things we didn't understand, about how nothing was simple but death. Mostly it was Stan and Estelle talking, and me listening but feeling as if I did understand because of the little I knew about death and because of the lot I knew about not knowing where anyone was or how anything would be really ever again.

Yesterday there was me, feeling already that I could not go back to where I came from but thinking that it was because of the drink, and the new chair that would be coming, and what I felt myself to be understanding.

But then again, there was me, not knowing yet what I know now today from watching the news about my father on TV, not knowing yet that the roar would not ever leave the shell, but would stay in it and glow with a sound too dry to wilt.

# Jeremiah

Of course, he had known always somehow that this was where the whole thing was going, had planned it, even, in a way.

Break a law, be cut free.

Free was the thing he had imagined, not why he done it but certainly not reason enough to stop him from doing it. Why he had done it was to have one thing his father didn't. Even for a while. Why he had done it was her red hair and oak skin, the same color as a stick whittled naked of its bark. And it was done now, and it had gone to where it was always going, but now he was here Jeremiah felt like maybe he hadn't a planned it, hadn't a known it, or had but that it was a trick, the way he saw it being and the way it was now all happening.

What he hadn't a known was being dropped off not even in town. A good five miles at least from anywhere. What he hadn't known was the way that would feel. Not relief. Not some unholy exuberance. But lost. Lost in the desert. And hot. And thirsty.

That first evening, after he walked a while, he waved a truck down with an old man driving who let him get in the back of his pickup with his two yellow dogs and ride to the edge of town, one dog trying to lick his face the whole time and all the while him hearing his Pa, telling him it was time. He could still hear it after he got there and walked for a bit until he got to a town he'd been to, with his Pa, picking up things, but had never seen this way before; it had always been part of a zoo he was looking in on but now he was one of the animals. He could still hear

Pa's voice after the sun had gone down, and long after he realized in this place you need money for food and after he remembered that he knew no one, not even one child, and even heard Pa's voice still as he curled up under a big cottonwood in the town park and fell asleep.

He woke up freezing before it was light. The grass was wet underneath him like it had turned to sweating in the night. He thought to get up and move, warm his blood. He walked the town, only two main streets really. Wide streets with old brick buildings. On the corner a café. A bank. An antique store. Spread out from there, small houses the shape of boot boxes. He felt like he was walking through a place where all other people in the world had vanished. Leaving just him. He wondered if this is what it was like in the after after. If you don't have the wives to get you to the right heaven, to your own planet in the Celestial Heaven. If purgatory was just you walking around alone at night in a town nobody lives in and you got no money to buy anything even if they did.

'Course that wouldn't be for him, neither. He knew where he'd go, a child of perdition. It would be worse. But probably not so cold.

He walked to the far edge of town. There was a church with a cross on it. Not his kind, not even close. The white brick of the building was lit up on the sides from lights stuck in the ground around the church, this light and all the shorter houses around it made it look tall. Taller than the gathering house at home. But narrower, more like a picture. Jeremiah hugged his arms to his body, and looked up at the big oak doors. He took his arms and tucked them inside his shirtsleeves and walked up the steps. He would huddle by the doors because there no one would move him. If someone ever came and cared.

So he huddled up even though he had been taught to stay away from these places, one of the havens of the wicked. But now he was one of the wicked. There was no use trying to stay on the right side of every rule he knew anymore because no matter what he was on the wrong side of it. He left, so no matter what, it was over.

He would live out here until he died and then when he did he'd burn. His head fell into the crook between brick and door and he sniffed.

It didn't any of it feel real.

*Time to get out now*, his Pa had said.

It was a still a dream, but different than the one he thought he'd have if he ever got out.

# Emma

Even after I was married and my belly was growing with child, I could not quit the loitering at my Mama's house, even though I had work and bed and sisterwives and everything else back at Josiah's, I did not have my Mama. My Mama has red hair just like me, which our people call matchstick, and her temper too is that color and I like the way she sassed me or Annalue or would tell us that He like to destroy our whole house for the smallest of our idlenesses and also the way she would crow or towelspank me or pull my braid and all of this bespoke what was not yet in my new home. Everyone there was polite or rude to me, but never just plain loving or plain mean and it was these two things I missed and also my Mama's apple bake to which she added ginger, her matchstick secret.

When my washing and work was done for Lizbeth, Josiah's first wife and Jeremiah's mother, I would get me down to the house if I could and my Mama would look at me when I come in and say Well I see you plan on refusing God's good graces once again, and cluck cluck with her hen mouth, but I knew by the way she would always soon after I come in push over a bowl of peas for me to shell or corn to husk and then set down with me to put our hands to work together that she was not really so riled to see me.

Mama never gave me no married lady talk, the night before I left she said she would have but it seemed I had already reaped that knowledge for myself and why, by the way, on God's red earth I would sin so would be an everlasting mystery to her. I, she told me, was a pious woman who did not even lift my eyes let alone my dress before being married to your Pa at sixteen devout years of age. So I do not know but that it was an unlucky day whence we baptized you, and we should have known it would take a team of plow horses to keep you from sin, and yoked you up right then, right there.

And so over peas or corn she would tell the story again of the unlucky day of my baptism when I was seven years old and memorizing my tenets last minute because I was the kind of child who'd lose my hair if it hadn't had the good fortune to be growing direct from my head, and it was a foreboding morning with dark thunderheads in the southern sky and first things first Mama went to get my white gown from the washing line and wouldn't you know it had blown right into the trough and was not white but gray with horse water and wouldn't that be hardly worth remembering if not also at the same time a sandstorm begun to blow fierce, and shut down all doors and windows and wasn't everybody so busy battening down the hatches that the oats on the stove we were to eat before House time boiled all over and made a mess on the floor and burned Levi, who crawled over to eat them and scalded his tiny palm and then was screaming to raise the dead before their time, and then to top it all off, my Mama, said, While we was waiting for your dress to dry, quick as can, Annalue came in and lift her own dress like a harlot to show me her body plagued with enough chicken pox to fill the night sky and so Jenna, who was not married to your father and I but a year, had to come and watch your poor ailing siblings whose bodies had been touched by the Devil the very day we dressed for God, while we put you in a damp dress only to get wetter in the waters of Redemption and finally we made it to House, and you were cradled in the blue of the sacred pool and were blessed but just as soon as your sweet face emerged, the wind that blew the dress blew the power and the House was dark but for the red whirlwinds outside the tall thin windows of the baptismal and all went quiet, a sign from him, perhaps, until you, who were dripping wet with His waters looked up at us all and said Amen. Everyone was laughing, then, and remembering Nephi, "even babes did open their mouths and utter marvelous things," because we did not know that you would take that utterance into a life so stained by the Devil's brand on your neck that you like to destroy us all when He come again.

And here my Mama would touch the birthspot behind my right ear, a raspberry-jam color shaped like a melting quarter.

My Mama would say things about that sacred day and now I think looking back it was not some forecast of a sinful life but a pious one I read: How my dress was stained to keep from vanity; How I did not get the chicken pox though Annalue and later Levi did; How God struck the power when I accepted him into my heart. These, I see now, are signs that though tested by the Devil, I would be later among his most devout. But then I believed Mama my inherent evils and almost liked the way she talked about the trouble I got to, exasperating, but gentle-like, and though I knew she was not liking what I had done, and how it had turned out, and how I left my work in her kitchen some two years early, I also did not think my Mama would be like to damn me to hell, if it was up to her. She would just sigh sad and either blame the baptism or the woman, Hannah Sanders, who took over the primary school from my grandmother once she got so old her hands went stiff. That woman, she would say, taught you to read silly books about manners and hair pinning when she should have been teaching you scripture and tenets. Who cares what you serve with potatoes, in fact I'll tell what you serve with potatoes, MEAT, and any good wife knows that and knows you don't need two cents to know that men like a sweet girl, with good grooming, and what a waste of time when you should have been learning the stories of our faith. And if Annalue was sitting with us, which was some afternoons, she would always say, but Mama, aren't you glad I know how to read your colors? And laugh at the old joke about the most ridiculous lesson that Hannah ever taught us out of her Guide to Homemaking, because there was only hand-me-downs in our house and so to read one another's colors we said this: Well, now, Annalue, with your hair so light and your eyes so blue, it's best you wear: OLD.

And Mama would tisk, tisk, and say a waste of time but no matter because hadn't she sent her daughters there and at least they could read, and God willing maybe one day we'd even read the Book wherein lay the salvation we both seemed so intent on thwarting. And wouldn't she pray for it lest she be all alone with only Pa in her Celestial heaven, childless as the day she was born and wouldn't we just know the suffering we put her through one day when we were older.

And Mama would say that we would know one day, but even when her tongue was loosed like this, she never gave no mention of the growing bump under my dress. I know she saw it because she stopped and looked at it sometimes when it was getting to be noticeable and sighed but never said a word and I do not know if it was because she worried in her heart that it might be the son's child and not the father's, like I thought God hath ordained, or if it was because when she saw it, she just saw one more sign of our ill-fitting, too big to hide from the eye of God, like Annalue's chicken pox, or Levi's burnt hand, both who still bear pink specks of scars. And though at that time I yearned to talk to Mama, to tell her Josiah had just been with me just the once and then said not again until I was older and I wanted to ask her if this made me a bad wife. To tell her and then to hear Mama's words and the shoring up I knew she could give about that and this coming baby, but that I knew I would not hear it because I had broken with the plan she had for me, and I had loved Jeremiah and had gotten dirt and grass on my dress and so was married and having a child these two years early, and that my punishment, if not before God, would be before her and that was to bear this my burden all alone, with no soft words to ease the child out into this world, and even though this my Mama's silence gave a glow of sadness to my visits home, I still went most every day because I knew that once that child came, I would not be able to go so much, and also was not sure I would be welcome.

*Listen. Sometimes things are already over before they begin.*

*In Jeremiah's case they were over the minute he was born a boy. His birth a death, a fall that prescribed to him a lifetime of waiting for it to be over until all of the sudden it was. Over and he was out. Exiled.*

*In my case they were over when I met him a second time. He called my name in the hall and caught up with me and told me his name again in case I had forgotten but I hadn't and he held out his hand like an old man, and I laughed and liked his blue eyes, and I shook his hand and his palm was sweaty, and then someone spun me around and he was calling my name again only now I was there at that party on the back patio.*

*We will get there, to the back patio, to the end, but once we are there, I'll be right back here in this chalky land. I'll start all over again.*

# Jeremiah

He wasn't done at the Home, even after the night when he felt Duke's throat. Not yet. That next morning, he woke up to Duke standing over him again.

Shit, he said. I'm sorry, Duke. And he was, he didn't have anything against Duke. He was nice and he'd had a rough time and he'd been real kind to Jeremiah when he first got there.

Man, no worries, I was an asshole, I deserved it. Duke stuck out a balled hand, and Jeremiah bumped his fist against it.

We're cool, Duke said. Then, Hey you want to go to school with me?

You go to school?

Sometimes, yeah. When there's nothing better to do. Where you think all the girls are at? Duke rubbed his hand on his jaw like he was stroking an invisible beard.

And so Jeremiah had a reason to put off leaving.

At the school, it turned out Jeremiah had to be a visitor and just go to Duke's classes with him. Duke told the women in the office that Jeremiah was a cousin who'd be moving here from Texas next year, So they, as he explained to Jeremiah, don't get all over you. The woman who helped them had a pin in the shape of Utah on her sweater and said All right, Texas, Sweetie, here you go, as she handed him a badge that said VISITOR. Don't forget to sign out at the end of the day, now.

Jeremiah nodded and followed Duke out of the office.

Jeremiah couldn't believe how many kids were in the hall. Kids their age, making noise, laughing, pushing each other, touching each other, girls in super short skirts, some without tights even in the cool of late fall, boys in T-shirts and baggy jeans. The space was hot with bodies, it smelled with bodies and echoed with voices and laughs and screeches of shoes on the tan tiles. Kids everywhere. Kids with headphones in, with braces, glasses, hats. Kids slamming lockers, high fiving each other, shoving past each other, someone kicked a soccer ball down the hall and hit a girl in a yellow sweater and green skirt in the butt. She turned and yelled, Asshole! The skin, the voices, the very vibration of the hall as the bell went off and through it all Jeremiah could hear the voice of the Prophet: Wickedness is like water in their world, that they drink from its well each day, and it courses through their bodies like blood until it is their very nature.

The first class they went to was History. The teacher asked students to turn to a chapter in their book on the start of the Civil War. Neither Duke nor Jeremiah had a book. Duke turned and winked at Jeremiah before moving his desk closer to a girl with long brown hair, looking at the page over her shoulder. Jeremiah just sat there and tried to listen as the teacher read.

He'd been to the schoolhouse in Redfield until he was nine or so. He could read some. He could write his name. He hadn't heard of the Civil War but it sounded interesting. The two sides were the North and the South, he gathered, but he didn't know of what. He'd ask Duke later, maybe.

He felt a tap on his shoulder. The girl in the yellow sweater from the hall was motioning him to scoot over, share her book. She had a curly auburn hair to her chin and bright green eyes and she smiled at him and he tried to smile back. He moved his desk over a little and could smell her. Like strawberry jam.

The book had a lot of small print words, so Jeremiah tried to look at the pictures. One was of a bearded man that looked like an old Prophet. The other was of a black-skinned man in chains.

When the bell rang, the girl held out her hand, her eyes grass.

I'm Haley, she said.

Jeremiah. He shook her hand.

Where you visiting from?

Duke stood over them. Texas!

Haley looked at him and squinted. Where are you really visiting from? She lowered her voice.

Duke leaned over and got real close to her; she didn't flinch.

This boy's a runaway slave, Duke said, and slapped Jeremiah on the back. They got up, and Haley stood too, looking with raised eyebrows at Jeremiah. Jeremiah shrugged and went to follow Duke but Haley grabbed his shoulder.

Really, where you from?

Redfield, he turned again to see Duke give somebody a high five as he walked out the classroom door.

Wait . . . that polygamist place? You're from there?

Yeah, I . . . he looked again to where Duke was going but Haley put a hand on his arm.

Why don't you come to math with me?

They had reached the hall, and it seemed even more chaotic than it had an hour ago. Duke was nowhere to be seen.

Come on, we'll find him after third period.

He let her guide him down the hall to another classroom, almost identical except for the décor. This one had laminated posters of shapes and graphs all over the walls. During class he tried to listen to what the teacher was saying but Haley kept elbowing him as she wrote notes on the side of her notebook. He tried to read them.

*Did you run away?*

Jeremiah shook his head.

*Are you just visiting then?*

He shook his head again.

*Did you get kicked out?*

Jeremiah read this slowly. He stared straight ahead once he understood what she was asking and tried to listen again to the teacher as she talked about the angles of a triangle she'd drawn on the board.

Haley tapped the question with her pencil eraser and gave him an exasperated look. He stared straight ahead again, but shrugged.

The teacher asked them to take out their compass and draw a circle and find the radius. Haley pulled out a sharp gadget and showed Jeremiah how it worked. You put the point in the middle of the paper, and it's sharp so it could go right through, then you move the second part around like you are winding a clock. He tried it himself, and tore her paper but she laughed and put her hand over his. Together they made three circles, each one smaller than the last.

She didn't write any more questions on her paper.

After the next bell, Haley said she had a free period, which meant no class to go to. Jeremiah said he should find Duke.

Haley led him out to the parking lot and into the far corner where there was sunny strip of grass. It was getting cold up North, colder than it would be in Redfield.

He usually hangs out here.

You know Duke, then?

A little, from parties, and he used to go out with one of my friends. Haley pulled a pack of cigarettes out of a pocket on her green canvas backpack. The pocket had a patch with a smiley face. Want one?

Jeremiah just looked at her.

Wait, have you ever had one?

Jeremiah blushed and looked down. Haley squealed in delight.

She lit two and handed him one. Breathe in slowly, she said and then watched as he did.

He coughed immediately and deeply. His eyes watered and she nodded, That happens to everyone the first time.

She inhaled her own cigarette gracefully, and Jeremiah liked the way she just barely held it between her two middle fingers.

Where was the Civil War? Jeremiah asked as he tried to inhale the cigarette again, this time softly, barely getting any smoke down.

You're kidding.

Jeremiah blushed again and Haley quickly spoke. It was here, in the United States, between the North and the South. The South had slaves, and the North wanted to free them.

Jeremiah looked up again at her and nodded.

He watched her smooth her skirt with her hand. The North won, obviously.

Jeremiah said, Oh. I mean I heard of slaves. Like in the Bible.

Haley laughed a little, You're funny.

Jeremiah looked at her sideways, he couldn't tell if she was making fun of him.

I mean, it's fun hanging out with you, it's like you're an alien visiting our world and I get to show you everything.

Jeremiah made a face, one his sisters always made to make the babies laugh, by putting his fingers into his eyelids and pushing them up, sucking his cheeks in.

Haley giggled and gently reached over to tap Jeremiah's cigarette, a cone of ash fell off into the grass.

Duke found them there after the next bell.

Did you learn anything, shithead? He grinned at Jeremiah. Let's get out of here already.

Jeremiah stood up and reached down to help Haley up, she took the hand. See you later, thanks for the cigarette . . . he turned toward Duke.

Duke stared at him, then motioned his head at Haley.

Jeremiah just stared back. Duke cleared his throat.

Haley picked up her bag and grabbed a notebook out of it. She tore a corner of a page off and got out a pen. Why don't I give you my number she said, and wrote something before tearing it off and giving to Jeremiah.

In case you have any more you know, history questions, she giggled and turned away, walking back towards the building.

Man, Duke had his hands on his head, that was *painful*.

What?

Never mind, dude, you got her number, that's what counts, man. That means that this was not a total waste of time.

As they walked toward the bus stop, Jeremiah realized he still had his VISITOR badge on. He slipped it off his neck and into his pocket next to the slip of paper with Haley's number.

*I become so good at being a ghost. At whispering, at becoming the dream that someone has that gives them an idea they think is theirs. Is theirs.*

*I went back to their sad little house when the sun was almost down. The mother, Beth, was napping on the sagging brown couch like a leaf curled with wilt. She was with child, I could see. Could see the two heartbeats pulsing. There was jam stuck to the coffee table like glue. Manti and the little girl on the floor dozing, him cupped around her. I knelt next to them.*

*I wanted to brush his shaggy hair back out of his face. He reminded me of a little cousin I used to babysit. Who used to fall asleep on my lap. Call me Hay Hay.*

*I placed a hand on his head. A hand he couldn't feel or know, and I wished I was full of kindness and love for him but I only had one thing to do here.*

*I bent down so that my mouth was smoke in his ear.*

*Ladybird, ladybird, fly away home, I whispered my song.*

*I heard Beth stir.*

*Your house is on fire, I whisper sang.*

*Then she sat up and I looked up. She looked right at me. The whites of her eyes rising. She grabbed a pillow and hugged it, pushing back against the couch.*

*She looked right at me. She saw me as I turned back to Manti's ear.*

*And your children shall burn, I sang, my voice rising.*

*Beth screamed then. Get away! Get away from them!*

*And so I knew, as Manti started awake, swearing, I knew her secret.*

# Cadence

My husband who I share with three other wives was gone. Gone out because something warn't right among the men. And the four of us wives were sitting around a table trying to find a thing to say to make everyone else feel at ease bout it. Also at the same time it seemed we were trying to convince everyone else that we each loved him more than the others in case the feeling we all had was right. In wives, I was no place near the top. Even less than Emma who was barely thirteen. An outsider, and they all somehow knew that I had been with other men before I was married. Heck, Tressa still acted like I was a danger to her kids or something. So I really wanted to tell her that I loved him maybe even more than she did, since I chose him and warn't assigned him by no Prophet. But this warn't the time with a black car, just like the one they say took Holden Brown sometime last year, driving all slow until our alarm bell was ringing and the day stopped.

I saw it. The car. It looked like an oily dark eye just taking everything in, gazing all through town, staring too long, with no apologizing. For a second, the hair on my neck stood up and I wondered if they could be looking for me. If my Ma had called someone to say I was runaway. But then I knew it warn't. Not a car like this. A runaway would mean a cop car. This looked like the feds. And my Ma wasn't looking for me.

And then that evening Josiah was meeting with the other men, and Tressa whispered that they even met without the Prophet himself. So the whole place was quiet like the dusk was meat and everybody got their mouth full.

So I sat there and didn't say anything about how I loved him, or about what I knew of these outsiders that had come looking in at us. And I just let Lizbeth's baby sitting in my lap suck my fingers, his empty gums clamping in that baby-mouth way that nothing else in the world feels like expect maybe a finger gnaw from Bitsy, that toothless old horse of Josiah's that he say he don't have the heart to shoot. And though I was just sitting there and not saying anything, it warn't that I hadn't learn to love my husband. Josiah had made me a better woman and a mother come next summer, if this one takes. And I did, in my own way and right, see my God more clear. I think He really did mean for me to be Josiah's, and I know he was trying his best to remove temptation from my path.

But still then and even now, I miss things like good black coffee and potato chips. And sometimes early in the morning when the light is just beginning to get a little up in the sky, I think about taking Josiah's old Ford and heading out to Broadview and getting a hot coffee and a pack of cigarettes and some Cheetos and candy bars. Being back before anyone missed me. I haven't gotten the courage up yet to do it, but just thinking about it gets me drooling. Even though it was that very temptation to eat and drink and smoke and get high that brought me here.

And when I was first married, you'd a thought I was a dog. Tressa kicked me around so much with *do this* and *do that*. And always the last worst jobs, cleaning toilets and bathtubs and then the last worst burnt corners of casseroles for dinner. It's better now, since Emma came, and she's got someone new to hate. And no matter what it's better than what I had, but still I'd like to visit that old life sometimes. But I am ashamed to admit it, and would never tell my sisterwives this. Not now and not that day while we sat waiting.

While we sat there, I did say that Josiah wouldn't do no good in prison. (But I did not say I knew this because I had done my own small time in jail.) And at first Lizbeth glared like she was mad I said it but then

Emma, with her own baby bumping under her dress, said that No siree, nobody would match his socks for him and we all got a quiet laugh. Lizbeth said Helpless, that man is.

We nodded at this and I remembered the day Josiah sat on the edge of my bed and tried to sew a button on himself 'cause he said I didn't do it right and so I told him, well then do it yourself. And I thought he might scold me for my mouth, but he tried. We laughed when the button pulled right off clean as a scab: the plaid fabric a spot darker where it had just been. But I didn't say this to my sisterwives, 'cause I didn't think I could stand their looks if they knew I had dared make him do it. Especially after a day like this one.

Lizbeth kept talking and she said, Sometimes I know God show us the darkness when one least expects it, but seeing that black car today was like an omen.

When I was a child, she said, during that last famous raid it was very much like the end had come. They came before dawn, we knew they were coming. The Prophet Lehi, and a holy, holy, holy man he was, had heard from God. So they came thinking they would find us in our beds still sleeping, but no, we were all in front of the House, we were singing our hymns. Singing while the littlest children played around us. They came into our collective body so strong and broke us up and arrested everybody, and took us children away from our parents in milk delivery trucks and we were afraid, and we slept in a school gymnasium for some days and I waited for God to strike the building down, for the walls to come apart and fall to the ground and free us from the policemen guarding the doors, and the nurses passing out cartons of milk. It was cold at night, and I slept next to my sisters on the hard floor and I prayed and prayed. For three days we stayed quiet and pious and in the end, they put us back in the milk trucks and drove us right back here and no one, not even the Prophet, went to jail, and all returned to the way God intended. But it was a test, for certain it was, and I fear that soon there may be another test: a reprehension maybe, and a test of our faith and of our people.

When Lizbeth said the word faith, we all got quiet. I looked out and saw that the day really was getting on. Saw out the small uneven window the sun drifting down like a lazy eye.

Persecution, Emma said, but she too was looking far away, patting her belly lightly in a rhythm too wild for a heartbeat to follow. And I knew that Emma had been through a lot for a child so young, and that her youth was a crime, her belly the evidence. And I knew all about that outside world and what they accused us of, could see it plain as day in Emma. And I thought about how to tell this to the others, how to explain why it was seen as wrong and I opened my mouth once but then shut it. I had become friends with Emma, and I thought she was wiser than her years. I had listened to her all the time about Jeremiah in those first days she was here and married to us and didn't tell no one about it. So I thought we were sort a close. So I didn't want to tell them that it was her that would really do us in if they came to look hard. I didn't want to give Tressa more reason to hate her.

Tressa was more sure than anyone that she loved Josiah best. She's got dark hair and mean eyebrows and a big bosom and big hips and big everything. She thinks her body was, she says, made the most right by God for wiving, and she liked to tell Emma and I, who are not old enough for her figure, that we are sad excuses for wives. She pokes at the bones that show below our collarbones. Like a couple a skinned birds, she says. And she had been hanging her head and crying a lot at this time, and we didn't always know why as she only talked to Josiah. But that day I knew it was because the big black car that drove around slow and left. Then after we came out and stood there in the dust cloud, and then the men called a meeting and left us wondering if our lives would change. That was why she was sad that day and why while we were sitting there, around the big pine table in Lizbeth's kitchen, she let out occasional wails to wake the ghosts.

But then she said, If God is testing us, I am not unsure that one of us will not pass, and she glared at Emma and mouthed Jer-e-mi-ah, as if Emma didn't know the name of her own sin and then she looked at me also.

So Emma grabbed my hand and squeezed. Lizbeth said Have Mercy, Tressa, times like these we be a family, the way Josiah would want, then, as she let her voice fall off she said too, The way Jeremiah would want. This part surprised me and I looked up quick but she was looking away and shaking her head. So I thought maybe I didn't hear her right. I hoped for Emma's sake that she did say that. That she could see like I did that Emma was a child who didn't mean no harm, and were only doing what she felt and being young and stupid. A place I knew well.

But now that she had a good old baby belly to rest her hands on, Emma already seemed much more grown up and Lizbeth treated her like it. Lizbeth, who, as we sat at that table, started saying what we had all been thinking. If one of those gone boys talked, she said, but she didn't finish. She was looking at her hands, old with washing, as she talked. Like she did when she was trying to name all the prophets past which Tressa made her do from time to time. Tressa was always testing Lizbeth, just like she tried to do with Lizbeth's new little boy. She picked him up one day from his cradle when he had been fussing just barely, and she got out her boob and pressed him to it for a drink even though she didn't have any milk, or shouldn't a. When Emma saw her and screamed, Lizbeth came over from her washing and asked Tressa what in the Devil's name did she think she was doing? Tressa looked then like a kid who'd stole some candy, her eyes all big and her lower lip all wet and quivering and she handed the sweet baby back to her. Since that day I haven't trusted her. But I also feel bad for her and the way things don't seem right with her. Her oldest is three, which seems old for no new baby. And I don't know why but I prayed to Him that it was not because Josiah had not done it with her, because I know that would break anyone's heart. Not just mine.

Outside it was getting darker early, and the day crickets of fall long since hushed. Even the desert knew the signs of winter. It felt much later in the kitchen than it was.

Telling-on is bad luck, Tressa said then and Lizbeth looked but no one said anything back to this because the boys that might have told, that might bear witness, already knew bad luck. They'd already fallen from the Prophet's graces, and had left with no reason to save us. Worse luck than seeing a coyote, Tressa added, almost whispering. I thought it was a weird thing to say until Lizbeth told me later that Tressa was always invoking the beliefs of other desert people until Lizbeth like to scream.

But right then I thought about the way a coyote howls, like a woman screaming, and I got the taste of sour milk suddenly in my mouth. Then Lizbeth said, Cadence give me the child, he fussing, and you go get some of the Lord's air in your heart.

So I handed her the baby and she took it and I felt the shadow of the weight of the child gone, and the heat where his body been against me, and the stiffness in my arm from crooking it to hold him. And I walked out the door and into the evening where the sky looked like a nectarine, all beautiful, as if it was making jam from our troubles.

As soon as I stepped off the last porch step and felt the earth under my bare feet, I smelt a little smoke in the air. All smells were so strong to me now that I was pregnant. I turned toward the center of Redfield and saw our world different than it had ever been, like some great altar on fire in the dusk. I saw Josiah far down the road walking home and I thought how much I loved him. And how it was he who knew my secret name to whisper when end times come and whose soul would be with my soul for eternity but who right then had other duties while I had this newly growing child. A plum hard in my soft.

I waved at his figure against the peach sky, but just then I had a bad-like feeling watching him.

I whispered my secret name, my password into paradise, and knew no one else heard it out in that yard with the world all pink and orange. I felt like the black car and its memory had seeped a well inside me, and

I could taste the deep dank water in my mouth just beyond the shape my tongue made round that ghost name.

But before I could get to crying or feeling even scared, I finally saw what I had smelt. It was a wavering line of smoke and I understood for the first time that nobody was burning a field, because that's something the men do and they were busy, and so something else must have been on fire. I saw then that flames were bucking up into the eastern sky, near the Prophet's house, and the first thing that I thought, ashamed as I am to admit it now, is Good Riddance. I didn't much like that Prophet and I couldn't really say why. But I didn't take my eyes off the smoke dusk sky being peeled by the night, and I sidled up the steps and pushed open the door with my heel and I yelled Lizbeth,

Something's on fire out here.

# Jeremiah

Everything was loud, all the time. In and outside. Then one night the city, the Home, his blood, seemed to boil up and around inside him so that his skin was so hot he couldn't tell the inside of it from the outside. Jimmy had come over, and Jeremiah was drinking a beer, and he could feel it and he was having a good time watching Flynn do an impression of some tough guy from TV that he hadn't heard of but it was funny anyway, Flynn so small and all. He was sitting on the big brown couch and laughing and then he saw that Jimmy was watching him from across the room, a red flush on his pocked cheeks, arms folded, leaning a hip against the kitchen counter. He looked away quick and took another sip of his beer but could feel Jimmy looking at him still. It reminded him of when he was sitting at Pa's early morning prayer circle with the rest of the family and he could feel Pa watching him, making sure his own eyes stayed low and reverent. If he looked up now or then it would mean trouble. So Jeremiah finished his beer and then went to the bathroom down the hall so that they'd all think he was coming back, but after he was done he ducked into his bedroom and shut the door as quietly as possible.

This time it didn't work, though.

A knock came at the door just as Jeremiah had started to pull off his T-shirt. He yanked the shirt back over his head and stood still, staring at the door. None of the boys knocked. Ever. He saw his folding knife sitting on the card table that sat between his and Duke's beds. He grabbed it and put it in his pocket before opening the door halfway.

Jimmy stood there grinning with a clear plastic cup of whiskey in his hand. Jimmy brought over whiskey for himself when he brought them beer, but he didn't let anyone else have any.

Super Mormon tired already? Jimmy leaned his arm up on the doorframe and his head dropped toward Jeremiah.

Jeremiah could tell he was drunk.

He could also hear the boys go quiet down the hall; he could hear them trying to listen.

How come you never stay up late? Jimmy dropped his arm from the doorframe and took a half a step toward Jeremiah. Jeremiah didn't take a step back; he kept his hand on the doorknob. He was maybe one inch taller than Jimmy. *Stronger, for sure.*

I'm tired. Jeremiah's voice was hoarse. His mouth was all dried out in a way that reminded him of the air at home. But he was so far from there, *I am here among the wicked, and it turns out, they are wicked.* He was, he thought, really very tired.

He could feel the weight of the knife in his right pocket.

Come on, how can you be tired? Jimmy reached into the room and playfully pushed Jeremiah on the shoulder. Jeremiah felt some dogtail inside him want to curl under with shame. This must be what the others felt, this closing, this nauseating surrendering.

*They are wicked and now I am here among them.*

Jimmy had dropped his hand, but Jeremiah could still feel the touch. He felt like it was making him spin.

*I have to get out of here.*

Jimmy took a step into the room and toward Jeremiah, but Jeremiah was faster. He sidestepped around him, pushing Jimmy against the doorframe with his shoulder, and ducked out of the room.

He took a few quick steps back down the hall to the kitchen. The boys sat gaping at him.

*If Pa knew. If Pa saw.*

Jeremiah cleared his throat. What? Thought I'd have another one.

Duke hopped up to get him a beer from the cooler he was sitting on, the red and white cooler Jimmy had brought over.

Alright, the polyg kid wants to party! Finally! Dude, I've been waiting—Duke stopped talking and Jeremiah could feel Jimmy behind him. Hey—and then the hand was on his shoulder. Again. The second time he'd touched him. Same shoulder. His fist tightened, and then Jimmy gave his shoulder a little squeeze.

Why don't you just relax, mo-man? Jimmy's laugh was high, and across the room Flynn echoed it with a sound even more unnatural. It reminded Jeremiah of the sounds coyotes sometimes made after a kill. A wheezy round of squeals. *Night there, so open and flat.* Not like this room, a closing hand.

Jeremiah turned around, shaking Jimmy's hand off him.

Don't you ever fucking touch me again.

Jimmy's smile shrunk and for a brief instance Jeremiah saw a pitch change in his eyes, saw the way he wanted to kill Jeremiah, to do worse maybe. Their eyes stayed locked for what seemed like might have been a time outside of time.

Seconds that were really generations.

He didn't look away but finally Jimmy did, gave another forced laugh. Flynn echoing again, from closer this time. Jeremiah noticed then the way the room was moving, the boys were shifting. Duke had taken a step closer to Jeremiah. Flynn was slinking around behind Jimmy's back. A big blond kid named Brett was leaning forward in his seat, and two others, a pair of brothers, were pulling themselves off the floor. *Dogs in the night.* Jimmy folded his arms and snorted.

Man, someone is touchy tonight, Christ, are you on your period or something? Jimmy looked around at the other boys, they were all giving the same laugh now. Not Duke, though. Not Jeremiah. Flynn, too high in his sound again. Jimmy laughed again, louder now, trying to force the room to relax. Brett leaned back, and Jimmy, brimming, reached over and clapped Jeremiah on the back. Just joking—

Jeremiah felt the touch and then felt his body push against Jimmy's as hard as he could. He didn't remember thinking he'd been touched again, and his brain deciding to do anything. It was like Jimmy's handprint had just moved his muscles automatically, his muscles not being told but knowing what to do.

He plowed both hands into Jimmy's chest until Jimmy fell backwards into the cheap wall, right into the laminated sign that read *No Shoes in the House.* Jimmy's eyes were wide and Jeremiah kept one hand on his chest and pulled the other one up to punch him when Flynn, little Flynn, swung onto his arm. Jeremiah went to grab Flynn's thin face when he saw Brett leap at him from the side, his large arms catching Jeremiah as he tackled him, and Flynn too, to the ground, Flynn landing on Jimmy, and Jeremiah's face landing next to Jimmy's socked foot. So much weight on his body but his neck and head were free, Brett turned to slap at Duke, who was trying to pull him off Jeremiah, Flynn now shrieking: He's fucking crazy!

And so Jeremiah made good on that and went for Jimmy's baby toe. Jimmy caught, too. He got his molars just below the knobby bone and bit down as hard as he could.

The scream was loud and shrill and othered.

The boys' motion on top of him now froze, the bodies taut. Listening.

Jeremiah felt the little ball of flesh in the most satisfying way in his mouth, and worked fast when he hit bone, grinding his teeth into it, wanting to finish what he started, to tear the knubby meat in his mouth free, he could feel a salty desire working his jaw clenching harder as Jimmy tried to pull his foot away. The boys still stopped by the scream.

He's got my foot, the shithead has . . .

Jeremiah could taste blood now, a warm wet.

He's trying to bite my fucking toe off, stop him, stop him!

Brett's hand was the size of Jeremiah's whole head, and used it to press Jeremiah's face down, Flynn pulling on Jimmy's leg to try to free his foot, Jimmy swatting at him.

Jeremiah felt the heft of Brett's hand press into his skull, felt the way his skull could give, but he didn't care. He would not let go, couldn't at this point, his body long since acting now without him, without his own mind.

*This, maybe, is revelation. Divinity. Watching from outside, inside.* Jimmy's blood, a toe gone, could be an atonement maybe. The bone finally beginning to crack now.

And then he felt two big fingers push into his nostrils, smashing his nose up into his brain, his airway blocked, his eyes turned to meet Brett, who had a wild smile now. He remembered now two weeks earlier, sitting on the couch, Brett telling him about his father working oil in Florida, a gator grabbing a kid's leg, the kid getting free by stuffing his fingers into the gator's nostrils until the creature had to open his mouth, and as Brett pushed his fingers in deeper to Jeremiah's nose, his body again without consulting him released his jaw so he could get a breath.

He did it, he did it, Jimmy was screaming but Jeremiah knew that the toe was still on. Barely, maybe, but still there. Brett released Jeremiah's head and it slapped to the dirty linoleum, smeared now with blood, his cheekbone pressed into it. Jeremiah spit out a mouthful of blood, a red foam.

Boys were pulling Jimmy up, carrying him to the sofa, Flynn was now yelling about ice, a bag of ice for the severed toe and pawing the ground around Jeremiah's face, Where is it? Where is it? Is it in his sock still?

Jeremiah could feel his own ribs bend with Brett's breath, their two chests still pressed together. He felt Duke kneeling behind, unsure whether he was there to make sure Jeremiah didn't escape Brett, or there to make sure Brett didn't hurt him. Jesus Fucking Christ, he heard Duke say. *The wicked.*

Jeremiah relaxed under Brett's weight, breathing hard but suddenly almost overcome with indifference. *Let them kill me.*

He felt his nose bleeding down his face, the heat of it, and only half listened as they figured out that the toe was still attached. Fought over how to treat Jimmy, Jimmy just wanting someone to drive him to the hospital, or maybe not, the pharmacy maybe. Flynn high and panting.

Jeremiah half listened and felt his jawbone anchored to the floor like a piece of furniture for the earth. He felt as if he and his whole body were only that one bone, all else vanished.

*An avenging angel. Maybe Pa would say that if he saw.* Jeremiah let himself think of them, his family, seeing him. Proud of him, Pa would be. *But Pa left me.*

Flynn, now, Jeremiah could see, was curled up on the floor crying, holding his ears. Duke was whispering to Brett.

Time stretched again, the closed hand of the room loosened with a kind of fatigue.

He watched Jimmy finally stagger over to him, held up on each side by the brothers. Out, you fucking freak, out, Jimmy said, I want you out of here right now. But his voice was shaking.

*No. If Pa.*

Jimmy looked at the other boys. You hear me? Get him out.

And the door slammed and the room was open and flat again. After a minute Brett gently rose from him, Duke's hands went under him, pulling him up to sitting. He took a breath, looked up just as Flynn came at him, digging his nails into his cheek.

Jeremiah let him, felt nothing.

He had dreamed it. He had done it. *I once cut out the heart of a calf.*

Brett flicked Flynn off Jeremiah like a fly. Duke pulled him all the way up and the three stood there. The other boys facing them now. Jeremiah wondered for a moment if it was not over yet.

Shit, shit, shit, Flynn looked like he was going to attack again, he was pacing, Shit, you fuck head, what if he kicks us all out now? Huh? Where we supposed to go then, huh? If you think I'm going to back to that redlight shit because you're a fucking idiot . . . He had his hand up against his one hearing aid, pressing, as he started crying.

One of the older boys, a skinny redheaded kid named Taylor who had come in the room halfway through it all, sat him down, tried to hush him. You're rolling, Flynn, it's just Jeremiah that has to leave, then it will all be back to normal. He rubbed Flynn's back in circular motions.

What? No? Let's stand by Jeremiah, Duke said, jumping up and down a little, Think about it, and I have, if we all agree, and Jimmy can't come over, then what's he going to do? If he kicks us out, then we'll tell the police. You know, we'll tell them. We'll tell them what Jimmy is and . . .

No one believes a fucking bunch of runaways.

Think, Duke said, he didn't want us to take him to the hospital. Because he knew there would be questions.

I ain't talking to those pigs, one of the brothers said.

But a few nodded. Looked at Jeremiah, like he knew the answer. Was the answer.

Whatever, he finally said. Whatever you want me to do.

*It doesn't matter. Every place is just as much a no place.*

Fucking have that beer, that's what I want you to do. Duke tossed a can of Keystone Light at him.

Jeremiah sat down on the couch and for a moment it was quiet except for Taylor shushing Flynn.

Dude, were you really going to bite his fucking toe off? Brett motioned for Duke to hand him a beer as well.

Jeremiah shrugged. Remembered the bone in his teeth, how good it felt.

You are one sick puppy, Brett laughed and his laugh was echoed by the brothers.

Jeremiah wiped his bloody nose on his shirt, avoiding Flynn's gaze.

That night he got drunk. All of them did. No one could decide what to do. They talked in circles, Flynn crying so much that for the first time Jeremiah realized how young he was. Fourteen, maybe. Duke had told him he'd been on the streets a long time, maybe always.

When the cooler was empty and the boys began to fall asleep Duke and Jeremiah went into their room. Nothing was certain, but it looked like

Jeremiah had better be ready to go in the morning, just in case. Duke watched as he put the few things he owned, a change of clothes Jimmy had bought him, in his pillowcase.

Dude, if you leave, and you shouldn't, because that'd be a pussy move, even for a fag like you, where will you go?

*It doesn't matter.*

I don't know. Jeremiah flung the pillowcase in the corner. Turned off the light. Flopped down on his bed.

Man, I know I'd get out of here, go to Arizona . . .

Why did you let him?

Duke didn't answer.

Why did you let him do whatever the fuck it is he does?

Silence.

Is it sucking? Is that what he wanted? Jeremiah sat up in his bed.

Silence.

Jeremiah realized by little sounds, like animal sounds, that Duke was maybe crying.

Dude, I'm sorry.

Maybe because I'm a fucking fag, maybe that's why I did it.

No, man, don't let him get inside your brain like that. Where I am from . . .

Jeremiah stopped. He lay back down on his bed.

Tell me, Duke sniffled.

Where I'm from, the crime stays in the body of the person, like in their blood. And if you get to be a victim, you could stop being a victim, maybe, by stopping the crime. So say, a lady cheats on her husband, like real bad, the crime is in her blood, and see like the people where I'm from they know that Christ died for our sins and all that shit, but sometimes they say, Christ's blood isn't enough. Sometimes the blood of the crime has to be spilt too. So if you kilt the lady, and spilt her blood, you help her atone for her sins.

Wait, you would fucking kill her? Why?

'Cause think about it man, it's much nicer for her to be redeemed and have an eternity of good stuff than an eternity of hell. What's the rest of her life compared to that? It's like . . . an act of charity or something.

Seems fucking extreme.

What the fuck do I know? Anyway . . .

Wait are you saying I'll feel like better, like less of a fucking fag, if I kill Jimmy?

No. *Maybe.*

'Cause I ain't fucking killing anyone . . .

No, I don't know what I'm saying. It's not your fault, I guess that's what I'm saying. It's his blood that would need spilling, not yours.

Wait, so did this actually happen? Where you're from? Did they fucking kill ladies for cheating on their men?

No. Jeremiah put his head in his hands. Remembering. *It didn't have to be a lady.*

Huh, so it was just like, a theory, or something?

No women ever cheated on their husbands.

Oh, but like, if they did?

How the fuck would I know?

But he did know. He knew what his Pa had told him about Manti's dad. He pressed two fingers into each closed eye until flecks of light appeared. The pressure made him feel more there than here.

Sorry, man, Duke's voice was muffled now by his pillow.

Jeremiah lay there trying to remember. It was back when he was younger, just starting to be let in on man's work and man's talk. Maybe thirteen. It was a real hot day.

We should get the fuck out of here though, if Jimmy comes back. Duke's voice sounded sleepy.

We will. *I will.*

He had been mucking the stables when his Pa came in and stood in the doorway. Jeremiah just thought he was checking to see that the work was being done the way he wanted it to. He waited for some correction. But instead his Pa said, Leave that, boy, and come on with me now.

But then his Pa just stood there, like he was surprised by his own words. He didn't even bat at the flies about his face. Jeremiah watched one land on his brow and he wanted to reach up and shoo it. His Pa was staring at the wall where the tools hung, until finally he grabbed a shovel and left the barn.

Duke was snoring now and Jeremiah turned on his side, buried his head under his pillow so that he could barely hear. Barely breathe.

Jeremiah had followed his Pa to the truck, where he threw the shovel in the back. They got in and Jeremiah thought they were maybe going into town, maybe picking up feed. But then they only drove toward the dump, so Jeremiah thought for a minute maybe they were going there, but the bed had been empty and Pa didn't slow at the turn in. They drove past the red mounds of waste, and out to Manti's small rambled house and Pa stopped there—a ten-minute walk at most. The Prophet's car was already there.

The Prophet and Emma's Pa, Brother Downs, were standing at the back corner of the house, arms folded. That woman with the raven nest hair, Beth was her name, who people said was crazy, sat rocking her little baby, little Manti curled around her feet like a dog. She was mumbling and looking far past them. Beyond the men, in the field, he could see their one skinny horse. And something else, something on the ground. A person.

Jeremiah's Pa had told him to open the truck bed and wait there. He and the two others walked to the body and Pa and Brother Downs lifted it. Pa got under the arms, and Brother Downs the legs. The Prophet stood and watched.

They carried him toward Jeremiah and the truck. Jeremiah kept looking for the face, not thinking dead but ill, and wanting to see who,

who it was. His brain was moving slow. It was hot for a fall day. He felt the sudden light of not being still in the dark stables.

He craned his neck then, stepping up a little to see the face and then he wished he hadn't. No face but half a face. The other half blood and some other gore. Jeremiah later thought brains, a bit of white bone.

Jeremiah didn't throw up. A little that he swallowed, maybe. He knew it was important not to throw up.

They tried to lay the body down gently in the truck bed, but some heave was inevitable. Brother Downs covered his mouth with the crook of his elbow after the body was in.

Get in, his Pa said. Even Pa was white, a sweating moon. He had a big red splotch on his sleeve that Jeremiah tried not to look at.

He sat between Pa and Brother Downs as they drove to the town cemetery. Not the House to be laid out, then. No laying out.

They drove in quiet and got there and then it was clear to Jeremiah that they didn't really know what to do. That was why Pa brought him along. He didn't know not to, maybe. They all got out of the truck and stared at the red mounds of graves. There was no waiting bed for the body but Pa opened the back of his truck and then stood another minute. Then he got out the shovel.

When Brother Downs spoke, words sounded odd. We're going to need more shovels.

Yep. Pa had said.

And maybe a few more hands.

Pa threw Jeremiah the keys, Go get a shovel, we got one more. Pa looked at Brother Downs.

Yep, go by my house, get Levi and Jenna's boy Willie and tell 'em to grab three shovels and hustle on down here.

Jeremiah nodded and quickly got in the truck, getting the saddle blanket off the floor to sit on so he could see better. It wasn't until he heard his Pa close up the back that he realized the body was still in the bed.

He drove down the road and told the boys all right, but he drove away before they got back from shovel hunting so that they wouldn't try to jump in the back of the truck. For some reason, Jeremiah realized, he felt some ownership over the grotesque vision, the man he'd been entrusted to take on a ride to gather up the means for his own burial. He drove carefully, and slowed for the potholes.

When he got to their own barn he looked around for a minute before realizing the one more shovel was the one he'd been using to muck. He grabbed it from the lean he'd left it in, then took it to the pump and tried best he could to rinse it off. It came pretty clean, though it was hard to tell with the roughed up rust of the blade if it was really without no shit on it.

He walked back to the truck and waited just a minute before he leaned over and set the shovel gently in the bed. Focusing on the man's feet. But he couldn't help but see the few rivulets of browning blood that had run down the hollows of the ribbed bed.

He had only spoken to Manti's Pa a few times, he was almost always gone. He drove a truck and Pa had made it clear that this was maybe not an honest way to live, away from the land like that, so Jeremiah had felt this man was bad, but interesting, too.

When he got back the Prophet was there and pointing out a far empty corner of the cemetery and the other men were nodding. Pa waved Jeremiah over and he drove the truck slowly through the narrow part between graves.

It wasn't until Pa started digging the thin grave that Jeremiah realized they meant to put him here. Not by his family. That they really meant to do it with no laying out. No meeting. No coffin, even.

Brother Downs grabbed the other shovel and looked at the blade. It was already almost dry. He looked at Jeremiah and then said, Why don't you go meet my boys on the road, make sure they find us?

Jeremiah nodded and walked to the edge of the cemetery, but the boys were already coming down the pink clay road on bareback horses. They had hurried. A dead-body hurry, and they met him at the bleached iron gate.

Jeremiah let up the pillow over his head. Duke was quieter now. But still he kept it lying loosely over his face.

It took a couple of hours. More men and boys had shown up. Taken turns shoveling. The Prophet hadn't even said any words when they put the body in even though everybody paused when it lay at the shallow bottom and waited.

He only said, Proceed.

When it was all done the Prophet said, Let his blood run into the earth, and run into Christ's blood, and shore up his atonement for his earthly sins.

And then they all backed away leaving a grave but no stone, a body but no coffin.

When they got back Jeremiah grabbed the shovels and went to get back to mucking.

Wait, Pa had said. I'll take those. You get the hose and wash out the truck. Jeremiah nodded and handed him the shovels and turned back toward the truck. As he did he heard the shovels drop and felt Pa's large hand as he grabbed his arm hard and spun him around.

So you not afeared of death, boy? Not afraid of blood? Is that it?

Pa pulled his face right close to his. Jeremiah could smell the sweat, and he thought, the iron salt of the blood on his shirt.

Jeremiah kept his eyes down. No, sir.

What you say?

No, sir.

No, what?

I am afraid.

Pa let him go. Good, he said, and wiped his nose. Good.

Jeremiah didn't move, waiting for Pa to tell him that it was all right, to go on. You go wash that blood out then, and as you do, you remember that that's sinner's blood, spilt to atone for the earthly sin of adultery, and you remember that good.

Jeremiah nodded, Yes sir, and waited till his Pa shooed him away. He went to fill two buckets at the pump and walked them over to the truck, laying them in the bed. He went to get a horse sponge from the stable.

Jeremiah hopped up in the truck bed. He stood over the bloodstain and thought it looked like the silhouette of a flying bird, one wing up. He tipped a bucket over it slowly and as the blood turned pink, Jeremiah swept it out of the bed with his sponge.

It took two more buckets of water to be sure. And when he was done he went back to work, but it was in his head all day, and for days after, even months when he used the sponge on a horse, squeezing water out of it to cool a mare the way he had squeezed blood out of it. He swore it was still stained, so it stayed in his head. Not only the half face, and the no stone or marker, but what little had been said. Jeremiah had only a vague idea of what adultery was then, and later he'd hear more about it from the other boys—Manti's Pa had been loose. Spreading his seed in sin outside of his wedding bed, they said. And in the years before Emma he would think about that sometimes in his bed at night, not touching himself as that was forbidden but rolling onto his stomach and rocking his hips, rubbing against his bed, back when he was still trying to be good. But more on Jeremiah's mind in those first days after was what the Prophet had said about how one's sinning blood might run down into the red clay earth, a stream of different red, and run down into what Jeremiah pictured as an underground river of blood, of Christ's and all atoning sinners, and that this would then make it right.

*Blood would get them back to that place, to that one place. Paradise. Home. To where it matters.*

But how could he have told Duke about that? And it wasn't about Jimmy, it was more about saying that what Jimmy had done, even if he'd done it with Duke, was in Jimmy's blood. *Could I taste it, tonight, the wickedness?* He remembered spitting out that red foam, he could still taste the iron saltiness he thought. He felt his lips in the dark, but they were dry. He wiped them with the back of his hand to be sure.

How could he have even begun to tell this story of Manti's Pa *here*, in *this* world? This modular home, this place where there was no river of blood underground, where there was no Celestial heaven where men ruled as gods, there was no hell even, just an empty husk of a word that people weren't afraid to use and without it there was only the immediate and empty days of cereal and television and sleep.

A heavy sleep that Jeremiah longed for as the night wore on.

# Annalue

After the black government car came belly-crawling through slow like a snake, there came the first fire. The men were all at the gathering House and we smelt town smoke, not fields burning but things built and made, Cadence running down the road and yelling for Josiah, yelling for everybody to come quick, and then we heard the bell and saw the house of the Prophet's wives was afire and exploding with children and the boys who are assigned to townfire, only three of them left it turned out, came with their hose to attach to the pump and the children were screaming and the whole town gathered as the back porch and one upstairs corner of the house burned, then smoldered, then sat like a black shell still smoked with fire's hunger but no flame as night began to come. One armchair sat in the yard blackened down to glowing coils in its seat, a pulsing skeleton tall among the clothes and dolls grabbed in haste.

It would be rebuilt in three days, as that is how things were done there.

No child was kilt, but one was burned some on arm and face, only on one side, one corner of the body like the house, but not repaired in three days. He was small and would carry the scars and their heat for years. He had been hiding under the back porch because he was in trouble with his mother. He would not say what for. He would not say if he knew how it started. He was already burnt and so spared a beating. The priested came in their line. Pa, Josiah and three others, wrested from their secret meeting that everyone knew about.

The Prophet looked on silently. It was only a fire, He said.

Then the next day was Sunday and there was House. And I went though I had not been. Had not been since I was wived by the heavenly speaker of God but not housed. Had stayed with Jenna's babies for a season of Sundays. Had watched the slow walk of everyone I knew disappear down the road from a porch while an infant half sister sucked my finger.

I did not go that Sunday because something had burnt, but because of the black car and the meeting interrupted and the priested standing there watching the fire but not even thinking about it. Because it made me feel we were being watched not just by them but by something else. Haunted, maybe, by Jeremiah's ghost. Because even me, with the Devil inside my cold leg and body too, needed the words of our place, though perhaps it was not the words so much even as the silent and pious story of us all listening together, hundreds of ears resounding with a hope, a harmony, a plan.

I came down dressed in the kitchen in my better shoes and Mama and Levi and the littlest ones were all there, and Mama looked me up and down and said well I hope you told Jenna that one of hers better watch the rest of hers, and then we stepped out into the heat and into the road where already many walked in woven pilgrimage. And Mama nodded her hellos and the littlest ones fell in with other kids and Levi waited to see if he could see Ellen Mai coming and I limped behind them and in front of him as we made our way into the thoughts and voice of God.

The gathering House was white and square and smooth against the red and wrinkled mesa like some dollhouse furniture placed carefully by His hand. There was colored glass in nameless shapes and rows and rows of folding chairs on the concrete floor and a painting of the last prophet past in his Celestial heaven with his wives and children at his feet, a halo of dawn behind him, his hands outstretched and painted too large for his body. Daniel, favorite son of the Prophet as he was, stood lighting candles and fingering the blue silken fringe of altar cloth and then He came out of the small stage door in a black suit and black shirt and all was hushed and the colored shapes splintered and stretched among us like they were also waiting and I warmed my hands in the red sail of light that had landed in my lap.

And I looked at this light and not at him. But that's not to say I didn't hear him, I did. I heard him as he told us it was God's behest to prepare ourselves for persecution. As he spoke words that contained not the stories of black cars and fires and boys taken before their time, but of older times of persecution and statehood and those who lost their faith, who turned the words of that original Saint and Prophet so as to suit themselves to the greater country of sinners. That we would not succumb. That since our birth and first death, our fall from heaven, we were sent to battle the armies of Satan and that we as a holy order of people would overcome in the end when the Lord cometh again to resurrect us brightly into this land which would then be our eternal land, to each his own, the men becoming gods, and the women Celestial mothers and wives and the rest of everybody else damned to Satan's darkness. And the proof of this was in the eternal geology of the mesas around us, the eons their layers bore for us to show us time as man had not yet been able to imagine it, an unbounded time that we should try to conceive of, for our lives would go on and on forever once we died our second death and He came and we were risen.

I heard Him as He spoke in slow summer cadence and incantation; as He told us of the lies of the outside world and its power of corruption, the colored shapes shifted and the temple grew warm and though the pious dared not restlessness, a haze settled in between the voice and the ears, and the dust in the light was a sleepy smoke, a nodding breath as that same eternal time bore on.

And then He said:

You, the priested people of his holy will, must be worthy. And I closed my eyes and heard his voice of that August afternoon.

You, you must be clean.

*So I will wed you.*

God turns away from those unworthy.

*And you will be raised up by this union.*

The heavenly father will not speak into the prophecy of an unclean people.

And I entered into his voice, as he had entered me, and I could feel the muscles of the voice gripping me, resisting me, until I was back on that long limp home, walking out the western field to the crick, taking off my shoes, standing in the cool water, staring at my naked white feet among the dark smooth stones that shone like eyes.

You must cleanse yourselves of those among you who have wavered in their obedience to God's will.

And I was lifting my dress, a dried dripping of blood on one thigh.

The revelation says that people that turn away from our great law will be destroyed.

Another kind of wetness too, white and eggy.

Our Saint tells us to atone with blood.

And I cupped the cool clean water, and the edges of my dress fell into the crick as I first poured, then brushed the coolness over my legs, afraid to touch the center of the pain until finally I felt a hot wetness from within, from behind my throat and eyes and also from where he had been and I pulled my dress all the way up.

Only through our laws can life continue forever, and increase.

And I lowered my hinds on the quiet stones so to let the water run through me, to let it carry away all that God had seen fit for me, to dilute my blood into the crick's unfeeling passage.

These are the words that were revealed to me as I slept, the words that I as His servant must reveal to you.

And as I was cleansed again, I pulled out of his voice and the crick and I opened my eyes in House as the Prophet began to speak not as himself but as God:

Now be ready and awake and not unto your earthly body, as I

am Jehovah and the Great I AM. I am the darkness and the light, the beginning and the end, and when the evil snake of the world finally consumes itself, I will make rise again your blood, and skin, and hair and remake you in death what you were at your finest in life. But only if you obey me, and obey my laws, and my servant your Prophet. Men, you must pray and pave your path to the Celestial. Women, you must bear the children, the fruit of our eternal tree. Questioning your Prophet, or being tempted by the evils of their world—their frivolity, their lust—mark you as unworthy. For I shall make rise only a people who are cleansed and anointed of all that is unholy, and who have taken the blood of all who have sinned as atonement for the blood I shed in that, my first earthly time. Now, go and be faithful as my servant your Prophet guides you to everlasting life, and be aware of the Devil working among you and within you.

And I felt Levi next to me, his flesh shifting slightly around his still bones. And the Prophet looked down, signaling to his people that he would no longer speak for God when he spoke again.

Our Heavenly Father has been clear. We must not rejoice until we are saved. And he disappeared through his door. And there were no songs as He had not ordered them. And the choir looked helpless, their hands still poised on open hymn pages. And the people looked around, and opened and closed their mouths, their tongues afraid of their own words as the call for blood, *Our Saint tells us to atone with blood*, lay wet within all ears like a fresh coat of paint. And the faithful obediently filed out into the desert winter of the world not yet eternally theirs.

And I walked in the sun on the road with the many but did not go home.

I went to the crick. I took off my shoes, and my dress, and everything and I lay quiet in the winter water so cold it made my back skin forget his voice while my front skin rose above the surface like a long white woman stone of one who once was alive but now lay waiting quietly for the time when that redeemer would come, and blood and breath deliver her to a world unmediated by men.

*Some things are always already over.*

*I watch little Manti start a fire, light up the woodpile stacked against the back corner of that holy house. His face a look of serious glee and giddy and after the pile has caught, has momentum, is brightening, he scampers away like a spirit, back into the fields. Back near the creek where he stops beside it and waits for his breath to even, his heart to let up its patter.*

*He rubs his hands cold in the creek water. Rubs off imaginary soot.*

*Does not look in the sky behind him for the veins of smoke.*

*Only breathes and says Just one thing right.*

*Just one thing right, just one thing right old Daddy.*

# Mercy Ann

After my father went to prison and not just jail, I got my own chair, and as it seems I'm not going anywhere for a while, Estelle asks me the questions she didn't before. She asks me about the community, only she calls it a commune like it's something different than is everywhere else and I know better than anyone else that it is, but I wish she wouldn't call it that.

One night, when we are done with the TV dinners and *Married with Children* comes on, which Estelle hates because she thinks Al Bundy is the ugliest man she's ever seen and what are they putting him on TV for, she says, if I wanted to see people like that, I'd just go down to State Street, so she turns off the TV. Stan makes a noise like a snort and gets out of his chair, saying no need to go ruining it for everyone else and he goes off somewhere and Estelle and I stare at the TV for a minute like it's still on.

Then she says, Tell me more about your family. It's funny she doesn't know that yet, but she told me when they gave me to her that they'd told her not to ask about my past, to focus on a future. She'd said this my first week and then paused, and said Of course you can tell me anything you want, though. But I didn't. But now I say I got two sisters and four brothers.

And she says that's it? Like she's been ripped off and turns from the TV to me. Well, those are the ones by my same mother. She waits longer and I pick at the plastic on the TV dinner box.

By my same father, it's a lot, he's got two other wives, and the oldest of them has twelve children.

Estelle shakes her head and clucks her tongue like she does when she reads something in the paper that she thinks is "A real shame."

I don't know what to do so I get up and take my TV dinner box, and Estelle's box, and Stan's which he left on the floor by his chair and I go into the kitchen and put them in the new trash compactor and shut it and push a button and listen to the sound of the plastic getting crushed.

But now that she's asked one question, the rest start coming, sometimes even during commercials. What are your sisters' names? And I think of Bess and Ziona and how strange their names are really, when even if I say the words out loud for the first time in months, nothing is really said about them that feels real. But I say the sounds and don't hear them answering me back but instead I hear Estelle asking me what they are like, if they look like me.

So I tell her, I tell her they are older. I tell her Bess is not someone to get in the way of, but now is married and Ziona is by far the smartest of us all, even the boys.

I never told anyone about my family before, because no one who didn't already know ever asked me. I don't like it. I wished I could say I don't want to talk about it, but I don't know what would happen to Estelle's face if I said that. Stan never stays in the room to listen and when we are done I get into my bed and dream about what I feel I never should have said. Like the color of everybody's hair was some sacred secret belonging to I don't know who.

It's hard to go from then to now and back, even if it's just talk. Here, I got school to go to, and I got homework, and no kitchen work really. And I got to figure out which are the nice kids and which are the not nice kids and it's not like home, where there are families of kids, but it is like home, the way the kids still group up even though not by brother or sister or mother but by things they like or something I don't quite understand, and since I don't even know how to play tennis, I am an outsider through and through but then there are other outsiders, so you never go an entire day by yourself, anyway.

The thing about Estelle is that she's trying to get me to say something. I'm not sure what, but I can tell that some of my answers are not what she is looking for. It's like she wants me to take a stand or something, and these little conversations after a few weeks really make me wish they'd cancel Al Bundy's show and put on something Estelle likes, so we can go back to just watching all together. It doesn't help that Redfield is in the news all the time since my father was convicted, and that everyday there is some *Polygamist Community Under Investigation* headline and it seems they want to prove the Prophet doesn't treat kids right. I start to dread when the TV goes off and Stan grunts and leaves the room, and I sort of feel angry at him, especially because I tried to follow him once, and Estelle said Mercy Ann, stay and chat a while, so I had to sit back down.

I start to feel like the condo and its green shag carpet and butter color walls is too small, like a sweater you're growing out of, itchy.

And then one night Estelle asks a question that she will later refer to as "the wrong button," which I'm not sure I understand.

She asks me if I believe in that Church still. She says it while a commercial for missionaries in Africa is on TV and they are showing tiny children with bellies like they are pregnant and asking for money to feed them. I watch the whites of the eyes in the black faces for a moment and pretend not to hear her. Then she starts to ask again and I surprise myself by saying, I heard you.

I feel my face go all sun burnt then turn to see if Estelle is mad, but she's not, she is just looking at me, waiting for me to go on.

I don't know what to say. No one ever asked me if I believed it because it wasn't like other beliefs they talk about outside, like Stan's politics, it was just the way we lived.

Estelle puts it this way then, as if she's trying to help me, she says, Do you wish you could go back Mercy Ann?

And this is when I get up and walk away. I don't even pick up the TV dinners, I just walk out of the room and down the hall to my little bedroom and I imagine when I open the door I will be doing just that, going back. I will open the door and see the big fields, and the chestnut tree we played under, the road down to Old Ephraim's place, and all his legendary twenty-two wives and past that the House, and Levi's house, and then the Prophet's house; it will smell like sweating sage and then I'll walk into our house and it will smell like bread. All yeastlike.

I don't see my trundle bed, and the card table set up for me as a desk, and the Mickey Mouse lamp Estelle found at a garage sale and bargained down to eight dollars. I don't see the world as made of two entirely separate places and if I did, if I could see the way things got divided so completely, with nothing between then and now, then I would understand, and believe, and even tell Estelle, that there is such a thing as heaven and hell and as far as I can tell you are either in one place or the other.

*I heard the Prophet thinking again about the basketball, heard him think about the unsmooth rubber, color of old blood, gripping into the hands.*

*When he is finally listening, I tell him about the dry, dry desert, how it will creep into his ill heart until the sand sticks to his slippery arteries. How it will kill him. How I will go on and on talking like this until it's over, until there is nothing left to sow the seeds of my already-done death and I will tell him that no one who ever means evil is good at it.*

*Your heart is black, I will say. And when the time is right, I will tell him to punish himself. Tell him to atone for his sins.*

*You can hear the future, I tell him.*

*Just listen harder.*

# Jeremiah

None of the many possibilities the boys had talked about that night, the night that Duke began to refer to as "the night Jer went all gangsta on Jimmy" ever came to be. Probably because the one possibility they hadn't talked about happening was nothing. And that's what happened. Nothing. Jimmy stayed away for a week and then showed up like nothing happened. He patted Jeremiah on the back in the kitchen and said he was sorry things got a little crazy. Booze, he said, booze and shook his head back and forth. Jeremiah stared back at him and then just nodded. He didn't retreat to his room, just kept his distance.

That first night Jimmy didn't disappear with anyone. He didn't even stay that late. But the whole time he was there Jeremiah felt like a dog, edging one of Haley's perfect compassed circles, always keeping a full diameter away from Jimmy, hack up.

After he knew he wasn't maybe leaving just yet after all, time moved faster. The days were shorter and colder now. One of the other boys from the Home, Taylor, helped him get a job where he worked. Pizza Hut. He filled out the application for him and put down "refugee" under work history. Trust me, he said, this lady hired me because I was homeless. He told the manager that a "lost boy" needed help, and the manager, a thirty-something woman with a round body and bleached-out hair interviewed him. He was soon working five nights a week, putting pizzas in and pulling them out of the hot ovens. Shimmying them into boxes. Closing them and folding the corners. Trying to smile.

He went to school with Duke when he could. He still had his visitor's pass and if he went in the sidedoor so he didn't 'have to walk past the office, no one seemed to notice. He talked to Haley more. He invited her to come see him at work. He gave her a free pizza. Pepperoni that someone had ordered but never came to pick up. He had kept it warm for three hours under the lamp hoping she'd come. Finally, she did, and smiled and made him laugh and touched his shoulder when she left.

Duke helped him buzzcut his head, like his own. Jeremiah didn't know if it was the pizza or the hair, but the next time he saw Haley in the halls, she invited him over to her house after school. She only lived a couple of blocks from the school, in a mustard brick house, stout and long like all the other houses on the street. He met her mom. Her mom was young and had a nose ring. She poured him a Diet Coke into a glass with ice and wanted to know *everything* about Redfield. Haley had to pull him away while her mom still fired off questions. She pulled him to her basement bedroom that had pink walls with black posters of different bands.

Down, there, *she* kissed him. *She* stuck her hand down the front of his pants. *She* pulled off his shirt. Not just that first time but then almost every day after school, they went to her house unless Jeremiah, Jer as she called him, had to be at work early. She always started it. At least for the first month, until she made him feel an ache, a want, that seemed to soak through from the back of his mouth into his brain and that would start as soon as they walked into her house and he smelled its smell, a sweet, lemony smell. It was a pull and an ache and a need and it was all the time right alongside a guilt or something like a guilt. Part of his brain, the Pa part maybe, still spoke to him and told him this girl was bad. She was it. The wickedness. *The harlots of their world*, the Prophet had said. This meant then that he was bad for being with her, but that made the want part of his brain even louder.

Sometimes as they kissed and petted he had to push away just to get a breath and when he did it was the kind of breath you take if you've been underwater.

Then without meaning to, he got used to it.

He got used to that part of himself that was like a shadow slipping up under his skin. The bad part. The himself that lived out here in the place only the Wicked lived. On his way to hell, he could do these bad things. Should do them. While they heard her mom move around upstairs they could fool around, pressing their hands into each other, rubbing, grabbing, tugging, fingering until they came and he could breathe the whole time and the Pa voice was still there but somehow now he could ignore it.

It was a coldness that let him do it.

But not an indifference, more of a removal. A distance. Like it was someone else that would open his eyes when Haley came and watch her face close up and then release open, her jaw going slack, her mouth making a soft yes. He would think of this face as the mask of her desire and he knew no woman wore it where he came from. No righteous woman.

Even Emma, erring as she was, as they were, had lain with her eyes closed and face still, a sweet smile on her face like it was a holy gift she was receiving instead of his quick thrusts.

He didn't like to think of her.

Haley never talked about love. Or being in love. Or marriage. Or any context for what they did that would make it right. Sometimes in his coldness he looked at her and thought *Slut*. Because, he thought, she always just wanted it.

Until she didn't.

*I watched Annalue by the creek. After House, I watched her try to clean herself of him again in water not yet muddy from the rain. This was only the second time. After this, when she saw Him, crossing the road, standing on the porch talking to her father, she again started to squirm. Like she had an itch. She'd wash her hands, again and again, scratching her skin raw. I'd watch her wipe her hands again and again until finally she'd slip away for a bath, the water so hot it scalded her skin red, and only then would her body release back into its natural state.*

*But this time, the second time, was more ceremonial. A deep exhalation, like she hoped it would be a closing parenthetical to what had happened. A baptism of its own. I watched her and I watched little Manti watch her. It was in the time people left the House and his mother said for him to go since she knew He would be coming. Even after the fire, the day after the fire, he would come? He gritted his teeth and left, wandered far up the creek where usually it was quiet. Where he'd washed his hands after he lit the fire. He watched her figure approach on the other side, just upstream. He knew her, her limp gave her away even before he saw her face. When he did see her face he moved back into the bushes before she saw him. He had left Peapod sleeping in her bed. But he didn't leave, instead he crouched and watched her and sucked a knuckle and when she took off her clothes he looked good and hard at that leg. He saw what I saw, that it was a little bluish and thin, but regular otherwise. She lowered herself down into the cold water and Manti raised his shoulders to his ears. She sat her body down slowly into the water and then lay all the way down like she was dead. I watched as he noticed her dress on the bank and shifted forward in his weight a little.*

*Was he thinking about taking it? Or of jumping in to save her from the icy water? Or of pushing her shoulders down softly until her blue blue eyes opened wide and forever? And did he see three ghostly versions of himself do all of these things? In the end he did not move, but watched her stillness until finally he just quietly crouched to the down-creek water and cupped the cool that had run over her skin, held it dripping, dripping her, to his mouth and drank. Then he wiped his hand on his pant leg and squinted at her figure, still as stone whispering so that only I could hear.*

He's afraid of you, and afraid of me.

*Then he crept back, into the willows, up the sandy path, through the fields and into Josiah's barn just before it started to rain.*

*She stayed until she was much too cold. She got out shaking, but her face held a peace that I knew wouldn't last. I knew that she was already getting back in as soon as she was getting out into the cool air. Was beginning to know her own circle, the one she had stepped into that August day.*

*Jeremiah*

The dull, the ache became something brighter, sharper after they had sex for the first time. In a motel room before the Valentine's Dance. They drank warm vodka because the ice machine was broken and he didn't ask her if it was her first time and he knew she thought it was his. Still, he looked in her eyes the whole time and after she lay on his chest and traced letters on his skin with her fingertip for him to guess, spelling words. *V-a-l-e-n-t-i-n-e*, he said the letters back to her and let her sound the word. Do another, he told her.

*P-o-o-d-l-e*. For no reason, she said, only the first had been too obvious. They lay there until they almost missed the dance.

After that he wanted to see her every day, *had* to see her every day.

And the cold part of him went away and she made him feel good. Not lonely but whole. With his paychecks from Pizza Hut he bought her things from the drugstore next door to Pizza Hut. Like a stuffed bear holding a shiny red heart. Like a pair of bird earrings.

This all looked to him like love. Being *in* love. Though that whole story was relatively new to him. He'd only seen a few of the movies where people fall in love. It wasn't a word people used much back home. Not like "I love you," and "you love," but rather *God's love*. Always through Him first. But not with Haley. With Haley is was just the two of them and that was the most all right he'd been since he left.

He was in school officially now too, thanks to Haley's mom. He stayed most nights at Haley's. Her dad wasn't, as Haley's mom put it, "in the picture," and her mom didn't seem to care as long as he paid her in stories.

He had to tell her something about Redfield every day.

After they talked in the kitchen, each sipping Diet Cokes, Jeremiah would sneak downstairs to where Haley was but before he was even out of the room he could hear her mom dialing the phone. She always told her sister what he said.

He told her mostly mundane things, like about school there. *Mostly priesthood history. No geography. Girls and boys separate after age ten, if they stay in school. If not, they work.*

Or about marriages. *The Prophet performs them, mostly in his own house. He chooses who marries who.* It was an arrangement more than an event.

Never the stuff that mattered. *Everybody helps each other out. I can never go back. I had my own horse and sometimes I wonder who takes care of him now. I left, so I will burn in hell for eternity. According to them, to everyone.*

She did ask him one day—when she was out of Diet Coke and he'd reluctantly accepted a Fresca, which Haley said tasted like cancer when he later went down to her room with the can still three quarters full and warm—if he had always known that he would someday leave.

No, he answered quickly, too quick, he realized by the way Haley's mom paused in opening her own can of Fresca and raised her penciled eyebrows. *I used to imagine having my father's land, I used to sit in Sunday House and pick out my wives.*

Well, then when did you know? What did it?

*I knew when I saw Emma's Pa standing there in that field. I thought, this is the end, and walked right up to it.* He took a sip of his Fresca, even though he didn't really like it. It was still cold. *But no, it must have been before that, before Emma. It was everything. The Prophet. The changes.*

Easter, he said.

Easter? Which Easter?

When He cancelled it, a few years back.

Who? Prophet Ellis? He cancelled Easter? How could he do that?

The Prophet can do anything he wants, and technically it warn't him that done it, but God. It was too hedonistic, he said. Too idolatrous.

The bunny? Haley's mom had her elbows on the kitchen counter and was leaned forward towards him, her eyes big. *Why does she find this so interesting?*

The bunny, the eggs. Too praising of ourselves in Jesus' resurrection or something like that.

Did you really dye eggs before that?

Yeah, Jeremiah laughed, With beet juice and spinach juice and raspberries, things like that, I think. The women always made the bowls of dye and then all the kids, we'd get to dip and roll and bathe the eggs in it. They were so pretty, the eggs. They would hide them in the small town park. Always a raven or two would be squawking in the cottonwoods overhead, waiting for us to leave one. And it was always a nice day, not too hot, and we had House late, so we could get the eggs first and then after House there was always a big meal and some special treat, homemade caramel or fudge or sometimes both. And then all that was gone.

So, the Easter lover in you said enough is enough? Haley's mom stood up and laughed loudly before she caught herself and brought her body back down onto the counter, posing herself like a teenager, a confidante. I mean, seriously, though, she said, That's sad. Why did he do it?

Jeremiah shrugged, Prophet Aldridge Ellis died and his meanest son took over and a few years later he said on the Sunday before Easter that God did not like our festivities in light of his Son's suffering. That we were to pray in the quiet spirit of forgiveness that Easter and that was that.

And no one argued?

You can't argue with God.

Haley's mom nodded.

But that was just the beginning. Then it was the holidays. Basketball. Children's books, even ones about the Bible. All of it was banned. *But it warn't even that, really. That was part of it, yeah, but it wasn't what the*

*Prophet said but the way they obeyed him. Even big men, even Pa, had ignored his wives' pleas and went through the house with a trash bag, collecting puzzles and books, Pa prying one with a torn cover about Noah and his animals out of my own hands when I was eleven. Removing my fingers one by one from my grip on the book, open to the best picture, one where the ark sailed under a rainbow with all the animals on board. Prying so it hurt and I cried out at Pa and when Pa finally yanked it from me, ripping the rainbow in half, I threw the rest of the thin books in the room at him and he just stood there, hands at his side, while pages flapped like broken birds in the air. Pa just stood there and waited for me to calm down. But I never really did.*

Geez, that's extreme.

I know. That's why I'm never going back, Jeremiah said and took another drink of his soda, *a swig, Duke would say.* This time he made a face.

Another day Haley's mom tried to explain to him the legality of the situation, how they should get him fixed up with an "emancipation" as a minor so he'd have rights. She worked in a law office as a paralegal and had already talked to her boss about it. He liked this idea. But he didn't like it when she talked about his world back to him. She started to scoff at the fact that his Pa hadn't given him any money, had not even driven him all the way to town.

Sometimes she went so far as to bring up his mother. How could she do this? She'd ask and shake her head. If someone took Haley away and said she'd never come back . . . I'd never let them . . . and she'd trail off, never sensing the cool shadow that Jeremiah felt slipping back into him when she said something like that.

First, he wanted to say, Of course you wouldn't, you don't live there. But he never did. He knew she'd argue that it didn't matter where she lived but that was the one thing the Wicked, as he called them without always meaning to, always got wrong. That it'd be so different. That they'd never do the things his people did, no matter if they'd been born where he was or not.

And he knew they were wrong about that. If they heard the story, about the Celestial kingdom, where man is God. His own king.

Second, he wanted to say, none of the things that you think or see or do here mean the same as they do there. *You wouldn't let Haley be taken away, because it wouldn't mean anything for you to fight for her.*

For his mother, it meant everything.

Not just her other children. Her home. Her safety. But on top of that a golden stairway. One that was so shining and magnificent and they'd heard about so much that Jeremiah was sure that not even Haley's mom could refuse it.

Not even if they took Haley away.

Which no one ever would, because the rules were different here anyway.

*But what of the Prophet? Did He feel when He saw her sitting in his congregation again? He did not see her, no doubt, as often as she saw Him. But He did see her. Get up from her chair that day. He saw her limp down the aisle to the door, her blonde braid swinging, saw her presence after an absence, as it was His job to notice these tokens of impiety with everyone. But especially that one. That one had plagued him since she was born and then more and more as she got older. He bit the corner of His lip ever so slightly, a twitch almost no one would notice but that I could see meant He was thinking.*

*Thinking like He'd done the night after He took her, said He'd marry her, meant to marry her, but then did and didn't. Meant to but stopped. Something had frightened Him in that ghostly flesh. Disgusted Him, maybe. He'd meant to get her up and send for a witness and her Pa to make it official. He had already spoken to his third and favored wife about her, and the quiet threat she clearly was, and his plan to subdue her and make her a regular wife. But then he hadn't and that very night after he'd let her walk out the door—that night he had wavered, had let her walk out, had kicked at her undergarments until He finally bent down, picked them up, and put them in His pocket, that night when his third wife lay asleep unworried beside Him —He deigned to speak to God.*

*He reminded God that He had meant to kill her when He became Prophet. He remembered aloud to the darkness and me that when she was born with a blue twisted limb they tried to straighten it by binding it to a board, but it would not take, and her Pa had looked to His father, then Prophet, and His father had said, Let this child be and then He had known that His father was too weak. He knew, He told God, that they hadn't built a Great Peoples in the desert by being weak, by allowing this clear sign of witchery to thrive just because it was attached to a baby girl. He had vowed He would cut her down and when He came to power He watched her. Watched her for five years. He was not surprised when she became beautiful, a creature of the Devil would embody temptation, but He was surprised how much harder He found it to hear God on the subject of her. He asked God, why didn't I hear you? I did not hear you tell me to kill her. And He knew He had to be sure on that point, to kill a young woman was different than a babe. So He just watched her and in fact didn't hear God at all on this (Why?) until He had the dream when He was doing to her exactly as He did that day in His parlor and so had woken up that very morning and had sent for her Pa to speak to him about it and then later that day, the dream image so fresh to Him, had sent his son to fetch her, and readied Himself for a new wife as He always did. I had watched Him clipping all the hair on His body, even in His nose and ears, and He told God in the darkness how He had felt completely sure even as He entered into her. Felt sure until He stood up and saw the leg there before Him, saw closer than ever before what He had not dealt with. His own weakness. He gaped and saw that weakness grow only stronger as she walked out the door. Now that He remembered, He told God, He could have sworn she did not limp as she left. He had thought He would conquer the Devil in her leg by bringing her into His house, thought the dream would answer itself, but instead he knew it was the Devil that had spoken in dream, not God, knew by the look in her eye.*

*He had lost.*

*So that night after she came back to House, He tried to speak again to God. He tried to ask His forgiveness. He asked God for a plan. He knew he could send for her, He knew it was careless to do what He had done and to not bring her into His house. She had a father after all and her father, along with that Josiah, were not entirely without power. If He did, He could keep her close, He wouldn't have to touch her again, it would mean she would be there, among his most pious, and He could tell the Devil to submit daily. Now with His third wife snoring behind him, used to these conversations as she was, He asked for confirmation from the whitewashed ceiling above His head, from the moonless night outside the window.*

*Was God silent on this subject? What was the later dream of the orange mountains? Did I whisper, Let her go, Let her be? Did He also feel to wash Himself the next time He saw her at House, after He watched her limp away from Him? Him on His pulpit, wavering ever so briefly in the world of words He lived and heard and spoke for God, wavering so that His people looked up from their folded hands in brief surprise.*

# Jeremiah

She wanted him until she sometimes didn't. He didn't remember the first time, or if he thought anything of it. But when it started to be a few days, a few days that he would show up, drink his Diet Coke, go downstairs and get a "I'm trying to read," or "Not, now, Jer, Jesus, not now," he noticed. He would back away a little, play with the small troll figures on her shelf, but it was never long before he was back, pulling her hair, trying to tickle her. Once it worked, she laughed and rolled over onto her back, and let him kiss her. But eventually she'd kick him out, say Don't you have anyplace else to be?

Even though she knew he didn't.

She started to change, too. Her hair, her clothes. Darker. Black fingernails. And then one day black hair, the color of raven feathers. When Jeremiah saw this that voice, that old voice spoke up inside him again. *She is wicked.* Still, he told her he liked it even though he didn't.

When he went to school, less and less now that the weather was getting a little warm again, winter waning, he saw her hanging out with kids that had black hair too and didn't say hi to him. A couple of guys in black jeans and T-shirts and piercings all over their faces. She didn't carry her backpack with the smiley face anymore. He would see her laughing with them and then she'd see him and her smile would disappear.

But she always came over to him.

He never approached them. They looked mean. Like they wouldn't care where he was from or who he was.

She came over to him and was kind at school. She let him put his arms around her waist and kiss her neck.

Until one day, not even that. She squirmed away.

What? He threw his arms up in the air. What's wrong with you?

She said she needed a break, she told him not come to her house for a while.

She said this in front of the school building. She had to go back in for class. She said this and then went to hug him, and he pushed her away.

Whatever, dick. Is what she said and then she disappeared into the building. Jeremiah didn't know if he was angry. He wanted to break something or kick something or hurt something but he wasn't sure that it was anger behind it. Confusion maybe.

*What did I do?*

*He told me he had a dog once, even though dogs were not abided, he said, and the dog would meet him in the creek brush and he would feed it scraps of hide and bone until the dog, who had honeycomb eyes he said, allowed him to put his hand atop his matted head and so became his.*

*He told me this in the dark, how the Prophet watched him one day while he cooed the dog and that the dog suddenly growled and bristled and he looked up and the Prophet was there, watching, from nowhere, like a true body to some God. That day was the closest he came to believing that that man had some kinship with the Celestial.*

*But the next day, he unbelieved again because he came to the soft bank where his dog would find him and instead he found his dog, throat slit, heart cut out. He put his hand atop his fur-matted head again. The honeycomb eyes were dull and blood teared down into the water, so it was as if the dying had the same sound as the creek.*

*He told me he wondered what He had done with the heart, he thought maybe He'd taken it back to his house, still warm and wet in His hand, heavy. He thought maybe He'd taken a knife and cut a flap of His own skin and pressed the heart in below His own ribs, under His own heart, and as he told me this in the dark he traced a line on my ribs with his finger, a stuttered line where the cut might be. He told me he thought that maybe his dog's heart was inside the Prophet, so that He had two hearts, one beating, one still, but both listening.*

# Jeremiah

After Haley said she needed a break, Jeremiah left the school and walked back to the Home. The house was empty when he got there but he kicked his bedroom door closed anyway and left a caved-in spot on one of its cheap panels. He lay on his bed and thought he might cry but didn't. He could taste the salt of crying but there were no tears. What would he cry for anyway? *Slut.*

He'd already lost family, home, horse. So what was she? Besides she'd be back. She just said a break. A pause. A moment. *Slut. Bitch.*

And why? He sat up and punched his pillow. Again, and again. For a long time he let rhythmic blows hit the pillow. It didn't react. No feathers, nothing. Finally he gave up, put his head into the well he'd punched and fell asleep.

Duke came in sometime later, it was almost dark.

Whoa, Dude, I didn't know you were in here. Dude, what's wrong, your face is all . . . are you okay?

Jeremiah told him: Haley said she'd needed a break. What does that even mean? He asked Duke. When girls say that?

Oh man, hold on, and Duke reached into his backpack and he pulled out a pint of Jack Daniels.

First, it means you should have some of this. He twisted open the plastic cap and handed it to him.

It burned in Jeremiah's mouth and he had to cough a little. That's strong, he said. Tastes like gasoline.

'Cause you've drank gasoline?

*No, but I've tasted it.* He'd left the gas can cap only loosely screwed on once, in the back of his father's truck on their way back from town. They drove over a pothole and gas sloshed onto a box of peaches. They rinsed them well but some of the peaches still smelled like gas. And tasted like it. He knew because his Pa had made him eat all the spoiled ones, *Lest you forget again.* It took him over a week. He never ate a peach again. The sweet yellow flesh still burned his throat even the next summer.

He didn't tell any of this to Duke, who was now saying not to worry: Girls get moody, they be one way one day, and the next day all over you like nothing happened. Just wait, you'll see. Just leave her alone and she'll come right back. Besides, man, you guys are like super intense. As a couple. You guys like practically live together.

Jeremiah nodded and took another drink from the bottle Duke held out. It was less hot than warm now. Medical.

Man, I've got something to show you. Make you forget all about her. Duke pulled his black backpack up on to the bed next to him and opened it. He pulled out a magazine and tossed it at Jeremiah. The woman on the cover had her head tossed back and her bare breasts jutted forward. She was on a beach and had nothing on, even on bottom. Her skin was the color of the butter caramels his Ma made every winter. The magazine paper was wet with shine and Jeremiah could hear the Prophet, *They will profane every possible thing, the wicked, and abuse even the act of procreation in their lust for obscenity.* He kept the magazine closed, but resting in his lap.

This, man, this is what I've been looking for. My girl. Duke pulled a bundle of dirty T-shirts out carefully, opened it, and laid the gun on his palms to show Jeremiah.

It's a nine-mil. Always wanted one. Then suddenly this week a guy I know was looking to get rid of one. His girl got knocked up and now she's tripping about having the gun in the apartment, so he says, and decides to sell it to me for cheap. Well, maybe not cheap. A good deal. You want to hold it?

Jeremiah nodded and Duke handed it to him. Careful, it's loaded.

It felt heavy in his hand. Maybe not heavy. Substantial. Like Haley's breast. But no, not at all. Just kind of filling in the same way. It felt, maybe, like the answer to a question he had never thought to ask.

He wagged his hand up and down to feel the weight of it. Shit, he said, that's cool. He handed the gun back to Duke.

Well, man, let's get drunk and forget that bitch of yours. Duke tucked the gun into his sagging jeans and handed him back the whiskey bottle.

It wasn't until a couple of days later that Jeremiah and Duke tried firing the thing. They went outside on the back patio, if you could call it that, of the Home and set up some empty beer cans. It was just past dark, and you could feel the way winter was starting to lighten up, the warmth of the day lingering. They'd been drunk for almost two straight days. The other boys had been pretty much ignoring them, with Taylor joining in last night but gone back to work tonight. He told Jeremiah he'd better do the same or there'd be no job to go back to and Jeremiah had said, Fucking, Boo. Hoo. No more pizza making.

Taylor had shrugged and left. Jeremiah felt something in him wanting to feel bad, bad for not working, bad for not doing better at a job Taylor had gotten him but it didn't quite get there, this bad feeling. And he forgot all about it when Duke suggested they try out Cinderella.

That's what Duke had named it, Cinderella. A rags-to-riches thing, he said but Jeremiah didn't know that story. Duke had been keeping it under his pillow at night in their room the past two nights and it seemed to Jeremiah like some sort of pulsing heart. He felt that everything in the room that one couldn't see seemed to tilt toward the small black shape, and Jeremiah always knew, even when he wasn't thinking about it, he was always aware of where it was. It reminded him a little of a story his grandfather had told him long ago. About a golden arm. The arm was buried with its owner, a woman, and then dug up by a poor man and taken home to his dark cabin where it shone, Jeremiah had imagined, like a small fire until the dead woman came looking for it. The kind of thing no one could really own. It always being part of another world, and that other world was always going to come looking for it, and maybe take you too.

But they set up beer cans on a turned-over garbage can and a few on sticks about twenty feet away. Jeremiah had shot with Pa maybe three times, but Duke never had.

Duke fired first, and Jeremiah couldn't believe how loud it was. With his Pa, they'd had bits of cotton in their ears.

Three quick shots. Duke kicked over a half-broken lawn chair after his third miss. I thought this was supposed to be fucking easier. He handed Jeremiah the gun, and shook his hand out. Thing kinda fucking hurts, Duke said.

Jeremiah held it and felt all that other, unseen world tilt toward *him*. This thing, its pulsing energy, reminded Jeremiah of the way the Prophet was to Redfield, you always knew where he was, could feel it. *Wonder if this is how he feels.* He held it up, letting the black extend his reach, he took a breath. A streetlight had come on behind him. He looked into the shadows of the scrap of yard just beyond the patio toward the cans stuck on sticks like marshmallows. He looked down the length of his arm, of the gun, like he was looking down the long road at home and for just a flicker he saw it.

Like a channel had changed and then changed back, he saw flash an image: The red road, Emma in a blue dress, a large belly, she turned to him and his breath drew sharp, a weight in his chest.

He fired.

Dude, that wasn't even close.

No, Jeremiah said. And he handed Duke the gun, looking at the small and lilting beer cans, the absence of the road. In the dark yard, a lit square where he'd seen the light of that other world still wavered on his retinas.

Not much later Duke finally hit a can and then Jeremiah hit one and was celebrating with the same little dance he'd watched Duke do when he turned and saw Jimmy standing in the back door. Arms folded.

*I could kill you right now, motherfucker, just a simple point. Click. Pow.* He let the gun fall at his side.

Put that away and come inside. Now. Jimmy's voice was gravelly. He turned and went inside.

Jeremiah looked at Duke, who nodded. Jeremiah handed him the gun and Duke put it in his pants, pulling his T-shirt over it.

Jimmy was sitting at the kitchen table, hands clasped in front of him. Cool. Sober.

Jeremiah didn't sit but stood. *You love this, love being the boss.*

There's no weapons allowed in this house, Jimmy said, and he pointed to a laminated poster taped to the kitchen wall behind him. "Rules for a Safe Space" it read in bright green marker. Right under No Drinking or Smoking and No Roughhousing was No Weapons.

You've broken the rules twice now, he said to Jeremiah. I'd say third strike you're out, but I think we are past that. Jimmy stood up. I'll be back next week. I better not see you.

He turned to Duke. You should know better. Get rid of that thing.

Jeremiah wanted to punch him. Grab him. Choke him. Wanted to yell, what about no fucking sicko touching? What about that fucking safe space? But he let the message travel from his brain to his mouth and muscles and then just sit there, echoing, twitching. His Pa would say: he's not worth it.

*But worth what? What do I have to lose? And it is worth it sometimes, isn't it? To have the last word? When someone is really wicked? Isn't that the least you can do?*

Duke put his hand on his shoulder after Jimmy walked out of the room. They heard the front door close.

Come on, man, Jimmy will chill, he knows what we got on him. Ain't nobody kicking nobody out. Not on my watch, and he lifted up his shirt to show the gun and grinned. Yeah, bitches, and he held up a hand for Jeremiah to slap. Am I right?

Yeah. Jeremiah nodded and hit Duke's hand; Duke clasped it and pulled him so that their chests were touching. That's my brother!

And it felt good, briefly. Even though he knew he would leave, it felt good to hear someone call him something besides his name.

# *Manti*

Murder. Blood. Fire. These are the words I know, words I know, words I know are bad in my head all the time now like fruckin birds flyin round.

It's the Devil, my bitch mother say when she hears me when I don't even know I talkin out loud but it ain't, it ain't, it ain't.

It's since the Prophet came to our house to do what he did when I wasn't there, except I was there. It's since then my heart burned until it made birds of fury and they cracked their shells in my chest and then my anger taught them how to fly. Then they flew up, up to my brain when I was sleepin and built a nest in my brain for me and my Daddy to see.

God Damn. Damn God. I hate God. Fruck him. Stops the bounce, kills my father, makes my mother's heart clay as corpse. And now she is seein a bloody girl. A ghost. It's the Devil, she says now.

The town will burn. I already burned one thing, His house.

Up, up, up

will go the smoke.

And the black car people will see the smoke and they will come again and won't just drive around like they're sightseein, but take everybody's father too and then no families will be pushin and pullin and laughin and fruckin scoldin after House.

And we'll be all right, Daddy, we'll be all right.

And still He came to her after the fire I started.

So the new and bigger fire'll spread fast in the yellow smellin grass and then up to the sandy old wood dry as bone and then everybody'll be sayin Fire. Murder. Fruck. Everybody will be saying these bad words.

The birds will fly from my brain straight into their fruckin pious mouths.

Then the black car people will be back, back, back for us, just like they came for the Browns. The women and children and me though I a man now, and I done things to prove it to other men. I make Levi mine with my mouth, and also I seen a girl naked. Swimmin. Nobody else here fruckin like me. No. Even though I was sorry when I watched the girl. I know He hurts her, too. But I wanted to see her leg.

Bounce.

But when the black cars come, they'll give Peapod and I to a new mother more like our old mother, the one who made corn biscuits. I hate my now mother. She smites me. She tells me now the Devil is in me fierce with my bad mouth and got to be beat out of me. She puts a spoon on the stove and heats it up then burns me with the hot smooth back of it when I swear. She puts it against my ribs where Jesus bled. Then she cries for the whole day like it was her that hurt.

Fruckin whore.

And once they take me away to someplace better, I am going to tell everyone bout the Prophet. Who he really is. I will save my little sister, too, because she dig a hole to find cold dirt then hold a fist of red soil to my skin and cool mother's burns. Love, she, to the bone and marrow.

Bow and Arrow.

I will save her from the old man with melting skin who I hate because he stopped the bounce but even more because he killed my Daddy and done what he do to my mother and I know he will marry my little sister off before she even not a baby. Not even bleeding down below yet. I know he will and do to her what he does to mother.

I burn at him.

Yes, I will get the whole town to burn next. It will make me happy like last time when I fruckin did it. I watched it burn and the birds in my brain flapped happy, their fish-egg eyes looking all over my insides for one thing not right, but everything was right.

But this time it will be the whole of it and Father, I will say, Lord Father I burned your world like it was my stomach and I a spoon. No cold black earth for you though, because you and your fruckin man shot my Daddy's mouth out while no one watched. You will just have to burn to the bow and the marrow, to the bone and the arrow.

And I and the birds will fly free.

# Jeremiah

So if he wasn't back out on the street already he would be soon. He would go back, went back, maybe. Back down south. Where it stayed at least half warm all year in the daylight. He would take his pillowcase, he took his pillowcase, filled with three extra shirts that Duke gave him and an LA Dodgers baseball cap Haley had given him months ago. His blade in his pocket.

He'd hitchhike back to Pine Mesa. He had been aching for the red sand, the green valleys, the bone-colored plateaus. The giant sky. Maybe he'd get a job. Someone was always paying someone to do something for them out there, his Pa had told him once. Maybe he'd run fences. He'd stay a few weeks until he ran into someone. Pa, maybe. He had to run into someone sometime. Maybe Levi. Maybe Levi would see him, maybe Levi saw him as he moved through the town. Just passing through, he'd say. He'd say he'd never go back. Even though Levi would tell him how much everyone missed him. You couldn't *pay* me enough to go back. He'd hang out and wait and then get Levi to come back here with him. They could be in this wicked world together. *He* could show Levi the ropes. How to buy a bus ticket. How to get a job at Pizza Hut for a while. How to ask a girl for her phone number. How to call her and hang up and then call back. How to use a knife you found under the seat on the bus. How to really get that girl to be your girlfriend and really want you and you really want her.

How to get her back. That's what he'd do. He'd go away for a few weeks and she'd miss him and she and her mom would worry sick about him. That he was dead on the street, or in the desert somewhere, and then when he knocked back on the door she'd jump up on him, wrap her legs around him, tell him never to disappear again.

They could get a place together. He'd get that emancipation.

He'd just get away for a bit, head back down to the country he missed. He'd do something. He'd get back in good with them, good with Pa. Or he'd get someone out. He'd get someone who could speak the language of perdition to come with him. Just like Lucifer, the fallen like company.

They could travel back to *this* world together. He would be in charge, and he would soothe that someone.

He would say.

*It's not that place. It's never going to be that place again.*

*It's all over now.*

*Now you just get used to being lost.*

III

Emma felt the first pain at night and thought *Good Me what's all the fuss this really is none too bad* and even said so aloud in her solitary bed for me to hear. She, stubborn redhead, did not call for help for the first hours of the night. So I watched her sweat and smile and decide she could do this alone. She would come out of the bedroom at dawn with a sweet new baby and never again would they think her a child. She didn't think of the danger, only the pain, what was right before her.

And what help could they give her? They had only wet rags and hot bags of dried corn. But then the time came when she could not keep quiet, an animal sound erupted from her. A contraction came and our sweet Emma yelped, she jumped up, she tried to walk out of it like she was on hot coals, tried to run from the pain. Panicked, she ran straight into Lizbeth's round body coming in her door whose strong hands flipped her over, bent her over her bed and pressed her thumbs hard into the bottom of her back, the seat of the spine. Emma's yelp slowed to a whimper as the contraction passed but when the next one came she grabbed onto Lizbeth's arm and dug her fingers in, her eyes wild, until Lizbeth flipped her back over and again pressed the two points where her backbone met her pelvis until the pain turned into something else that didn't drown but just soaked. When that was over Lizbeth said *This baby is early, I'm going to go get help* by which she meant the Prophet's fifth wife, an easily forgotten number to be when wives six and seven came along, but she had learned to distinguish herself by practicing midwifery. But Emma screamed *No*, afraid of being left without Lizbeth's thumbs and so Cadence was called to move like a ghost through the night to get help that in the end was not needed. And I knew it wouldn't be as I could see then a little spirit like a puff of smoke start to collect over her body, waiting for its time. Its beginning right here in my end time.

The baby small but breathing. Crusted over in blood, boy. Here a boy, like extra change, would scatter. Cadence crying tears of joy, at seeing such a *miracle as this, she kept saying that word, miracle. Lizbeth cutting his cord with her kitchen scissors and smiling and wrapping him up.*

*Josiah now up, outside under the window, waiting to hear the first cry and out of superstition, as he had with all his other children, even the one that had died, as soon as he heard its tremor he praised God and picked up a rock for his dresser. This one was a purple-gray stone with chunks of white quartz.*

*The girl on the bloody bed, torn open and crying: the pain hadn't made her a woman but reminded herself she was a child, and the idea that this thing needed her now and would forever always was plenty to cry about.*

*And I burned at the way this would never be for me.*

*Annalue*

Emma survived that child's birth and when I went to see her, she saw me come in and rose up and sat like a queen holding that baby. And it was a little boy and I did not think of his fate but only his small breaths as she held him out for me to hold and I held him and first thing I reached under his bundle and I did squeeze each little foot and could feel their warmth, their untwisted perfection.

What a thing, to have a body born exactly as it should and Emma was talking about getting up and sewing some things for him out of old fabric, so bored was she with lying in, and I listened to the crick of her voice flow around these two little ears her body had made, perfect in what they had not yet heard. And I listened and wished for him the world would be a song never broken into words, but flowing always.

# Levi

I was good for the longest time after that night in the barn but there came a point when I had to get out of the square: the square of the field I was in each and every day since Pa had decided that work that breaks the back might keep me best out of trouble, the square of pen and barn and room I shared with two too-small brothers, the square in my head that was beginnin to edge into the roundness of my pupils and corner my eyes themselves so that I saw unbodied angles where there was none God intended.

I had to get out so I got out one night, took the car and left note 'cause if I did not I knew they would take me for real gone and grieve and then in the shock of seein me live again 'pon my return would probably kill me so as to keep the dignity of my after-grief.

I took the old Skylark and pushed it so quiet out from behind the barn and down road a bit and then I started her up and rolled out of town with no lights, off into the night in that car I'd driven since I was ten, natural as can be, and drove flat out for those miles of dust road flanked by desert and toward the only town nearby which is called Pine Mesa and which is where I had my first coffee and where I saw that ghost of manchild called Dead.

The sun was comin up and I woke in the car with face pressed on the cool morning wetglass of window and felt so relieved to see somethin other than curvature of my own pillow that I did not mind the crook of my neck pullin 'gainst itself with car slept ache.

I opened that car door and felt the cold desert and saw I parked in the lot of some bright good store with the word *Smith's* above it, and that a worker from there was tying a red apron over her black shirt and pants and lookin at me strange as she walked from her car to the shiny suckin doors of the place.

I thought about goin in but the way she looked at me like I was somethin other than what I was, which was a man on his own, made me decide I would just walk 'round on the streets for while outside, and watch the sun come up and shadow different buildings with the relief of new.

The main street only had a few bodies movin slowly 'bout it, and only two lit windows, one was a window full of pictures of houses for sale with all dark behind the display, and the other was a diner with people sittin in there drinkin from mugs and not talkin much. One man was eatin eggs, too. I stared in at them, wonderin what it was like to order your food, as they did at these establishments when I saw my breath obscurin the glass and as I went to wipe it off, someone opened the door and said, Well honey you going to come in or what? She was wearin a peach dress with white apron and was as old as Ma but was beautiful so I nodded my head even though I didn't have but four dollars in my pocket that I warn't even really supposed to have, but won in a bet with some boys, most of them gone now, maybe from stealing money from their mothers jars, and I went and smelled the warm sapped sweetness of a place like that, with red leather cushioned booths and tables with rounded corners and small sparklin flecks in their clean surfaces.

Sit anywhere you like, you strange little bird, said the waitress in her maple-voice that sounded scratchy and deep but was still somehow smooth so I took seat in the back, way from the window, not rememberin but not forgettin that I was still a fugitive in the temporary and that my Pa would be up by now, milkin in his hand teats not smooth but hot, waitin to walk around the barn and see the place where the car should be, or maybe first the tire tracks in grass-scabbed mud.

Maple-voice gave me a shiny menu then that you could spit on and still wipe clean and I read it like it was the newest Book, and was not even through the first half of three pages when she came back and said Well? When I didn't answer she asked me if at least I didn't want to start with some coffee and I nodded, made deaf and dumb by her and her sound.

She brought me the coffee and I kept readin, almost through to the section where the coffee and other beverages were and she set down a thick-rimmed mug the color of teeth.

Looks like you're still looking, sugar, but you let me know, she said and then walked away to chat with an old man who kept calling her "toots" loudly, so that that was all that anyone could hear of what they said but I didn't care; I was still feeding off *sugar*, her sayin it, like that, to me, in that voice.

I put down the menu and decided with none to no money I better stick with what I got, and so went to take a sip of that dark steaming water. It was hot and bitter and at once worked against what I thought 'bout it, thinkin it might be sweet, for some reason, but I drank that sip slow and natural, imaginin to look like I did it every morning. And I sat there like that, sippin slow and watchin Maple and the old men come in and out, talking about weather and news and singular wives with names that were at home and I sipped until I began to feel a little pulse, quick, in my head, behind my eyes, and my mouth started to feel coated with the sin of coffee and I highed it, but I highed it most when Maple came and sat down across from me and said, Now where you running away from honey?

I shrugged but couldn't help smile, and she slapped her red fingernails down on the table and said, Oh Lord Almighty we got the silent type right here in booth seven, maybe he's strong too, but he's not hungry. She laughed and slapped her red nails on the table when she said this so I laughed too but then she said, quieter, Or are you sugar? And when I didn't answer she said, I thought so, and slid out of the booth quick and easy and came back in a flash with bread, all buttered and toasted and cut into the shapes of folded handkerchiefs and double stacked, It's on the house she said, hate to see a silent type drinking coffee with no toast and she winked at me then and I knew I was in love and not so impotent that I did not say I do not have no money, but rather thank you.

I tasted the toast and its roughness and crystal butter crumbs and felt that I might truly be in some version of the Celeste. I knew back there, Pa was probably done milkin, and everybody else was already sweatin too with some kind of work, some expense of the body, back, hands, legs, eyes, these parts on them were already tired from carryin, hoein, diggin, tillin, feedin, waterin, pasturin, boilin, kneadin, churnin, seein. Only parts on them that wouldn't be tired were their ears, and my ears were tired, the fresh-breeded tired of horse just husbanded, full of all kinds of phrases but mostly *sugar* and *honey* and *Maple*.

When the sun was high nuf not to be coming anymore in windows, I asked Maple how much I owe her, and she said, If you got one dollar, then that will do just fine, so I pulled out my bills and gave her one of them and wanted to give her all of them but thought I might need the other three to put gas in the car in case the gallon in the trunk didn't hold up. I told her thank you and smiled my best smile, which is with my mouth closed 'cause my unpretty teeth, and stepped out into town where things were happenin.

Morning was full up and people were walkin fast, not a lot of them, but enough, they were calling out to each other and waving. There were cars waitin at the stop light and I wandered down a side street and wondered if people liked livin there, like that, and thought that I certainly would, I could go to breakfast every day and then wander around and say hi, maybe I could work at the *Smith's* place, and wear a black shirt, and stand around all day helpin people with different voices and faces buyin different things. Though now that people say end times are nigh, and with my own sins so recent, I am not like to go back to this diner life anytime soon.

But that day I was in the bellied dream of the beast, looking at the unreal of my surroundings, which seemed distilled by the coffee in my blood to colors possessed of something more than themselves, and my heart was beating fast, when I heard my name called in a place where no knew it.

Levi, I heard it again. And that's when I turned round and saw a Ghost. A ghost that looked like Jeremiah, with hair much shorter and skin darker and wearing not the black pants of us but baggy blue jeans with a T-shirt that said something I didn't read. But he was dead, not changed, Dead. The Ghost kept walkin toward me and even said Levi a third time bout the same time I said Dead, Ghost, get away from me, and turned to go towards where I'd been, the place where no one knew me.

But Jeremiah the Ghost followed me and I could hear his heavy feet behind me. Wait up, Levi, wait up, he said and I looked around to see if anybody else could hear him or see him and suddenly there was no one, so I glanced back and there he was walkin' after me, close to me, so I began to run, turning up a shadowed narrow street back up toward Main street, where I knew the livin be dwellin strong.

And that's when that Ghost did catch up to me, right as I came back into the sun of that sidewalk I had already been on, and that's when he near potato-sacked me tryin to get me to stop, and suddenly the Ghost was feverish, desperate, not how you thinkin the Dead, who have all of time and eternity, to really be. I said, but you're Dead. Prophet saw you in His vision, and you're Dead. And then he was talkin and talkin fast and as he held his arms around mine, leanin over me, I could smell animal in him and feel his warmth and stink against my back so I listened to him when he told me the story about how he warn't dead:

The Prophet, Levi, the Prophet lied. I ain't dead, just dropped. He didn't kill me and neither did anything else, not even God, yet.

And so I told him: The Prophet don't lie, his mouth holds the tongue of God which speaks in our language the truth of our times.

And when the end comes truly, I hope somebody remembers that I said that.

But Jeremiah said, Well he must a lied, 'cause here I am Levi, Levi here I am. He lied, Levi, he lied 'cause here I am. He tried I guess, Pa leaving me nowhere to die of anything but I wasn't ready, no I wasn't, so

I walked, walked, into the wilderness and wandered until I came here, and then I went other places, too.

I shook my head and told him no, no, pushin my arms out 'gainst his brace, when he finally let go me but kept hold my arm so as to give me Indian Burn. He twisted the skin of my forearm in counter motions like it was rope and I winced but did not scream because now people were watchin, and could see us both and this was in fact the same Indian burn that Jeremiah had done unto me since I a child so I understood as my skin twisted back on itself that whether it was true about the Prophet or not, it was true that this boy was not Dead, but Jeremiah changed over, unless maybe he was a ghost with a body, made corpse-real by the Devil.

Okay, I told him, Uncle, and he let my arm go all wrung and red with hands, and he put his hands in his pockets and said somethin quietly, he said Maybe the Prophet didn't kill me, but still he shouldn't said some-one was dead when they was alive, having hitched to Pine Mesa, trying to make by workin fences and saving to go back to the big city up north, where he said he already been if I believe him.

That's when I saw, sittin, rubbin his mouth, squintin into the sun, how dirty Jeremiah was, and a new kind of dirty, not the under-nails-sweat kind from field work, but somethin else, a more all over grime that seemed to be not just on top of his skin, but under it too, and I began to wonder what kind a life he lived now that he was not Dead and he must a saw me lookin at him 'cause then his face got bright and he put his big hands upon my shoulders to square me and he said, You're here Levi, and you run away and if you want to stay here with me, Levi, he said, you can. We'll have some fun, and we'll save better together, and then we can go to the city, where there are other boys too, we all help each other out. His thumbs squeezed against the bone of my collar and he said You ran away right? And he sat there waitin, smilin in a way that made me suddenly hate of myself and him, who didn't belong there among the wicked, but belonged somewhere else, where nobody lied and where my Pa sat in the corner at night and told soft tales of Moroni. So I said all quiet but stern, like I was talkin to a breaking-horse, No, I just visitin.

Jeremiah let me go with a little push then and laughed, covering his mouth, and shakin his body back and forth in a way that made me think he wasn't really laughin but tryin to get his body to do so before he stopped and said Look, Levi there ain't no visiting, you are either here or there and right now you are here with me.

And now when I think back on this moment I see Jeremiah with his dirty pale skin, and his weasely laugh and I think it was really the Devil there that I encountered that tried to buy me for one of his own.

But then it was Jeremiah I saw and I got mad then, 'cause I also saw the way Jeremiah was tryin to boss me still like we were little 'gain even though I fought him plenty and 'cause I still didn't know why the Prophet would name him Dead if he warn't so, I said, For all I know, you're a soot-souled Ghost I am crazy to listen to, even though I was quite sure he was not no Ghost and I could see it in that face of his, the way it hurt a little to think everybody think he Dead, even his mother Lizbeth and my sister Emma, so I quieted my voice then and told him I was goin back, even though I wouldn't a said it to myself ten minutes before, that's when I knew I had to and would.

I told him that and asked him then what in the world I was supposed to tell my sister Emma, and I asked him why he had not let anyone know he was not Dead.

Which is when I saw his shoulders crump a little and I thought maybe it was 'cause I had said Emma's name but then he said Well, I didn't know I was Dead. Then, That Prophet really would kill me if I told now, don't you see Levi?

And I saw that he was a pilgrim without ship as he said, Then I have to be out here without no one, and I was thinking I felt sad for him and was about to put hand on his shoulder and tell him that I would go back and make him live again for his people because I was feeling a bravery but soon as he saw some pity in my face, or maybe just because he was crazy he put his hands out and waved me away and then he began to laugh that same silent mouthy laugh, rockin his body back and forth 'gain.

Don't even worry about it, though, and don't get me wrong, little brother, I've had my good times. Real good times, not like back there, and I have learnt a lot, and I could teach you, boy could I teach you. Not just how to survive, but to have a little fun too, and then Jeremiah the undead put his arm around me and steered me down past the diner where I hoped Maple warn't watchin me yoked by the arm of a boy 'specially right then as I was blushin because Jeremiah asked me as I saw our reflections in the window I knew from behind, if I had ever gotten to any girl.

When I made no answer he laughed again from his mouth, a sound I did not like no more and I pulled his arm off my shoulders and started walkin 'gain, tellin him I got to be goin back.

I told him I was out for a trip, doing a favor for my Pa, and we both knew this last part warn't true so then I crossed my arms, wishin we were still in front of the diner now, and I said got no interest in becoming one them apostates, or even more like you.

Then Jeremiah smiled at me for the first time not mean-like and without that laugh and said only Oh, come on, you don't want to try it? I know girls prettier than Ellen Mai, he said, and easy, too, and I could even get you a beer if you want to try, and then you'll know what it feels like to be a man, not like our Pas, but a real cowboy.

And when he said this I felt like I had when Maple asked me if I wanted coffee, there was temptation in my face, different yes but maybe more smite-calling and so I understood that I was in fact in a place where the Devil could be anywhere, and he was in fact in front of me livin in Jeremiah and tryin to seduce me with the honeyed voice of promise, so I told him nah and so he asked me if I warn't afraid and punched my arm and so I told him to get on back to hell and started walkin backwards toward the *Smith's*.

Then Jeremiah said Oh little brother, hell don't mean a thing to me, and you can bet that that place you holding so high in your head will burn just as quick, everyone out here wants it gone 'cause it's so backwards. It will be gone maybe before you even get your yellowed soul back there, and believe me when it goes, it will smolder worse than hell itself. Jeremiah laughed 'gain and I began to think I was not afraid of him, I was bigger than I was when he died, having grown all winter by two inches, and it warn't the same as it was, and now I was angry for all he'd said.

I stopped walkin backwards then and told him to go away, get Dead again. You may be alive, but your soul is yoked by that Devil's ghost and his corporal pleasures, and he started laughin then and sayin, Don't you get it, Boy, the Devil ain't here, he's back where you going, he's running that place and then he paused and sucked his cheeks in before he said, but if you want to go back, suit yourself, just say hello to that harlot sister of you and yours.

So then I did what I maybe would not have done had I not started the mornin watchin Maple walk back and forth from the counter where she leaned, talkin, or to the tables where she put a hand on a hip and smiled, and I punched Jeremiah with the side of my fist which ached in the knuckles later but which buckled him over, surprised as he was, and which made a man run across the street toward me, yellin Hey Hey Now, and another woman and her dark-haired child stop and stare but that was all background because I was lookin at Jeremiah as the man and his plaid shirt came to stand between us and pushed back on Jeremiah who looked ready to hit back, and held him while he said, spittin on the man's shirt as he spoke, Levi, you be back, and when you are, we'll get back on this and then we'll have some fun because even if you go back, run back, coward, run back on down that road, you were here, and I saw you.

And so I turned and walked away, my hand shakin, still curled in its fist so I held it to steady it as I walked slowly down to *Smith's* trying to keep eyes dry and not yelp out the greater disappointment I felt: the thinking that the world was in fact so cruel as to resurrect a version of Jeremiah, who I never liked all that much, on the one day I was just trying to let some air in, trying to get some roundedness to the things I saw when I closed my eyes at night and felt the body so tired it would not even let the brain get to dreamin.

As I got in the car and drove back to the flat land of Zion, I was sad and angry also 'cause I didn't know what Jeremiah said that was right, but I knew it was somethin even though I warn't like him, and didn't want to be like him, but it was true that I had taken the car, and pushed it out oh so quiet and left. I had left the work that God had left for my hands to do and I had come into hell thinkin I was at the gates of heaven even though somewhere I always knew from the Book and from my gut that the land itself would not be any heaven in the end, nor would it be true hell, but rather the mediocre ground of cottoned-out mouths and suffering until a true change come, which may or may not be now but I hope it is not because I am afraid of hail and brimstone and also dogs.

And then I wished I could go back and tell that Maple who I really was, a follower and a believer and I wished that I could rewrite the note I left that mornin that said "I am not Dead, just Out, back later" because now I knew Dead was some other person to be and if you were that you were alive in un-hell and if you warn't you were runnin back to a place you didn't know anything outside of, really, or maybe really dead, not knowing it, and going home. And when on the road the farms turned desert, it was high sun time and so I knew that the work would still be there for me, and I would be left out to work into the night, with no one else nigh.

Indeed it was and I did, work, with the first star out and I did replay everything Maple-voice said to me and tried to cleanse the part about Jeremiah and I imagined that everything would be okay as long as it was Alive that I was and am, and that comin back, havin gone, had not rendered me Dead for writin my state of not bein it.

Though I also knew, muckin at dusk time, that knowin this thing bout Jeremiah, that he was alive, and that the Prophet was the first one to call the livin Dead, would save me somehow in a way that was like the world I'd just left, strange and full of real angles of light and other. I didn't know how to place it other than to imagine myself bearing a gift like I was some wiseman, holdin out until I had finished my work time and my Pa had finished his silence and was ready for belt-back father-son speech and then I would look at him a way and he would know I have somethin for him, brought somethin back.

And I did and he did listen bout Jeremiah not bein dead and about what he said about why the Prophet say him so and he looked up past me, and slipped the end of his belt back into the loop doubling it over so the leather was two layered thick, fittin, and then he nodded and left. He left to go think, or confer, 'cause he and Josiah were building somethin, I didn't know what at the time but maybe an ark of some sort. One that curved and sailed and winded away from the Prophet and one that I hope now may lead us all into a better promise for those shinin rays that come to lift us once this land becomes frostbitten again. And hearin with witnessed certainty that the Prophet had lied on behalf of God was somethin my Pa listened to with his face graven, and I knew the part of him that was listenin and he would know it was the same part of me that made me leave with that old Skylark and write note sayin I still continuin life and it was the part in him and me too that wanted change and new air and I told him what I knew and he understood and I was helping him, being a part of something big and nautical but not yet navigable and this made me feel somethin over everybody even though.

Even though, I knew that if I ever let on that I knew that that's what he was doin, or that that was why I was doin my tellin, my throat would like to be cut like a pig and my desert death would not be no lie, but the corpse truth, 'cause as my Pa said when he first started takin his belt off that night, he's got plenty more sons.

## Manti

It goes worse. No curse in my mouth, no nest in my heart, no rubber eye in my hands.

He came again. He fruckin came again and came again and each time after mother with her spoon burns me and cries and then she got big in her belly so quick with His coming in the afternoon that I knew he'd been coming at least since early last fall. In the Sunday afternoons. In the time after House. In the time after He talk and talk to the fingers of people below the steeple palm and even Peapod and I are fruckin there.

He come come come.

He bringing God's word to my gone mother but that's not all he bring.

Worse and big. Her belly.

Worse enough to read the Book. I know a fruckin Book that starts I, *having been born of goodly parents, therefore I was taught somewhat in all the learning of my father.* I know this book but I want to write my own since mine can't start that way, no. Having no Daddy, no. No goodly parents.

Better to start at the fruckin end. *I soon go to rest in the Paradise of God, until my spirit and body shall again reunite, and I am brought forth triumphant before the pleasing bar of the great Jehovah, the Eternal Judge of both quick and dead. Amen.*

So mine will start: aMen. A. Man. Quick.

He comes six times that I know. Six slices of Him. Mother fruckin smiles like a sick dog. He shuts the door and makes the meanness out of her. He prays into her. I hear him purifying. Thump thump thump. I take Peapod outside and show her again:

Rock. Paper. Scissors.

No sound now. No collar straightening. A. Man. Quick—walks away. And all his talk of seeds. I watch him and with my eyes I burn burnt burn the trail he walks. He fruckin knows it, too.

Fruckin whore.

Rock.

Paper.

Scissors.

*Dead*. Dead. Dead, Mother says we'll make the bird her belly hatches. She'll be quiet, she says.

She'll be quiet.

# *Emma*

When Levi let spill from his mouth that word dirt that was so damp I knew right away it must have the same truth as God's good earth, I did not know what to say. I opened my mouth and then shut it like most never because there was nothing that came due to the layers of him all in my head, not only him as I remembered, and the way we were together in a love of such ethereal proportions and his mane hair and his bluebird eyes, but also him in my memories as the image I had made of him dead, and it was a less pretty shape of dog-bitten sun leather skin rotting, his body a sacrifice to our figtreelove and these images were both real to me and so to learn that one might not be real only made me wonder if they were both not real, so that in hearing he was dead once, and now alive again, it was as if there was some cancellation of his existence in my life so that I had dreamt our whole sweet error.

And it's true when he told me I did not yet know God's great plan, and it's true I did not know what to say but it did not take long before I knew what to do. Levi stood there outside my Mama's house, leaning on the horse fence, still talking, all about him, how he looked now, what he was doing, and trying to make some new image in my head but I had enough Jeremiahs and so was not inclined to listen and besides there was a tightness growing in my chest and making its way to my hands and so I leaned toward Levi and pressed my first finger into his dry lips even while they moved so that they stopped half open and then I pressed Levi's chin until they were closed and then I turned around and I walked the dusk-prostituting road back to the place I deem home, where I thought Jeremiah might come back to now that he was alive, out there in the big black world doing things I did not know and things I thought that I would probably not ever know because I could not go, with a child feeding off me most hours and even if I could have gone I would not have, I would not have because he had not come back.

Even with no words for Levi I still had a certainty and I felt to know what to do with the tightness, with the feeling and it was like some other body I moved in as I came into the kitchen and told my husband who was then washing his hands I needed to see him in the west, which was where my room was, and I walked up the stairs and into my boo dwar without pause knowing that he would be behind me, hearing before they were there his booted steps, and undoing my dress fast, a button pulled loose to the end of its thread so that I already had a later and something to do in it, but for then I took off even my underthings so that I stood naked as I never had before him, hoping I was healed from that early birth, when he came into the door. His face made a look like surprise and then his mouth twisted as if to laugh or cry and then he went all last page and asked me plain as day what I was doing and that is when I should have known what to say because the answer was there and simple in my hands and my chest and in the mouth of Levi but instead I did not say anything but walked toward him with my still small hips and udder breasts and I went to kiss him and I put my lips to his, trying to start it, to be a wife for a second time, and he put his sarsaparilla mouth back into mine, and I put my hand on the back of his head and pulled him to me strong as I could and with my second hand I went to the button of his black pants and as I put my fingers between his hot grown man stomach and his pants to make space there, he pushed me back.

He pushed me and I did not fall over backward and then he looked at me, his lips red from mine, and then he hit me across the cheek.

I felt the mark as maybe something I wanted more than the other: a reason to hate him. And the sting woke me up and I bent over and Josiah said something I didn't hear, and didn't listen for and then he left the room and I fell onto the thin red quilt and held my hand to the heat in my face and let the water and salt come into my mouth, my eyes, my nose as I let myself hear Levi for the first time when he said Jeremiah was dirty and so I saw him in my mind, a third Jeremiah who was not skin-eaten dead but was somewhere I could not picture, and he was whole and he was dirty and he was making his way north and here I was naked and south stuck.

And now I picture myself at this moment in my story as God must have seen me, in need of reminding of the light that existed outside of the body, that someday transcended flesh, and in need of reminding that if we listen, and listen hard as I know now to do, the sky is always singing in rounds.

*I whispered to Emma: If you turn your mind-dirt over to where it's dark, where you don't often go and it smells cool and mineral, then maybe I can teach you to listen.*

*Listen, really.*

# *Mary*

M y brother is alive and I knew this before it was told by Levi whose
mouth gave news of him in Pine Mesa or before anyone said he
was alive and up to bad. And I don't believe this last part because I did
not dream it but I know it's true he is alive and have known it longest,
before anyone, because I dreamt it and also because I prayed to Him, our
Lord that art in Heaven that he would not be dead so that he could be
saved whilst walking His Green Earth.

When I pray I do not stutter, the words are clear in my head for God
to hear, without my epigene mouth to make them tremor. It sounds
like this:

> *Father in Heaven, in the name of your Beloved Son, I speak unto*
> *you as your humble girl servant setting my faith upon your ears and*
> *also to ask for your blessing upon my brother who they say is gone,*
> *and with you, and if he is, to ask you from my small place in your*
> *brood to take care of him, and if he isn't, take care of him too so as*
> *to keep him always and eternally within the softcloud fleece of the*
> *Lamb of God.*
> *Amen.*

This is how I know that when I get to Heaven I will not stutter. I will
speak clear and I will know what has happened without having to wait
until Levi bears witness to my brother, who he says has fallen from His

Good graces as the Prophet tells it, but is in fact not dead, but alive, like I knew him to be from my dream. And while I know he is, alive, I also know the Prophet had his reasons for saying otherwise. He got to.

I had a dream like Lehi's dream in the good and holy Book. Lehi had a dream and he was in the dark and dismal wilderness like our desert but he was not hot but cold and fearing of where the caverns of his own dream soul would take him and then as in a revered miracle, he saw a golden tree the color of hay and it glowed with the moon fruit of God, and he knew if he ate it he would be happy. The fruit was magic and so that it made the throat so sated one had to feel nice in the eyes and heart and spleen. You would feel all this, but first you had to get across the vast and baleful darkness, and follow an iron rod which was cold to touch when Lehi grabbed it, and he saw the other people of the path, following the rod, and you had to have the faith that the cold pole would take you to the tree and Lehi had faith and so he got there and he ate the fruit and in my own dream I got there too and the tree was bright like noon water and there was a sound of womanscream like the coyotes make but I ate the fruit and was happy and full even when I saw the people who didn't eat the fruit because they did not want to, and they were the dog howls, swallowed in the darkness or drowned in the errant river of sin and in my dream I saw my brother standing there waiting to take a piece of fruit but not moving. He was pale with no more muscle and I thought him dead, he need not eat fruit but then he said, No, I just already done ate some, but I saw he looked hungry and not sated and so I knew he could not be truthing. And so I remembered unto him that in the dream in the Book, the brothers that don't eat the fruit fare not well, and they are bad, bad, brothers of Laman and Lemuel and in the dream he nods like he remembers and then he walks away with triste face, and old in it too, leaving me with the sticky supernal fruit in my hand, half-eaten and unsad and so I woke sweating and thirsty for wanting a sweetness in my mouth that would be like that in the dream but then I thought.

I thought: I want no brother of mine swallowed by darkness.

I had this dream and so knew he alive and told my Ma Lizbeth and she near slap me because she said I was mixing backbrain dreams with God's good work and she wouldn't listen past the part of the dark and the tree, telling me not to steal old prophets' dreams, neither, and pressed my lips shut for me with her fingers. All this until she found out that it was true, that her boy was living and then she hugged me large and asked if I remembered my dream that I told to her, and I said, Of course, and she said, the Lord doth truly guide us and then she let me have a bowl of cherries and it was like the dream was His Beloved Son's truth in all ways, except I hoped now that wherever my brother was he would eat the fruit already and not be amongst the openmouthed drowning faces of purgatory and so I set to dreaming once again so I could see him and I lie in bed thinking of his bony face and tried to make him come in my dream so that I could tell him Not to harrow up his soul, but to get amongst the straight place where hands were not idle but in prayer. But he would not come to my dream, even though he was alive for certain and working the world over in atonement, so they say, he would not come so I turned to Him instead in hopes of making the other him hear me that way.

*Father in Heaven, in the name of your Beloved Son, please bring my brother back from the land of Gentiles, so that he may repent, and not bring down or up the full wrath of God to himself or to his family or to the inhabitants of Zion. Bring Ether to him and convince him to eat your fruit. Bless him and me and the fruit eaters and deliver my brother from the venison of the universe. Quit them folks from saying he's bad to the core, gone to hell early. He sometimes hit me but I know he wouldn't do nothing so bad really.*
   *Amen.*

And I been saying this at night before bed, and when I sleep I dream not of my brother but of other things more reptile that I don't remember, and I hear nothing back from my prayer and so there are only my blank sleeps and silence for an answer and it makes the dark darker, even darker than in my dream.

And I wake sometimes thinking I hear his steps outside, coming home, coming to help turn the field and speak not of the forsaken path of flies and it's not never him in the sound but I know he should get back here where the people like us, soft babies of His Beloved, belong. Because out there, there is no tree, no straight iron rod to follow, no fruit and no one to remind him bout his hands.

*I saw the Prophet on his knees asking. It was morning for he could not wait until night and so he waited until the house was quiet upstairs, all playing outside, someone doing dishes, an infant banging a table with a chubby fist, a squeal, the house upstairs full of morning sun. Then he knelt by his bed. I saw him asking Why?*

*What had he done wrong?*

*That Downs boy, another one that bothered the way a splinter under a fingernail bothers. That boy telling his father that Jeremiah was alive. Hadn't he dreamed him dead? Hadn't he seen a boy turn into a vulture with black wings for arms and red neck sagging like testicles? If that did not mean death, then what? Perhaps he had wanted it too much as now he wanted this other one. He must be dead. The other one lies. For God would not deceive him such, would he?*

*There was one Prophet long ago, I whisper, Remember him? Lied in God's name and the people saw fit to help him atone. To spill his blood into the already red earth. It's his blood that stains the road, the rocks, the mud in the creek, I whisper.*

*Don't be wrong, I whispered. Even as I knew he was.*

# *Emma*

Then after the news of Jeremiah alive and not dead, the black metallic sinners came through town again, following hot on Levi's trail back from town and making two visits from the authorities in one year. I actually saw it and did not just hear it told through the mouths of others or through the hollow siren of our sounding bell. I was out front of the house, in the green green yard that Josiah had just replanted for us after winter and that he was mighty proud of, seeing as it was only the lawn in Redfield, save the Prophet's, and he even had a mower to keep it trim. I was out sitting in the spring weather on a blanket with my babe, watching Lizbeth's littlest two playing in the grass, crawling around and sticking every little stray blade straight into their wet little apple mouths so that I could hardly take my eyes off one before the other one was up to something new, what with their four little hands. But I did hear the sound of wheels on the gravel, or I must have though I don't remember it, because I looked up and saw the sleek black car with mirrors for windows reflecting the blue sky like shimmering snakeskin and rolling slowly through, like it didn't want to get itself all red with our dust. Like it was taking its time to see what to eat first.

When I first saw it, my mouth turned baby just like the rest of them, and I was gaping too, and I didn't move, nor try to hide my child nor Lizbeth's two, nor did I get inside quick as can, something Lizbeth would later scold me for. No, I just sat there and watched at how much this thing didn't belong among us. It was low to the ground, not like a truck, and it was clean, clean, like it had just been shined up three minutes before I seen it. The engine, too, was quiet, with no sputter nor sign that hands had worked on it ever. It looked *bad*, like the evil in the Book, in the way no body could be seen driving it, and that slow creeping, wide and low, the bumper like a hungry mouth. I just sat there in the grass and watched even as it drove right by, slowing almost to a stop not far from the edge of our lawn, and I just sat and watched when one of the windows rolled down part way and the lens of a camera stuck itself out like a mechanical dog's nose but instead of flaring its nostrils it click click clicked and even then I did not say to myself *Run*. Rather, I wanted to see the face behind the camera, if it was a man or a woman and what they might be wearing and how old they were. I had always imagined faceless beings in white shirts and black pants, men I guess, though perhaps women, women dressed like men and this is what I pictured when we heard the stories of them taking the Browns away, or questioning the men. But when I saw that mechanical apparatus like an extension of a hand of a will of a mind, I wanted to see the face. So I did not think to cover my own face, another thing Lizbeth would later scold me for, nor the faces of our children. Rather I sat looking curiously and did not think *they are taking my picture* but rather while I waited to see the face look out from behind the camera thought *will they at least wave?* And it was this last thought and the realization that they would not, and that they were not here to be friendly, which finally propelled me off the grass, and so picking up my infant Warren Jessop and Lizbeth's little Sally not too hurried like and netting her little Jacob with my dress between my legs as he toddled and we made our way back into the house. I did not look back again, and felt my face to be flushed.

It was on the third step of the porch as I waited for the toddler to crawl up it, that the bell finally did sound and I heard the car drive on behind me and Lizbeth's heavy steps making her way to the door, her stout figure through the screen a ghost in the shade of the house, then fully embodied as she opened the door for me and held it, already with a look on her face like you should have been in before now, as if the bell echoed not only after it rang, but also before it rang, and it was these first faint intonations that I should have heard. I should have heard, smelt, tasted in the air the blood of those not ours.

And she didn't even know I'd seen them, that they'd seen me. She did not see them on the far end of the road as she bent down and picked up her youngest by his arms, the black car turning down toward the Prophet's house, its tail of dust hiding its dark head just so briefly.

She did not know I had not really felt afraid of them then and am still not now, knowing as I do now that they can never take eternal salvation away from us, and try as they might, they only drive us closer to the time when we are all reunited.

# *Levi*

My life is complex in many ways, and most specially after I had my special trip to the lips of Hell's mouth and felt the Devil's breath on me and learned that some death is really a poor life. At this time some half-truth cloud was a hangin o'er my head and making the ground all muddy round my feet 'cause Pa came into the barn one night as the birds were singing their day over and the sun was bedding down and I'd just turned on the naked bulb crusted over with dead bugs and he said he had to talk to me and so I quit my cleanin of Star of Celestial, a pregnant white mare with whiteblue eyes who makes it her business to get dirty. Rolls in mud even, kickin her legs up toward heaven like she fightin her own holy name. I quit pullin at clumps of mud in her hair and then he told me not to quit, just keep working, he said be good for us both to do something and then he picked up a horse brush and started pullin her greased mane through the wires.

There's some trouble, he said then. And then I looked at my Pa over the horse's lowin neck and saw he ain't lookin at me. He said then that the Prophet said it was a lie bout Jeremiah, that he dead like he done spoke months ago and that the mouth that says otherwise is full of blasphemous teeth spouting the Devil's gangrene mind.

I heard Prophet's lilt and knew Pa was speakin His words and I kept at work at the horse but I knew my hands were shakin and sure enough Star of Celestial trembled under my touch.

It was getting warmer every day, but at night you could still feel that fresh bite of winter on your neck. I hoped Pa would just think we was cold, me and Star.

Pa soothed her then, speaking softly while I tried to think of a way to tell my Pa he gotta believe me and then he just said it, like God heard my own clenched thoughts, he says: I believe you. And I found a breath in me I didn't know was there and I let go and Star of Celestial stomped her hoof and I wondered how she knew my relief, but then Pa said, Still, though, we in a fix.

I nodded but couldn't see him 'cause the horse's head and I put my hand to her warm snout to feel her iron breath and we groomed her a while, not saying nothin before my Pa spoke again to ask what exactly was the nature of my business with Ellen Mai.

I liked that one since Mercy Ann left and liked her black hair I did 'specially since my horse was taken and gifted to Cadence but I never did see her all that much and the only time I saw her lone we went on walk and I found a geode broke open and gave it to her and she laughed and asked me if I thought that all the stone in this world were broke open if it would look so lovely and I told her I don't know the secrets rocks keep, but probably. Except for gravestones, I told her, and that was the one thing I wish I hadn't said that whole long walk because her face changed and she just nodded and did not laugh. But that was it, so I just told my Pa: Barely seen her.

You got to tell me if there's anything, he said. And so I wished more than ever there was somethin, because there I was atrial before my Pa and probably the other men, somewhere, too and certainly the Prophet was speculating on how I touched her, and even if it meant the exile that was maybe comin anyway, at least I would have. Touched her.

But I worked a burr out of Star of Celestial's matte tail and cleared my throat and told him I talked to her sometime but only once took her on a walk and nothin happened and my face burned hot when he said That's it? So I told him about the geode and he walked around to my side of her flanks and nodded with some musement and maybe relief.

Still, he said, you know she's meant to marry our Prophet, right, you know you can't do those things. And I nodded and hoped my eyes would not water for the heat behind them and I swallowed and felt my tongue to be not a part of mouth but somethin in it, instead.

My Pa took the comb from my hand then to work at a knot in her mane and I thought it was strange, him helpin me, and he gave me the brush and I started my strokes along her dirt-white body, makin her shiver all over again and turn her head towards me so as to aim a marble eye my way.

We did this for a while and I knew my Pa had work and business, and so I knew there must be something else to say and I could see in his face he was workin toward it and when I was done brushin and waitin for the comb to do the rest her tail I saw my Pa was just combin through straight hair, like he was one of my sisters bout to braid.

Outside the light was gone, and the barn glowed like it should be warm but it was not, the evening birds quiet now.

I waited and did not say anything until he saw me standin there, my hand restin in the gap of Star of Celestial's back, low with colt weight, and he turned to me and the light from the barn door backshadowed him so as to make him a dark shape rather than some exact face and then he said:

Levi, thing is. The thing is, Levi, is that I believe you. But someone here is lying, and according to everybody, and I don't mean Josiah, but I mean our Father who hath helped elect Our leader, the situation is this: Someone is not truthin. Someone is lyin. And it either got to be you, or Him. Boy can't be both dead and alive, see.

I started to argue, saying But you said you, but then he turned his face so that the light shone on part of it like some midmoon and I saw what he was sayin.

Star of Celestial shifted her weight.

And He thinks you been disrespectful bout Ellen Mai.

Star of Celestial swatted at a fly with her tail.

And He knows you took that little trip to Pine Mesa.

Star of Celestial blew air out her lips.

And He wants you out.

She did not move.

I turned way from the door-shaped light and picked at somethin on her hind. I put the back of my hand to my nose and felt the cold wetness of it from workin in the barn since dawn.

Pa coughed a little and put his big cat hand on my shoulder and I did not turn toward him.

You ain't to go, he said.

Not just yet, let's wait it out. Josiah is Jeremiah's father and he don't want you to go just yet, whether that boy be dead or alive, he said. We got to wait a while, he said. We know what's right, and we got to trust the Lord will help that be seen. In the near-time, though, you stay out a town, don't go to House, and nowhere near Him, and just do your work right round here, in the house or in the barn, don't tell no one, and if you got to get out, go quiet to the woods.

I turned half to him, keepin my hand on Star of Celestial and he dropped his hand from my shoulder, and I met his father eye and I nodded.

Only to the woods, ears up.

I nodded 'gain, keeping my mouth closed and my tongue high up in it. And no word.

He held the comb toward me and I took it.

And pray like you, and then he trailed off and kicked at some hay and turned and walked toward barn door, stoppin to look at a bent nail on the frame, pushin at it with his thumb and saying Huh, before walkin out and leaving me to tail, still full of mud and burrs. Leaving me to do as before but in secret, to try to make myself invisible like I had left, like I was already with Jeremiah, ridin in cars and workin fence lines, not there at all, but someplace else where I could be seen but only by those invisible to God.

I kept at my work and knew I'd stay till dark, feelin already that my presence was some callus on the community, the beginning of an end, where the river of the Prophet's voice would no longer be one fluvial sound but would fork off in part, with me in some small logged-up eddy tryin not be seen. And even in these later days—I still wish it was never me that no one wanted here.

# *Cadence*

When you grow up with people that drink and get high and get mean, you learn to smell the change in the air. It's like a slight shift in the light, not so loud as a cloud over the sun, more like that sun still shines bright but has looked away from you. Changed from yellow to white in its rays. You get to be real good at knowing when's a good time to take a walk. To get outta dodge. And I hadn't felt that in a long time. And then, suddenly, in Redfield. Long before the day when the FBI or whoever they are came for the second time. I felt it in the air—in the past months as fall blackened to winter and then winter exhaled spring. A first visit from these sinners as they call them, a fire at the Prophet's house, an anger stuck like dirt under Josiah's fingernails, and then his dead boy back alive again by witness and then dead again by prophecy. That wild woman on the edge of town, Crazy Beth, growing a belly for anyone to see and I saw it when Lizbeth sent me to her house with a box of spring lettuce. And the Prophet. Silent. Silent while his people sit pawing in the darkness. And then this second black car, a faceless force of no-good evil. Well the car means I better get together my plan for getting outta dodge because I'm no fighter. But a survivor. And sometimes that means running.

So if they take Josiah away I will go home, not home to him or home to my stepfather or home to my mother, I will just go home to the people I belong to, the ones I know ain't better than me 'cause half of them I know are worse. And when they take him, I know if I tell anyone that I am leaving that they will surround me, other wives, all Sisters, all will surround me if I try to leave with them knowing. Their gums will pull back and they will fold their arms and I will cave in and stay and be alone in a place full of words, but not him. And I won't even be able to say how I will feel when he is gone from here so I won't stay, and I won't tell anyone I'm leaving. I'll sneak out at night and I'll ride my horse back to town, with baby or no baby. I don't know yet because since I lost that last one I still ain't betting on this one.

I'm gonna ride my dark horse out of here because without Josiah I got no place here. I cannot work like this, in the dirt and flour and wood, without his hands at night rubbing my back, or his voice telling me how good I am. I can do it for him, and not any wives, not Lizbeth, and certainly not Tressa. Not even sweet Emma, really. And I felt God's love for me but wasn't sure what that love was without Josiah and *his* love, *his* favor. It was him, really. Even as I fit in here, and I will stay until he goes and then I'll ride away into the night.

Lizbeth thinks he won't be taken, ever. She says we worry for nothing. But I remember the news, the frenzy over the conviction of Holden Brown, and I know they will tear this place apart if they get the littlest chance. But first, they will take him. And I will be gone, gone with my horse.

When I first came here, and he first give me that horse, I was afraid. He thought it was because the animal was big and strong but no, it was the color of its blackness, the real absence of any light whatsoever and the way it was alive with that dark, that shining eclipse in the silhouette of a horse you could see from just bout anywhere. Looking at him was like looking at a hole in the day, like you could fall into him and come out in a place stranger than this one. My body, even as it carried that first unborn sadness, felt like paper next to his.

But when I first rode him I understood what everyone said when they said he was an angelic animal. He was big, but he was also smart and gentle. I didn't have to be a good rider or dig my boots hard to get him to go where I wanted and so I loved that horse, and loved riding in a way I had never loved anything back home. And so I'll take Blackie with me, and I'll go and have something new in that old place. And he and his night body will keep me from smoking and drugs and drinking and bad men.

Maybe I can get a nice job at the post office or somewhere else that is clean and automatic-like.

But I won't stay here, providing as a place as it is. There is too much dust and work and drabness in color and me and my new baby, God willing, will find somewhere else. The horse, the baby, and I, we will all be all right, like he says, I am one that has survived the Devil's breath hot in my face and though I don't tell him this, it's been elsewhere too. He breathed in my mouth and on my boobs and in between my legs so that my body was all his ashen mark before Josiah found me and brought me here and washed me clean through and made my blood red again and gave me that dark horse.

No Josiah don't know how fallen I was, just like he don't know that I will leave when they take him. Just like he don't know for sure that they will take him because he doesn't know them. Josiah doesn't know that they been talking about this for years in Pine Mesa: When is somebody going to take them down? They're breaking the law, someone got to do something. And this chatter, from high school locker rooms to gas station trucker talk, has been spinning and spreading, and all that being said for so many years has to gather up and get something done eventually. And now that they been for yet another visit, this time to ask questions—making us sound the alarm, which is really a cowbell and tells the children to say that Lizbeth was their mother, the ones too young to do that kept silent by their elders, and all the wives but Lizbeth had to hide away in the dirt under the house while people walked above us not smelling us, not hunting us, but wanting us to be in their sight—they will be back. Because the one thing these people and my people have in common is the dislike of anything halved.

And when they came this second time, the car stopped in front of the house. It had driven by once and seen Emma outside, and so Josiah gave Lizbeth a look and went out to invite them in while us other wives went down to the cellar. The interview took over an hour, they asked questions we couldn't hear, and Josiah answered words we didn't know. Emma and Tressa and I sat down there quiet and still, smelling the earth and the ferment of winter's food. It was cold and we shivered and were sitting hunched forward but when I tried to move just a little, slow, hushed, Tressa shot me an accusing glance. She thinks I'm a spy, an outsider, someone come in like a weed to take over even though I've never stepped on no toes and done my best to avoid the whole foot. It's gotten worse since I got pregnant again, so it was kinda a good feeling when I found out that it were one of her children, Josiah told us later, that almost had ruined it because he ran out to look at the detective's car and the lady officer just getting ready to leave crouched to him and pointed at Lizbeth and said, Is that your mother? And he looked at her with his true mother's fat cheeks and shook his head, and Lizbeth turned white and Josiah yelled for the child to leave the people alone and when they tried to ask him again Josiah had to tell them to leave that child, he deaf and dumb and don't need your pestering to boot, before he picked the kid up by the arm and swung him back through the doorway.

Lizbeth waited then to make sure half hour after they left before she opened the hatch and the daylight came through to us so that we understood how used to the half dark we'd gotten.

So we came out of the pantry all cramped from our hideaway, and Tressa brought a jar of canned pears up to open and eat while we listened to Josiah tell it all. I didn't know how she could eat that country candy at a time like this, and wondered that no one else accused her of that she always said I had: disloyalty.

But we sat there and Josiah said it would be all right, that he had answered their questions and even though Tressa's child had nodded in that most crucial of moments, he didn't think they had any probable cause. And he used this term with deep seriousness and he laid his head in his hands and rubbed the skin of his forehead against his skull.

He said it would be all right, and there would be no meeting like the time they drove through before, and no fire to put out, and we would all sit and eat and pray together. And he looked years older and when he put his hand on my knee, heavy and warm, I began to wonder why I'd thought him younger. Wonder why I'd thought it was a good idea to come out here and into this place where just like every other man, he would leave. But he would leave me to wives, one who was just then licking her chops with the stick of pear juice, and another who was too young to do anything but play like a grown up, and another that was too good to share her husband but did for some reason I'll never know.

That day turned to night and day again and each minute since I've been waiting to hear the sound of some car. The wheels on the dirt road spitting into town, lights off but still churning our hand-laid gravel as they come to take him.

I've been waiting and so will be ready and, in the commotion, I'll go soft-footed to the barn. Go with only a gray sweater that Lizbeth knit me and a necklace Josiah gave me when we were wed—an arrowhead he found tilling the field that is as black as that horse only cold and heavy on my breastbone. I'll go as he goes, so that I may even go first and even if I don't, I won't be left behind. Go and not be left, and the baby if he's here by then will ride with me, bumping along on my boobs, ignorant as sin of how fatherless this world really be.

*I saw Him ask, and I saw Him cry, bent over silence like it was the body of a dead lover.*

*And when He could squeeze no answer from the sky between his open hands, He felt wet in the back of his mouth and made good on a promise to himself.*

*He called His boy Daniel to him in his parlor in early morning and whispered in his ear, and Daniel's mouth turned ungodly upward carve, a grin that disturbed even his father as he said right Father, and took his lurking and lanky teenage body (a boy I could have been in school with) out of sight and the Prophet stared after him. And when he was gone the Prophet suddenly noticed that leaves were erupting slowly, tender curled pinches from the branch outside His May window and He thought this was a sign, a benevolence, and sighed.*

# Manti

*Too much trouble, daddy.* She will be quiet she said.

Worse: dawn. She was *fuckin* quiet as she said. She waked me and give me a bundle with a sleepy swollen small face. Shhh she tell me. Put this bundle in the crick. Put this bundle in the crick quiet. No splash. Float it way to Jerusalem.

No, Mother.

Yes, Manti.

Worse. She says it will be for Peapod. For me. For her. More burnt spoons. Less canned beans. For me.

Worse. She begs and I want to *fuckin* hit her. I hit her. I push her away and I take that bundle that weighs nothing and I walk past my own meanness and it follows me like a goat outside into the smoky blue morning and across the back field toward the crick and the deep part and the water that will carry away all His autumn and winter Sundays. *Fuck.*

The crick is rubbing its water wings together, gurgling and soft. The sound of all time, before and after fathers and thirst and swallowing.
    There it is.

Could be a drop, a nudge, a gentle bedding down of bird in water but not before I see what all those shutdoor prophecies of afternoons made. I fold back the white cloth and dig out the face in the bundle. Shut eyes. Tiny breath. White putty up its nose.
    Sister.

Worse. No pleasing bar for me. No crickdrop. No erasing.

I rewrap and set the bird by the big cottonwood.
                    The town will burn for this.
    The bundle between two root humps with a face up.
                    The fire will spread fast in the yellow-smelling grass.
Like a felled beehive.
                    We'll all float in smoke to Jerusalem.
But no buzzing just little wake-ups.

I look at it and think how fruckin little it is, how much life it don't have to live and maybe I want to cry and maybe I don't care and maybe I want to feel light for this thing that gets to fall asleep here.
    It's not that it's easy. Not for me and not for Peapod.
    So I walk away.
    I fruckin leave it by the tree and summer is comin again suddenly and I go back through the horse field where the beasts stand still.
    I stop and watch them and there they are, not carin. I stand rooted on the dry earth and feel the whole world comin up behind me. I can hear its heavy footsteps but I don't even turn around instead I just watch those tail-flicking horses staggered like candles on the altar at the House; flickering now and then, and burning, burning, waiting, waiting,
        and
        all the time
        dying down
        to the quick.

*Manti: A tree can be a mother, roots stir in their earth, awake as arms around a sleeping babe.*

*Too small to know this is not always how it is. It cries until shapes of light in the soft new leaves above lull it to sleep. How does it know that sleep isn't milk? That light isn't love? That the sound of water is not its mother's voice?*

*This place, this place, would break any heart. And when darkness falls, even the smallest knows that something is not as it should be.*

# *Mary*

Most of the time I don't mind my own stutter, most of the time it's my Mama and my Pa and other people of here that mind. For me, it's the way God made me, and I know the Prophet will see that when He comes back and it's time for me to be his wife.

But the day I found the dead boy in the field, I wanted to speak nice and clear. I wanted to go into the kitchen and stare until they all knew I had something important to say and then I wanted to say it crystal clear, all the words smooth and round as bearings, I wanted to say:

There is a dead boy in the field.

His name was Manti, and I knew this, but thought it would be better to just tell them that it was a boy first and foremost, shocking as it already was, but of course I did not imagine my Mama to slap me on my face and call me a tongue-torn liar, which maybe she wouldn't done had I said right out that it was Manti, out there, in the far pasture, his body folded over itself and his eyes looking up for Jesus and the blood coming out his nose in a small winding line like a river and his skull smashed in good right above his left temple.

I know all this because I looked at it close so as to memorize what God do to children who don't behave themselves. I don't know what Manti did to get this blow, but I knew he wasn't a good child, but even a bad child and was always trying to act all older than his twelve little lonely years. I looked so as to remember but my Mama didn't want to hear about it in the kitchen, she said Hush child just let's go get your Pa and show him where instead a telling it all over Zion, Go! She say, get, and I led my Pa then, out to the field, with no words but just a hand and we stopped when he saw the boy and I heard him say the Lord's name in vain and then he stooped and brushed a fly away from the face, but it was useless because flies were newly woke from spring and had found him and so were many.

Pa asked, with his hand o'er his mouth, hadn't I seen what happened and I said no, I saw something laying in the field and not moving and so came over, and he said then Mary, looks this boy's been kicked in the head by a horse, and then stood up and looked at the six horses there as if he deciding which to shoot but none were grazing and all were agitated as if they did not like this new dead flower on their green fuzz grass.

Pa told me then to stay away from them horses, give more distance than usual and go get a blanket and go quick. So I ran to the house but looked back to see my Pa whisper some words and then reach down and pick up that poor boy, whose neck flopped about, too, and carry him toward me, toward the house, too.

I brought the blanket from my bed 'cause it was the only one I could find I knew I would not get whipped over taking, and brought it down to Pa as he laid the boy on the kitchen floor and shut his eyes with his thumb and swore again and told my Ma to keep everybody out of the kitchen because she had just then began to say over and over again, Good me, good me and so needed something to do, and so stood guard at the back door and told me to watch the front and I did but I also saw my Pa cover that boy's bloody head with my blanket and for the first time that day I felt my soul to be a fear.

It's not that I hadn't seen a dead one, before, I had: my little brother by Tressa died not two years ago and though I don't remember much of him being alive I do remember him dead, because he was sick and in his room and we were all waiting and then he was dead and I went to his bed to pay my last respects with all the other children and I touched his little hand and it felt like sandstone not skin, pink and dry, not damp like palm.

Yes yes I had seen something like it before, but different because it was not a sudden thing I found in a field like a piece of old leather or even a Judas napping 'stead of working and I could not help but also think of my brother, a real sinner too, and his own end that would be forthcoming if it was really the time when God gets to setting the righteous up to be by themselves.

My Pa left to go tell Manti's mother Beth, who I was afraid of like everybody else and his baby sister, who looked to be covered with some sort of sugar or flour or dirt at all times and I waited there with my back to the body and my Mama with her back to me so we could each look out the way we were supposed to and watch that no one came in, and also that no spirit came out, though Pa didn't say that last part, I felt it to be true because I knew Manti and he was sneaky.

My Ma spoke then and her voice was shaking and she said, what you see child, what you see and I told her nothing Ma, just went to feed the chickens and looked out in the field and saw him lying there, so I went to look. But even as I said this I was already knowing what made me go over to the pasture and it was a horse neighing, high and hurting, neighing as if being whipped or fouling that I heard from the pen but as I came closer there warn't no horse jumping but all looked scared and that's when I saw that body down but I did not say this to Ma because, again, for the second time that day, I didn't want to stutter none especially when talking about a boy whose body I found and ain't no other witness but God and his six beasts know what happened.

So instead I asked Ma if Pa would shoot a horse now, and she said she didn't know. Be different if we knew which one, I figured and for a moment I imagined us asking all the horses to confess their varied sins, looking for the guilt bulging like a vein in their tethered necks, the eyes going big with the thought of the inferno God would surely send them to, because though I do not know, I do believe God punishes all mur-

derers, men and horses alike and now I wonder especially as I do believe
a large purification is upon us, what with a fire and Jeremiah most certainly lost.

We stood there for a while and my legs began to ache so I sat down
on the threshold even though Jeremiah used to say that be bad luck, and
as I did, I did look around to see the bump of the boy under my blanket
and for a moment I thought maybe he moved and felt my skin hair go
all cactus and made a note on exactly what floorboards he was on so I
would know for sure if he moved again. Then I turned back toward the
front room and said Ma, that boy's got my blanket.

I know, she said, but nothing else so we just waited there and I could
hear all sorts of sounds that were never before scary but were also never
so loud and rhythmic so I felt like the room had started to stutter, too.
There was a drip of something slow, like a wet rag melting its water off
into a bucket, and a shrill bird outside and somewhere upstairs the voice
of someone of our blood, probably Emma, singing a little song to sleep a
babe over and over again whose words we could not hear.

I heard my Pa returning because I heard Manti's baby sister crying,
crying like a baby does, not like someone bereaved does, but now she was
both so I didn't know if she already understood, or didn't, and she came
in the front door sucking her thumb and holding her mother's hand and
their ma looked frightened, her head a nest of blackbirds, and also like
she with child, but cleaner than usual and she mad, too, like she ready
to beat the Devil out of her son soon as she lay eyes on him so I stood
up and quick got out of her way and walked clear around the room so
as not to step over him and went to stand by my Ma but she was already
crossing the room too so as to offer a hand to her Sister, who did not take
it but was looking down stone-faced at the body under my blanket like
it was a shape of something besides her boy, then she very slowly knelt
down like she in temple though this was one woman never go to Sunday
House, which I thought in secret might be why she was having to kneel
like this, now, to see the face of her own misfortune and she went slow
and pulled back the blanket, a quilt with blue and white and red flowers

that my Mama Tressa made that had a white underside. I saw now with
more fear in my heart that it got splotched with the blood of the boy and
when I saw that I saw her face and it was still stone as she stared a moment and then reached to the boy's face and closed his lips which were
parted like he was about to speak, and she herself made no sound and
even the baby, who was already three or so and no baby really, stopped
crying, and everybody looked as if he might wake up by our own eyes
staring until the baby girl said it.

Manti, she said. Manti, Manti, Manti, and it was as if she was calling
not only him back but all the people of his great namesake and I heard
my Ma choke as she began to cry and watched my father pick up the little girl as she began to point at his face saying his name again and again
and Beth stood up slowly and stared at my Ma as if wondering why she
was crying and then she took her child from Pa and walked out of our
house leaving her son still uncovered so that the door swung back and all
we heard was Manti, Manti, Manti going back on down the road.

They buried the boy that very night in my blanket. It didn't make no
sense to take it off of him, especially because when my father loaded the
body into the cart he was all wrapped up in it. I watched as they disappeared down the road, going to pick up his mother, maybe his sister, so
that they could watch over the body till night.

I wished I could go too, as I knew the Prophet would be there to comfort
and pray words over him, but Ma said I had to get back and water the
chickens I had abandoned in the day's events and here it was the first
real hot day and them without water so I went back to work head-down,
noting that if I heard anything else not of usual I would ignore it, let it
waft through me so that I would not regret again my stutter, thus by
never having anything else of that measure to say again, and never wanting God to punish me thus, and never having to stand watch again over
something that may or may not be moving.

I worked in watering and feeding and in the smell of the wet wood troughs, but Pa came back and watched the horses in the field until dusk that night. He stood there, leaning on the fence for most of the day, but he did not shoot one or all of them. He saw when they went back to grazing, and at the end of the day he brought them all in one by one, cautious, speaking gently, not even checking their hooves for blood.

And I went into my bed with a new blanket that Ma had found in a trunk above the barn and it was a brown quilt and smelled like moths and hay and was heavy with dampness and it felt like it was not mine so I imagined I had switched blankets with Manti, and was then glad that it was only this blanket above my body, and not the freshly turned dirt of God's red earth enclosing my earthly form for all eternity within the shapeless arms of silence.

*Manti. I didn't listen when your skull fractured, nor to the quick footsteps walking away, the horses scattering like leaves in a quick gust. I didn't listen and so heard only my own silent scream that will echo all the way back to where I came from.*

*Haley*

*+*

*Jeremiah.*

*= Love*

*On my notebook. History class. He leans over and writes it. Grinning.*

# *Levi*

If I go like Jeremiah, I won't work fences but really I won't go to Phoenix neither 'cause I asked my mother and she said it's far, far way. Might as well be another planet, she says. And I don't think I'll murder nobody, not even some sinnin body, but it's hard to say 'cause once I leave here, if I leave here, I'm bound to get real bad. I'll hear the music and see the TV and the other things that will make me think evil, even if I am trying my best not to be. And I'll be among the bad, and getting bad, and set to damn in Hell for eternity for not livin pure and clean and havin lots of wives so I guess it won't matter so much what I do. And anyway, probably won't have much time anyway since I hear coyotes at night, yipping at me that the end is nigh.

It only matters if I can stay. If I can be still on high. But I got to be good, no joyridin and no thinkin, 'specially bout Ellen Mai. So for now I got to stay out of the way and be in purgatory, mostly workin in the barn, walkin in the woods, botherin the womenfolk since I can't get to findin the boys. And I can't be seen by those who might tell Prophet. Those beside Pa's and Josiah's. So I wait and I wait and it's my private waitin for earth judgment in the middle of all our together waitin as a people for the Redeemer and the Great I Am and our second death and our resurrection. And it is as dull as a spoon in the meat. But I have been good, was all good about it for nigh six weeks even as the weather got warm, and even when I saw Josiah with a body in his cart this morning and the body was Manti and this night a funeral and all got dressed, the

men in their black and the women in their white and I paced and I paced
and I dressed too, and my Pa shook his head, and then they all left and I
had to get back in my work clothes and sit at the kitchen table with a pile
of napkins to fold which my Mama had set before me like I was some
home-curled girl.

And I sat there with the knobby corners and the washed creases and
I wondered if it was best my only secret had died with Manti midst all
this trouble, even though I knew God still knew. And I wondered what
Manti did to get himself kicked in the head by a horse like a fool. Manti
should have known animals, but his Mama didn't have any more, poor
and widowed as she was. Maybe he didn't really know no horse sense,
probably not 'cause he barely had any regular sense.

And I was smoothin napkins against the wood table and I got a sliver.
A black seed straight in my pointy finger. And I sucked it with teeth
hard and gave up on the napkins for a woman's job; God signing me with
this table bite that I should be in the barn. His language only a small
wound, but I could read it.

But the barn was dark and dull. Horses out to pasture. Only three
shovelfuls to clean for Pa. No new hay to get. Not quite time to bring the
horses in for the night.

And I knew that the service would end and they'd head to the cemetery as dark fell. A warm day and now a warm evening. And they'd close
up the casket before I saw him. I wanted to see him dead. I didn't know
how they'd clean up a horse wound. I remember when a tractor rolled
over Hal Jens's boy and they had the casket open and the Holy come to
bury him all went green, his neck and half his face crushed like pound
meat and even though there was nice dressin and some quilt his ma had
made to cover him, it wasn't no quiet mark of death and the Prophet
had to speak to us of the absolute renewal of our bodies at resurrection
just to keep his Mama breathin.

And now it was Manti. I was bettin there was no hiding a hoofcrush
like that, skull like a caved pumpkin. I wondered if it was Blackie who
done it, Blackie who was mine no longer. Blackie wanting to get back

to me and my careful hands, smiting other boys. It might have been Blackie. And I wanted to sneak in, hide among the hundreds, and the hundreds would be there 'cause who would miss a funeral. Not here. Not in the boxing away of one of ours til the day when we'd see them again. Not even if it was a no count like Manti. Not even if it better his sad life with his mother and her no good head was done. Not even if he had started that fire at the Prophet's house, as is whispered among the children but not the elders.

We have our secrets too.

We have our secrets and right then I was one of them.

And Manti had his secrets, and most of them are now in one of the red clay mounds of the graveyard.

My grandmother says in Phoenix they bury folk below ground. But here the ground turns to stone not four feet down. Here we stay afloat for the time when he will come and be both the End and the Beginning and we will enter into wide-circle time; rock time.

But not me, not if I have to leave. And I was good that evening and thinking bout bein good and so I got to wipin Pa's tools with a rag. Shinin up the handles, layin them neat and rowed like silverware. Housework in the barn. But one can only do that so long.

And everyone, I knew, would be at the House. Listening to the departure. So maybe I thought I could take walk. I would still be good, but walk too. I hadn't been 'bout for weeks. Not since my big trip. So I set Pa's tools in a line, quietly, like I was already sneakin and took path on the far edge of the fields so as to stay off the main road 'fore I made certain all was still. And I walked east toward the mesa and thought I might wander to the top of the town, where the crick come down from the canyon, and no one would be. And I did and I walked past orchards hanging with fruit new and green, and it was still hot out, the heat the reason for the hasty burial I thought, and everyone was at House so I decided then I would take the road home since no one was 'bout to see me who shouldn't be seen. And I did and so I saw. The answer to the question I hadn't thought of. Who was pickin up trash with other boys and Jeremiah gone and now even me out. The drainage ditches on either side of the rosy road were stacked with white bags tore open. The first one I saw I almost went to pick up by habit but when I got close I saw it was tore up anyway, eaten through by somethin. A raven picking at one bag in front of Josiah's place. And I stood there for a minute on that hot road and squinted at this empty place, what with everyone at the service for a dead boy, and heard that raven squawk out a lonely broke song so that for a minute I thought the whole town was gone, and no one even pickin the tree fruit, like it was already end times and it was in this moment, where it seemed I was standing outside myself, in some other time, that I did not hear him comin.

Daniel. Prophet's favorite son. I was lookin at the dusk and then out of nowhere. There. He was in front of me. In front of me with a one-sided grin on his face. A head taller than me with hair so light it's like he got none. Why he was not at the funeral with everyone else I could not tell you. Maybe he was in fact supposed to be doin somethin 'bout the trash but instead he was in my face sayin, I got you, I got you and Didn't I know it? Didn't I know yer Pa hadn't a driven you out? You just wait until Prophet hears about this, my, my, aren't you gonna get it? And he rubbed his hands together, all lick-lippin and I thought for a minute if I had anythin to be offerin Daniel to keep his mouth shut but I knew I did not, as Daniel wanted one thing, and that was to be the Prophet's arm and hand and eventually whole body and this news would get him closer to that. Just like me tellin my Pa stuff made me more his son too. So I just looked past him down the vacant road, that would soon be peopling up with a procession to the cemetery and I thought a Pa, and how I'd disappointed him again and I looked back at Daniel and he was grinnin so I thought to punch him in his white teeth but did not but rather turned and walked away while he said things to my back 'bout how I better get packed and I looked good and hard at the fields and houses on the five-minute walk home because I knew it may be the last time. And

I went home and started this waitin, a waitin different from the first one since I thought this one was bound to end with my leavin.

And when I have to leave I'll be buried below ground and the maggots will eat me and no one will even say words over me because no one will know me and I'll be bound for Satan's darkness and my body be plagued with that oncomin journey and no one will want touch me.

Might as well be a murderer. And a bandit. And I could steal Ellen Mai away. But not yet. First I wait and I pray and I think about the menfolk and the Prophet who might find out soon and who might be right to banish me and I don't know. He might kill me too, or just say I'm dead.

Or maybe He will remember that when Jeremiah left it made trouble, someone following that trouble right back to us, and that makes more trouble. I heard my Pa say this after the morning when the bell rang, and someone tell us they were back—the black cars. Like black flies that buzz until the end is spelled. This is why I guess I am still sittin tight in barn-purgatory. 'Tween house and field. This is why Pa believes me. Never likin that one, but always followin, always obeyin even though they seemed to think somethin not quite right, like a door stickin in its frame. But Prophet could find out and take away their wives. But not their land. The earth has been cut up by older prophecy and God was good to Josiah. Josiah feeds a lot of us. He is why I haven't yet been driven out and if that's true I know he will make sure I stay.

But I will bring in the horses. A full moon rises over the red mesa like a giant horse eye.

I won't be no maggot food. I'll be in a pine box like Manti. People can look at me lying there, all old, and say their prayers to me while I go sleep for a while. I'll be tucked tight in a mound and the Prophet or somebody will dedicate it to my spirit and I'll be in a flood of Celestial water while all of me waits there in the red earth. Like when I return to the barn and wait for them all to come back, only for longer.

*He had told his Daniel: The last boy I let slip had thrived in the Devil's world, but that would never happen again. This one, this Manti, would not get away. We will not let malevolence fester. He had said: a wound, if left, infects and spreads until it streaks a red arrow right to the heart. We will not, he had said, gripping his son's shoulder, we will not feed Lucifer one more.*

*He had not told of his own adultery with Manti's mother, had said nothing of his own festering wound. For him, excused, perhaps, by all the work he did for God.*

*Daniel had no trouble finding a large crumpled stone and he palmed it against his thigh and set out. Even less trouble to find Manti, out in the back fields, with the animals, where he always was. And Manti had his back to him and he was crouched and he was looking at a big black horse like he was talking to it. And Daniel had his stone.*

*And even I, in my ghostly in-between, wanted to scream. To tell the strange boy to run. And I remembered what we are working our way back to, I remembered death coming up from behind.*

*But I didn't hear the sound that a rock makes on a skull. I wasn't listening. I was listening again to my own death.*

# *Annalue*

We came back from Manti's funeral quiet. No one had much to say about such a strangeness, both his life and death otherworldly but still I was sad. Sad for him, for the two he left behind like stray dogs. How could he, dark and light, man and child, be an anchor? But seeing mother and child it was clear he had been the weight that tethered them to us, and now they were unmoored. Sister Beth's oily eyes staring to one side of the grave, dark wells in a face so white it was like she seen a ghost and the little girl sucking her thumb with eyes large in her jaundice face. I watched them and thought I would go soon, bring them food, clean their house. If they let me in.

We walked home in the night, the moon risen, and came in, my Ma and I, and for a moment just stood there listening to the empty rooms that were supposed to house Levi who was here bound for his own good. We waited to hear him and as we waited, I felt the dimensions of our small farm kitchen to be changing. Tightening.

Mama cleared her throat. I'll boil some potatoes.

I nodded and went to sit but couldn't move yet. I was hearing something. A cry.

Full moon as it was, I felt the light shift its weight and undershade everything like a sunny wound, as if some unearthly presence no one would mistake for God or one of his angels had come to stand in that kitchen door.

My leg in its deadness throbbed. I sat staring at that cracked doorway as if waiting for some miraculous darkness to interrupt the strange brightness of the night when Levi come through the back door and scart us both into paralysis.

I meant no trouble, were the first words out of his mouth. But I got this, and to us he held a baby child, no more than a day old, still bloody from its own sinful origin.

Mama saw Levi with a baby and threw her hands out, splashing her freshly filled water pot and wetting everything, including this feral thing. Where'd you get it? She shouted in a whisper and put the pot down.

Found it, Levi held out the bundle and stuck his lower lip out a little as if still convincing himself of the reality of the thing.

What do you mean you found it, and Mama took that child from Levi.

By the big cottonwood, just lying there, Levi said as Mama laid it down in the middle of the water stained wood table.

I heard it crying when I was bringing the horses in, Levi said and wiped his nose with the back of his hand. It stinks, he said, a wonder nothing ate it yet.

We all stood, then, around that child who we saw then was awake and we looked at its small eyes, lined with the plump swell of birth.

There was a silence as one of the thing's small hands reached up into the heavy air and tried to grasp it and, failing to bring anything to its small mouth, let out a cry. This small maw made us all stop and look at one another and it was in this moment a cloud finally darkened the moon outside like the old eye was turning away from our unholy creche.

IV

*Haley*
*+*
*Jeremiah.*
*= Love*
*On my notebook. History class. He leans over and writes it. Grinning.*

# *Jeremiah*

And then after Levi and six weeks of working fences, slinging barbed line from a coil until his borrowed gloves had worn through, and two months of working outside in the new heat and two months of being lonely as a dead man would, he figured she would be missing him so then—then he decided to go. Back North. One bus ride later. She wasn't home her mother said, but wouldn't he like to come in for a nice chat anyway? No thanks, but another day, for sure. He did like Haley's mom. At least she seemed to care what happened to him. Even if Haley didn't. He left and took another bus to the Home.

Jimmy's car wasn't there so he went in and found Duke, who said All right, All right, Chill Out Man, let me see if I can find her. Her mom said she was going to a party? Okay.

Taylor was there, too. With pills. Taylor was into pills now and said, Man, if anyone needs one of these things it's you, dude. A Real Chill Pill. Take it. Just swallow it. Jesus don't chew, what are you fucking six years old?

Handed him a beer, washed it down.

Levi had said he was Dead. Dead to all who knew him. Already gone to that eternal burning place. And he said this, and Jeremiah knew there was no grief. Maybe quiet, secret grief his mother kept folded like she did her own mother's kerchief in her apron pocket. But no real mourning to stand in for his absence.

Duke was making calls and talking way too long.

Jeremiah kept nudging him, Ask Ask, if he knows where she is.

Duke pushed him away and Taylor kept him there, sitting him down. Dude, just give it a minute. The pill. Give it a minute and it will start working.

Levi said he was Dead and then to Get Dead. Levi his friend. A kid like him that liked trouble. A scrapper. Had said he should have told them if he didn't want to be dead. But he didn't. He never tried. *I was up here too busy being among the wicked. Inside the wicked.* He saw now that he'd had a chance, a door that had been open but that he'd never thought to look for and now it was closed. Now that they knew he had been alive and hadn't been trying to redeem himself he was truly dead to them. Dead to everyone and everything.

He was sweating. It was a hot night. Hot especially in the Home. Even with the swamp cooler on high. He drank a cold beer fast. Duke got off the phone.

Found her. He grinned.

Jeremiah jumped up. Okay, let's go. Let's go, let's go.

Dude, chill, I mean I found where she's *going* to be. *Later* tonight. Let's just get some pizza, hang here, preparty a little and then we'll head out.

Jeremiah drank another beer. He sat on the couch and fingered the spot on his cheek where Levi had punched him, the same spot where Levi's father had hit him that day after Emma. A red puff that had hurt to touch both times, but he had kept rubbing it this second time. Feeling it. Even after it stopped hurting, he missed the tenderness and touched it anyway.

Smudging his cheekbone until he was back under the cottonwood tree with Emma. He was watching her tell him how righteous their sin had been. It was like she was blind or something and he had been fascinated. He had watched her plan their lives together like they lived on some other planet. Not here, but not there, either. A place with her rules. Her God that she professed to know so well. He had not said anything because there had not been any reason to. He didn't want to tell her she was right, because she wasn't, but he didn't want to tell her she was wrong either. He didn't want to say No, here is what's going to happen. They will find out. I will be exiled or maybe even kilt and you will be married to my Pa. Maybe he didn't say anything because he wanted what she said to be true. He wanted her world to be the right one, the one where they could love each other in some Celestial light that would raise them above the power of man. Of men. Even good men like his Pa.

His Pa was a good man.

My Pa was a good man, he said aloud.

Duke looked up. Dude, what are you talking about?

My Pa.

Duke laughed. You're rolling. You've just been like spacing out. Here, drink it down. And he handed Jeremiah another beer.

Besides, man. The dude was not a good man. He practically left you for dead.

No, dead was Manti's father. A body. Dead was a body. A body that spoke in blood and asked forgiveness from the river under the earth.

Dead was him, but with a body unspeaking. Unspoken for as of yet. A body too late to ask forgiveness because he didn't know to claim his life. Didn't know to show up and state his aliveness. Out twice now. Lost twice now.

There's no going back, he said.

Dude, you don't want to go back. We've been over this. We're going to start a business. Make sweet cash. Get the honeys, J-dogger, the honeys! And speaking of, you have got to let this girl go, let's go do something else, go to another party, find you another ass to get all weird over. Besides, I think she might be getting around.

Duke spoke so fast.

What?

I don't know, man, but I seen her with this other guy of late. Some douche from Southside.

No. Jeremiah looked at him. No. He looked down. There was a river of light now below his feet, slinking around the torn-up sofa. No. Let's go. Is it time to go?

Dude, it's been like ten minutes since we sat down. CHILL. OUT. Drink your beer. You haven't even fucking touched that beer.

It was so hot. So definitely hot. Like he was already there. Burning in hell. He tried to focus on the label of the beer can. Read the fine print. Before he went back down South, before she said she'd needed a break, one of those nights at her house, she had made fun of him. He was trying to start something, and she was trying to read a book for English class, for a test, and she said, Jesus, just 'cause you can't read doesn't mean I don't want to. As soon as she said it, she felt bad, put the book down, tended to his wounds which he played up for her attention.

But now he felt it. How mean that was.

I *can* read, he said aloud.

Whatever, man. Duke tipped the beer can in Jeremiah's hand up toward his mouth. Duke, it was Duke. Duke feeding him beer. Not Levi. Duke had never been there. Duke didn't know any of them.

He would talk to her tonight, they would make up and she would be so sad that he'd gone away, so glad he was back. He'd hold her but then too he would write Emma a letter. Tomorrow he'd write her a letter and say, Maybe you were right. Maybe we were meant to be together in the Celestial light. I'm alive, that's how he'd start the letter.

I'm alive, he said aloud.

Okay, let's get you outta here. Some air. We'll drive around a little. Maybe go shoot some stop signs. You'd like that, wouldn't you, country boy?

Duke's hand pulled him up by the elbow. He stuffed another full beer can into his other hand. Roadies.

*The road. Pink and hardened sand. Two boys on horseback. Coming to help bury the sinner.*

Outside the night air was even hotter. Like the loft of the barn in desert summer. He got in the back seat. Rolled down the windows. He could see one star.

So many stars and they'd hold hands and spin so that it looked like that thing. That old toy they had before the Prophet thought they were a distortion of God's creation.

Kaleidoscope. That was the word for it.

Spinning until they let go and fell back on the grass of his Pa's lawn. Him and his sisters. Spinning and singing. Watching the stars keep going round and round even as he lay still until they would eventually stop and look set as ever in their places.

As if they'd never left.

He was there in the desert grass looking up and then he was inside a house.

It was hot, so hot. Bodies were shoving past him in a thin hall, bare skinny shoulders, tattooed forearms.

Watch it, asshole.

At the end of the hall, a kitchen, a lamp hanging over a table. Red cups everywhere. He could feel Duke on his arm. Duke was saying something but then he saw past the table and the bodies around it to the darkness and the stars and the light reflecting back on the glass of a patio door. Past the door he saw yellow.

Yellow. Haley. He was looking for Haley, so they could get out of the heat. Get some place cool. So he could explain to her everything. So she could explain.

So many bodies. *Crowd of wickedness.* He swam through them.

He finally found her, grabbed her arm. Hey, he said. Hey, look, and he showed her what Taylor had given him. He went to grab her some pills from the baggie and dropped it, and when he looked up she was gone.

Gone and it was so bright under the lamp.

He would find her again and tell her everything this time. About then and now and the great forever. He would tell her he forgave her. That he knew a way to undo all of their sins. He moved to the back door.

Steady man, he heard Duke say.

I'm going to tell her.

What? What are you going to tell her man? Man, don't say I love you, just don't. Not a good move right now. You got play a little hard to get, you know?

He reached to the shiny glass of the door, to get past it. To the cool air. The dark. Yellow.

He pushed out and sucked in a breath, like he was getting ready to dive in the swimming hole at home. He waited for the cool to wash over him. But it was hotter. There was no breath. The night hugged around him. Not stars but lights. *Wicked city lights.* He saw her again in that color he had first seen her in.

He reached out and touched her yellow dress.

Haley.

Not Haley. Another girl, she smiled at him. He couldn't breathe. He felt the weight of it. What was it? Tucked in the front of his pants. He remembered. Duke had put it under his seat and Jeremiah had reached under from the backseat and grabbed it. He let its heaviness center him. *Prophet.*

He stood on two feet. So many lights out there. A city view, the house on a hill. So many and each one glittered until it split into a million vertical fragments. It was beautiful. He wished his sisters were there.

*What was that song?*

Hey, you should sit down, you don't look so good.

*Who was this girl in yellow?*

Haley?

What?

You're not her.

No, probably not, but sit down, I'll go in and get some water for you. You are not Haley. He pushed at the yellow.

Her red cup spilled, he had something sticky and orange smelling on his hand. He wiped it on his forehead but it was warm, too. Not cold. Not like the ice that still rattled in her cup. He reached for it.

What the fuck?

She was so loud, this girl. He could hear Duke now, he could hear Duke saying his name from inside.

It was so hot. Hot like hell. He was there, already.

You are not fucking Haley, he yelled. Did he? He wanted to yell but his voice was dry. Gone. Nothing he was saying was coming out. *Or was it?* The lights seemed to pulse, like they were getting closer. Glittering. He spun around and watched them spin too.

*Ring around the rosie . . .*

Then he saw her. At the edge of the glow from the kitchen behind him, leaning against a cement wall, staring at him. A cigarette in one hand. The butt glowed when she breathed in and it looked like a small eye of the hellish snake the Prophet had warned him about. Why hadn't he seen it that first day?

That cool fall day in the parking lot. He hadn't known then that it would get this hot.

Talk, he would talk to her. He put his hand under his T-shirt and felt the skin on his stomach as cool and damp. Talk. He would show her Duke's gun maybe. She didn't want pills but this she would like. She would want to hold it. Together they could shoot at the millions of lights and make them fall from the sky like the fireworks they'd watched on New Year's. They would laugh. Hold hands. He would get her to see everything.

She met his eye and turned away, talking to someone, a shadow in the darkness. He walked toward her, he felt himself smiling. As he walked, he could feel another weight in his pocket. A rock from the roadside maybe, he had collected them for years. Always there, a weight bumping his leg then and now. But each step toward her he felt lighter.

Even as he remembered it was his knife, not a rock, he felt lighter. Like they were already home. Lights, lights.

He saw the beams of the city lights behind her swell and ebb like each was its own heartbeat. He could see now, they were definitely closing in.

*Pocket full of posies . . .*

Her name. He knew it. Yellow.

Yellow, he said.

She didn't turn, he saw the cigarette move to her face. The edge of her turned-away face. No, Haley.

Haley.

His voice sank in the heat. The air between them was so hot, it had burned up his sound again. Like in a dream.

Behind her, now, he could see the lights orange and pulsing, and now flowing into one current, enclosing them.

Haley.

She still didn't look.

Haley. He said it as loud as he could. Haley, look.

But still she didn't turn. Didn't hear him. The lights, the heat muted him.

Haley.

He was right there, and she didn't even see him. He felt the gun now in his hand like magic, he held it out to her. A golden arm. The river now at his feet again.

Haley!

She still didn't look.

Haley!

Didn't see. He was a ghost to her. Dead like Levi had said.

He opened his mouth to scream but then he felt the gun in his hand. Substantial and sure in all this melting air, this watery brightness. The trigger a lighter. *Flick.* Like when she lit his first cigarette the day he met her. *Flick.* I'm Haley, she'd said.

Haley. *Turn around. Look at me. I'm here.* He could hear his voice waver between his world, and hers. The orange lights now red. A current around them.

Haley. *It's time to come back with me, to the fresh air, the cottonwoods, the breeze, the creek, the blue sky, the red stones, the birds and the crickets and the voices of someone calling their own. Then you'll understand.*

Haley *look at me. Look at me. LOOK at me. I am alive.*

HALEY.

Haley. Look.

Haley.

*Flick, pull. CRACK.*

The lights drew back into their fixed and angry places as she finally turned to him. She turned right before she fell.

But she did not fall through the earth. She landed instead on the cracked cement of the patio where grass was growing through.

Haley.

He let his body fall and his knees land on the cement too. *No.* He crawled to her and knelt. He saw the red opening up on the back of her shirt. White, not yellow. Now red.

No. He had meant to talk to her. Not this.

A blood moon spilling, becoming a river right there on the patio.

Why so much? His Pa had told him: *You go wash that blood out then, and as you do, you remember that that's sinner's blood, spilt by the sinner to atone for the earthly sin of adultery, and you remember that good.*

He put his hands in it. He couldn't clean it up. He didn't want to this time.

*So are you not afeared of death then, boy?*

He was not. Not anymore. He was already Dead.

*I can't let her go without me.* He looked up from the blood and saw the lights had converged again around him. Stars and faces all shone on him, screamed their luminations soundlessly at him.

Something told him he should go. Out into the night.

*It's time to get out now.*

But he couldn't let her back there without him. He had to be with her. To show her. To teach her. To protect her. He had to be with her. He pulled his knife from his pocket and opened it, gripping the blade with his palm.

His hand opened for him like a fish gill, but he didn't feel it. He reached his bleeding hand to the wet flow of her back; their blood would run together now. He closed his eyes but still could not smell the creek. What if she leaves?

*Don't leave yet, not without me.*

He had to be with her. How to get with her? He saw her skirt had come up. A black skirt. *Slutty*, he would've teased her. He unbuttoned his pants.

This would be it. Emma was right. All this time she was right. He could feel what she'd said: *God's light in you telling you what you are supposed to do which is powerful and strangelike and makes you do things you usually would not do.* So this was the way to be together in God's light and the eternal Celestial heaven and there, there would be air and coolness. He felt his own limpness in his left hand and tried to make it hard. He pulled at her black thong, he would get it. He would get it. He would and then he would make sure he was dead too. He had to. He had to make it so that they would be together atoned in the light and the river and they could get out of here. He couldn't just leave her. Not now, he couldn't leave her. Not in all this blood. Couldn't waste this blood.

*Let his blood run into the earth, and run into Christ's blood, and shore up his atonement for his earthly sins. Her sins. His sins.*

He couldn't get stiff. Couldn't, though he tugged at himself with his hand an open wound. So hard it hurt. He couldn't because he could hear now that the stars *were* screaming, he could hear his name, and he could hear his own voice from far away, from the desert night on the grass, he could hear himself singing, but he could see only the lights. The lights and the red. He put his face into her back, next to the hole he had made in her.

*Ashes, ashes . . .*

He almost had it, his hardness, he twisted her thong strap out of the way and felt for her, her way out. Doing it now to undo what had started that summer day under a tree, to start them back all over at the beginning. He hurt now, but he would do it. He looked up at her face and saw then that she was staring. Just staring. Like she had given up. He slumped over her body. Was so tired suddenly. He didn't want to. But he had to, for her.

He just needed to rest a minute.

That's when they pulled him off.

*Annalue*

When the moon was high and shadowing everything in the reverse of its color, my mother drew a bath for the foundling we unwrapped like a dressed wound, so sticky and raw and then Mama started talking to me like she was mine. She said good lord didn't I know the child like to be hungry and hadn't I best go quick before the last lights are out in Jenna's who could give us some formula and wouldn't she just bathe the thing while I went and wasn't she too tired—by all the earth had shown her since the moon first rose like a vellum smudge on the good glass of the afternoon sky—to even wonder whose child this was. But probably some no-good townie from Pine Mesa thinking to rid themselves of their suckling sin.

But on the day of a dead child, she said. And a full moon. And everything else. Ain't that strange?

Now git.

And I handed her the girl, who she would gently sponge in the warm sink water while I was gone, and reswaddle in an old gray diaper and clean white flour sack, and I walked the seventeen slanted steps to Jenna's house and thought how a boy could get kilt, a baby left. Something was rotten all right because it meant someone had done these things. Wrong was among us. And if wrong was here, then right was not all here. So there was some great hold over the place starting to slip.

Jenna handed me the formula, two bottles and six diapers without a word, having heard everything one needed to hear already from Levi who was leaning on her porch, and her knowing not to say anything, and I walked back the seventeen steps, looking out for the shadow of a sibling, seeing none, and feeling my exhaustion as I once again hauled my dead leg up the porch steps and into the kitchen where Mama showed me how to heat a bottle in a pan of hot water, how to test the milk on the inside of my wrist, and the baby learned to take it, refusing it three times before finding the right mouth motions, the first muscles of desire.

Then awoke in her a fierce hunger I recognized.

And as she suckled I couldn't help myself from warming.

And that first night she slept in a fruit crate packed with towels next to my bed, Mama saying she would have Levi get a bassinet from the barn tomorrow, and the both of us knowing without saying that this baby was ours because ours found it, mine because even at sixteen I didn't have one yet, and the same thing that was making everything go slip, slip was going to make this baby stay.

Stay.

*And then things are over. My name, twice. Haley. Haley.* It's Haley, right? *Bodies shoving by, backpacks rubbing against my arm, the bell ringing. I'm going to be late to history class.*

Haley.

    Jesus, what?

    *He's like a dog tonight. Everywhere I go, he's there, he wants to show me something he found. He wants to give me a kiss. He's high, so high and wants to hold my hand with his sweaty hand, he says he got something for me. A plastic baggie with some more of that shit in there. Jesus, I don't want any pills. I'm in a vodka mood. I'm in a talk-to-my-girls mood. I'm in a leave-me-the-fuck-alone mood.*

    Haley.

    Just leave me the fuck alone right now.

    *I'm on the porch, putting a cigarette out with the rubber of my sandal, he's coming up to me again I know it. I just fucking know it. And I'm just starting to feel good.*

    Haley. Haley. Haley. Look. Haley.

    *The middle of my spine to the back of my skull is a stadium light. A sun. The patio cement is cold and I can see a thin crack right next to my face.*

    Haley. Haley. Haley.

    *He is on top of me and he's pushing it all out of me.*

    *And I was already late to history.*

    *All my life, all my voice, he is thrusting it out of me, and I don't even remember a gunshot.*

    *Jesus, now?*

    *And he wanted to shake my hand. And I laughed.*

# Mercy Ann

His face in the paper didn't look like him. He had shorter hair, first, and looked all yellow and unhealthy, but it was also one of those bad printings of the paper where there are two layers of ink not exactly one on top of the other so even the words look like they are moving.

I looked at it for a while trying to steady it with my eyes from across the table as Estelle sat reading the other side of the page.

My father's picture was not in the paper, ever, not even during his trial, but then again, he didn't shoot a girl in the back and then try to rape her as she lay dying in front of enough witnesses to fill a school bus but none of them present enough to stop him.

Estelle wouldn't let me read it at first, I saw the picture from across the kitchen table and I said I know him, and she said what, and I said I know him, well knew him, he's my cousin, and then I asked Estelle what he was doing in the paper right as I took a bite of my marmalade toast.

She began to look flustered and pushed her chair back and started looking around her feet like she dropped a pen or was looking to pick up that poor dead Rosie she still couldn't always remember was dead and so I leaned over and tried to pull the paper over to me but she slapped her hand down on it and said Mercy Ann, you don't need to be reading all this in the paper, it's . . . it's maybe not productive. And her voice seemed panicked and she called for Stan and he came in the kitchen, still doing up the buttons of his golf shirt. Estelle pointed, speechless, at the paper and then at me.

So I had to wait while Stan read the article, which he did standing up, drinking coffee, and Estelle kept interrupting to say, She knows that boy, her cousin or something, until he had to say Estelle I heard you the first time, Let me read, and then all was quiet except for the ticking of the kitchen clock and I ventured to finish my toast figuring Jeremiah had maybe gotten into some trouble like stealing. Or maybe he was dead.

Then Stan dropped the paper and looked at Estelle, This is God awful, he said and asked Estelle why she made him read it.

So then I dropped my L-shaped crust of toast on the plate and waited to hear. But they just stared at each other, Stan drinking his coffee still and Estelle waiting too.

Well, can I read it now? I asked and Stan said then She's going to hear about it at school anyway, so you might as well tell her. Estelle sighed heavily and said Oh my, oh my, before laying her head in her hands and beginning to speak into her lap so that no one could hear.

What? Stan asked, and then she raised her head with wet eyes and told Stan she did not think she could repeat the details of that vile story, and Stan said maybe he couldn't either, and maybe it'd be best to let me read it. So the warmed-up paper came into my hands and I pushed my toast plate aside and smoothed the words in front of me, not knowing if the thing I read would have the same effect on me as these two people, familiar as I was with Jeremiah, polygamy, and that other world.

And that's how I came to read that Jeremiah had been at a party, and had a gun, and was trying to talk to an ex-girlfriend, and then when she turned away from him he shot her in the back and then began to pull her underwear down and his own, like he might rape her as she lay dying, the party-goers gaping, no one moving, the girl dying. Bleeding out the back, and dying. Jeremiah softly saying her name.

Bystanders said.

When I was ten, before my father's fool of a third wife ran away and then testified in court against him, I lived two roads over from Jeremiah. I used to pass his house to visit Emma, which I did a lot because I liked her brother Levi.

Levi taught me how to make braided bracelets out of horse's hair, which he had a bunch because they'd had to shoot a mare that summer and then Levi asked if he could cut off the tail of the dead horse and nobody said no, so he did. First he tried with an axe, he told me, but swinging across the wiry black hair warming in the sun did no good, so he had to use the orchard pruning shears. When the hair was off he was surprised how it no longer held together but all fell flat, not a rope anymore but an unwoven rug. He also said the horse body looked so strange without its tail, with this broke off unburned end instead, that he had to look away though he was still happy to have the hair, and I was happy too because he taught me to make my own horse hair bracelet which I wore for two summers until Levi turned mean and then I buried it behind a dab of sagebrush with a prayer for him to get nice again.

And it was in those days, those horsehair summer days, that I knew Jeremiah most. I knew him because he was the only one who guessed my secret. When I walked by his house, he would singsong a little tease, Going to see your boyfriend, Mercy Ann? He would give me an over-wink of his blue eyes and once he even came into the road, saying in a woman's voice, Now let me check your hair, make sure you look alright, before tickling me until I could get loose and run all the way to Brother Downs's.

When I quit going to see Levi and had buried my bracelet, Jeremiah came to our fence one day and asked why I hadn't been down the road. When I shrugged he said, Well you can always come to see me and then scratched his hair and walked away. I was too surprised to call after him, child as I was, as he was, but as he walked off there was something stooped in his posture; it was like he was heavy with the sun of that day and shouldering its light. He bent over to pick up a pebble then, like someone that knows he's being watched, and I thought I saw a certain loneliness about him and so I briefly saw him not for a farm-worked kid like the rest of us, but for an old man weighed down by some unseen stone or past.

Estelle let me stay home from school that day. She said, No use going while the news is so fresh. It'll air out, she said, in a day. Tomorrow, someone will shoot someone else and everybody will forget about your friend here. She said this and then patted my hand with papery little slaps.

She had been talking a lot since Stan had left to go golfing. They had both watched me reading the article so that I felt like I had to remake my face into dry clay so as not to move. I felt if I cried, or even said Oh No, that the floor of the room would tilt and we would slide across into a corner and be stuck, all piled together. Or maybe I was just worried Estelle would cry, make that dog sound she did when her bridge partner died.

It was not hard to stay still. It was too strange a story to really place someone I once knew in it. I reread the interview with the girl's mother, who knew Jeremiah, and she kept saying that she was sad, and angry. At Redfield. At what they did to him. They, she said, had made him kill his own dog. Had put him, a child, out on the streets. She said she had loved them both, her daughter, and Jeremiah. She knew them both. It was terrible, she said. She was sad.

For some reason then I thought of a time, during my first couple of months here, when my math teacher asked me to stay after class. He had me sit down three desks away, as if calculating the distance and then he said, I just wanted to let you know, if you need any help to just let me know. He said this even though I was actually doing well in the class because Stan loved math and would help me with my homework, sometimes just saying the answers fast over my shoulder, as if we were in a race to do the problem. But this teacher saying this made me think maybe I wasn't doing so well until he said, Even if it's not about math, if you just need to talk, I am here. And it was difficult to picture this man who talked only in numbers and equations listening to anything so rounded and distorted-feeling as what I would say if I was to talk about anything outside of school.

I could picture him now, three desks away, saying, This is terrible.

After I finished reading the article, which was continued on another page in the same section I said, That's terrible. Because the word was strong in my mind, but also because it seemed like the kind of thing you say when you want to be like everyone else who doesn't know someone in the paper.

You okay kiddo? Stan asked then, but already seemed relieved as he turned and opened the fridge to find the small can of tomato juice he had every morning. And I nodded at Estelle, and couldn't find any more words and so heard myself say Terrible, again.

So that is when Estelle said I could stay home from school, even though it was almost out for the summer. That is when she started punctuating the day with small comments, some about the reckless media, some about assimilation programs for "Lost Boys," which is what they call Jeremiah, the exiled kind without foster families. His exile, I realized, was one of the things I'd missed, and didn't know. I didn't know he'd been exiled. I sure didn't know anything about a dog. There had been no dogs, they'd been outlawed by the Prophet. When our family was pulled out, he was there and so now I had a measurement for how much I missed, for how much of the world I left, the world that was still the same in my mind, the same people at the same age, was no longer real, and existed only in my memory.

Through the morning I was thinking all them, of him, so when Estelle said something about justice or inappropriate educations, I didn't always listen.

I saw him the day we left. I saw him, working out in the field. He was standing straight up, leaning on a hoe, holding his hand over his eyes like a strange salute as we rode away in those state vans that had come to get us. My father had already been arrested, there was no one to provide, and before the Prophet got a chance to remarry my mother and her sisterwives to other men, they came. We only had an hour to pack. Then we got in these vans and saw our town as never before, muted into sepia through tinted glass so it was like the last image of the town was our past already, driving out, and I saw Jeremiah in a field and put my hand up to wave before I realized he wouldn't be able to see me through that dark moving window. He would only be able to see the hot blue sky reflecting back.

Estelle asked me if I wanted to go to the mall. She asked me this from time to time when she felt the need to walk and look at things. We never bought anything, unless I needed new shoes or hair elastics. I told her I didn't, and I'd never said no before but thought it was probably okay to today, and she just nodded her head.

I want to sit outside, I said, and so I went out to the patio and she brought me a cold lemonade so I wouldn't get too hot even though it was plenty cool in the morning shade and then she went to get her purse.

I didn't want to even taste the lemonade at first because I'd never had anything like it before I got here, and I didn't want something of this new world in my mouth right then. I wanted to sit and stare and remember everything I could about that time. I wanted to remember and reremember Jeremiah as standing in that road, as tickling me, as leaning in the field, as if by thinking it I could keep it going; I could imagine into truth Jeremiah still there, not out here.

Estelle peeked out the patio door again and asked if it was okay if she went on without me, and I said yes, and was glad she was going though I felt it to be because I must be scaring her and she needed to get out the house. I imagined she might open up about her connection to the whole famous story to a sales clerk on break at the food court, and that would be all right as long as I wasn't there to hear it, to hear that truth countering the one I was trying to visualize into being, to recreate.

She called out again to me that she'd be back soon before she changed her mind and came out and gave me one more hand pat, this time squeezing my shoulder with her bird bone hands before finally leaving.

The glass of lemonade got warm as the sun got high and hot in the sky. The condo was empty behind me and its hollowness breezed about me from the sliding glass door, making me feel like I was moving even as I sat.

I remember before Levi got mean, the Prophet gave a talk at the House. It was the kind of talk he would give with a shaking voice, whether with anger or passion I do not know, but the voice would tremble as he questioned us, our people, and asked if we were pious enough. He banned the playing of board games in this voice. But this time he was talking about relations. He said then that reward for the faithful was marriage deemed by God through him, and no other commune was acceptable. I did not know what he meant then, but I remember it because he kept saying. The faithful are impotent; God grants potency in his own time. Impotent are the faithful. Chaste was Christ.

This last phrase stuck in my head, singing around for a few days, Christ, chaste, chaste, Christ, until I next went to see Levi.

A plane flew over the patio and I wondered if a person in the plane could see me, or if they knew what had happened. Maybe someone was coming to take Jeremiah away, away to a prison like the one they kept my father in.

Levi was cleaning a feed bucket when I walked up to the pen that day, but he motioned for me to come over and together we walked to the shade of a small oak, and looked for twin acorns on the ground. He had his hands in his pockets as if he didn't see the same fallen crop that I did so I picked up the funniest looking one first, which was our game, and it had two caps, one on top of the other so that it looked like a sultan from the Book. Levi and I stood looking at the thing in my hand, our heads almost touching when he said, I hate faggots. I looked up, scared, because I didn't know the word, and then he said I hate faggots, and I'm not one of them and I'm never going to be one. Chaste was Christ, but the impotent are faggots, he said softly, then he took the acorn from my hand and held it up to his face and said Christ was not no faggot. Then he tossed it aside and said Come on, Mercy Ann, let's go out for a ride. We had never done this before, even though once Levi had let me help him groom Blackie, and so I nodded and felt like we were true friends as Levi led me to the barn and let loose the stallion from the corral. He said This is my horse, and even though I knew I nodded and smiled because he was as proud as can be, so that his chest rounded out like the body of an acorn itself, and he kicked a bucket upside down so as to step up and swing one leg over the giant black beast. He held its matte mane then and asked me if I could ride bareback. I said Yes, of course and he reached his hand down and I took it and felt then where his palms were calloused from work, and I stepped up on that hollow bucket and lifted my skirts just enough to get a leg up and then Levi put a hand around my waist to get me on right and steady me atop that the most beautiful animal I had been on.

I was sitting there my hands hanging on Levi's back belt to hold on, feeling the animal raw beneath my legs, its great muscles starting to move as Levi clucked, pressing his heels, the backbone articulating beneath me as if to remind me in its own syllabic motion that I was doing something I had never done before.

We had taken a few steps and I was just beginning to breathe again when I heard Levi's Pa call his name. I turned and saw him, squinting and frowning in the sun and he said it again. Levi.

Levi did not answer, and even when I tapped my finger into his back he did not turn. Levi. He said again and I could hear he was closer and my breaths were closer, they seemed even to breathe back at me from Levi's warm neck, and then I felt my head pulled back and my scalp was burning and Brother Downs had the end of my long braid in his hand. Levi, he shouted. And I let out a small yelp, but he would not turn and the horse, still feeling the heels pressed into his side was walking again or still, so that I had to grab Levi's waist to keep from being pulled off the horse, and just as I thought my hair was being pulled out of the scalp which I could feel more precisely than ever Brother Downs let go and walked in front of the horse, grabbing his mane and stroking his nose to stop him. The horse snorted then and Levi's Pa said, Off. So I slid right off, and Brother Downs did not take his eyes from his son but told me to get on home and pray, and I ran then back to the road, but I looked back one more time and the two were still staring at each other, the horse non-party with peripheral vision, the three profiles in the same plane. I heard Levi say something, and only caught that one word of that day on the wind as I turned back down the road, past Jeremiah's and toward home where I did not pray but tried to busy myself.

When I got to Stan and Estelle's, in the second week, Estelle announced she couldn't take it anymore, we were going to get my hair cut so I could stop with my fishbone braiding, which is what she called it. She asked me if that would be okay, then, to be nice, but also said she thought it might be my only real chance at a normal life so I said yes.

When we went, the lady was named Sharon and she asked me in a molasses voice after she snipped it off the back if I didn't want to keep my braid. I shook my head no, but was thinking then of Levi and the horsetail, and how if he would have braided the hair before he cut it, and tied it at two ends the way Sharon had done with mine, it would have stayed together when it was sheared off the horse.

A couple of days later, when I could get away from chores and lessons, I ran back to Levi's and he was out working again, in the same pen, shoveling manure this time and blowing flies away from his mouth. I called out his name and he did not look up. I called it out again and he bent over. I called it out one last time before he picked up a dried clod of dirt or manure and straightened up and threw it at me. At first I tried to laugh like it was a game, but then he threw another one that this time hit me in the front of my dress and left a mark and so I began to back away when he said, Get out of here, Harlot, get out of here, so that I began to cry, hearing him still as I turned and ran away from that house again, tearing at the scratchy horsehair tied around my wrist, clawing it off, already digging a place for it as I ran.

At school this last year, a student wrote "faggot" on another student's locker and the principal said he would not rest until he found out who had done it. He called it a hate crime, and made it officially a suspendable offense for someone to say it or write it. Everyone seemed so bored with his passion that I did not dare ask anybody what it meant exactly. But I thought I knew something from the poor kid whose locker it was; the kid talked a little like a girl. He was sweet and shy. Nothing like Levi.

I did not go back to Levi's after that. I saw Blackie again, though. He was trotting lightly into town, and astride him was Josiah's new young wife, the pretty one from outside who had a different look than the rest of our blue-eyed army. She had white hair, and white skin and green, haunting eyes and a little scar on her left cheekbone, her navy dress a little too big for her body. She had a small child curve to her belly too, and so atop that regal horse she looked like a pale Mary riding in from the desert. I asked Jeremiah if that warn't Levi's horse and he told me it didn't matter, told me it was a wedding present for the girl. Cadence was her name, he said. Her whiteness a shock against the night of the horse. Chaste was Mary, I thought.

They never found out who wrote the word on the locker. No one ever really thought they would, but one boy leaned over to me in science class during a lab experiment where we were watching strips of paper turn bright colors in different chemicals and he told me that he did it.

I looked up at him, and his grin, and I wondered if he was a boy from where I was from. His eyes were blue, his teeth crooked so that I had to smile back at him even though I did not think what he said was true.

They gave the kid a new locker and painted over the word in white paint that didn't match the beige of the lockers and barely covered the shadow of the slur.

I sat on the patio as the afternoon came, finally daring to sip the watery electric yellow lemonade and feeling its grittiness on my teeth. It didn't matter if Jeremiah confessed or not, because of all the witnesses, but I wonder if he had said it anyway. If he could whisper, I did it. I wondered if he was sorry, and I wondered if I should bring the paper outside and burn it so I could watch the smoke twist and puff its way to nothing. Send a signal to him, maybe. To Redfield. Let them know we were out here, him and I.

At the House, on Sundays, Levi would come, postured badly with new growth, not looking at me. The horsehair still lay underground waiting, I thought, for our adolescence to be over. I could not bring myself to talk to him after being mudded at, but I still wished he wouldn't ever see Cadence atop his horse, Mary-like as she was, it wasn't a sight I thought he would find bearable. Emma came to my house sometimes, but I did not go there, and I thought there would be time for everything to return to what it once was, but I did not know we did not have time, that the place was for me and mine a spun ghost and in the end I did not even see Levi as we drove out, it was only Jeremiah's figure in the field.

In the end, I did not go get the paper to read again or burn. I just sat there, staring, sipping again. Knowing that another plane would be overhead soon, because Stan told me we live under a landing pattern, which I didn't know exactly what meant other than regularity. Knowing, also, that Stan would be home before Estelle, he would say something that had nothing to do with Jeremiah, then Estelle would come home, renewed. She would suggest I call someone at school to see what I missed. I would pretend to call someone from the sticky phone in the hall, which I had done before. We would watch TV at night, and Estelle would avoid the local news, glaring at Stan when he turned it even to the weatherman.

Tomorrow I would go to school, sit in math class, in the back, many desks away from the board.

No one would connect me with Jeremiah and his crime. This would make me feel something like disappointment.

I dumped the rest of the lemonade into a planter box made to look like an oversized boot, watched it become colorless in the pitched soil, and felt an emptiness. I didn't understand how it was possible that Jeremiah had been in that road, picking up a stone, but also in that article, doing what he done. I wanted to know if it had all happened because of the loneliness I saw that day in him: quiet, folded, waiting for the opportunity to hold something more than a small, misshaped thing from the road.

*And so here we are, back to my end.*
      Ashes, ashes. We all fall down.
*Haley + Jeremiah and then he wasn't the only one with a place to circle back to. I was there, too. But in a different place, at least at first. My grandmother's front lawn. In a pink Easter dress with tiny white flowers stitched on an itchy collar.*

*The patio is cool and rough on my cheek.*

*Spinning. My cousins' hands hot around mine.* Ashes, ashes. *They are going too fast. We collapse onto the half dead grass.*
      We all fall down.

*The smell of concrete. Lying by a pool on my stomach, drying off, my body oozing a shadow of water that darkens the patio.*

*The clouds overhead spin and I think I might be sick but I am not.*

*I am laughing.*

*I can feel him. I can feel him trying to get at me. His weight on top of me.*

*We sit up and brush away bits of dried grass.*

# Cadence

Then like a thunderstorm it came: a murderer they said, one of ours. And Tressa was howling like a wolf. And even Lizbeth was as white as me. She kept saying, I just don't think that's right. And Josiah even came in cursing. First thing he did was look at Lizbeth across the kitchen where she was keeping her hands busy and says, So he's alive after all.

Then he laughed like, ain't it the darndest thing? And then a cloud came over his face and started pacing and ranting: He's alive, and he done this? Strangled some girl, they said? He's alive, so the Prophet lied. He was *wrong*. If he hadn't made him leave this never would have happened. And where's that damn one that started it all?

He stopped and looked up like he just remembered her. His fists clenched. My throat clenched in answer.

We all looked around for the littlest mother.

She was gone.

*He's trying to get inside me as the lost syllables of his name appear on my*
*tongue like a burn,*
    *A.*
*as he thrusts my voice,*
    *MY*
    *sound out of me like a scream that will echo all the way back to you,*
*Emma.*

*Emma*

Then six weeks after they said he was alive, they said my Jeremiah had kilt someone. Strangled her they thought. Definitely murder, not at accident.

Said he had become death himself, and that the Devil's world had done ate him up and spit him out, and of course they said this and I did not believe it. Not at first. Ellen Mai's Pa came over one dull day to tell us he was in town picking up feed and the fellow at the hardware store told him: One of yurs done kilt someone. And he'd shown him a picture in a paper and it was definitely Jeremiah, and Ellen Mai's Pa got the story but not the paper and then came straight with it to Josiah and he told, yelled it in the kitchen for me to hear out the window on the back porch.

But whether it be truth or story I knew not. In the beginning when I heard I did not believe; I did not fathom that hands cupping over for the love of God and myself could do anything other than what they'd already done: work and hold and eat and touch, not kill, and it was Jeremiah who owned these hands, my Jeremiah who I knew better than anyone else, me left here behind him when he went to die and then did not die. I heard, but I did not believe it as I went down the backsteps.

It was a lie maybe that he was even still alive, because it ran counter to the Prophet, and then another lie about him on top. And at first I felt falsehood like an itch under my skin, and was blasphemed for more than three hours, and cried to Annalue and she shushed me and set me to calm so I went out and then later I got to lying down under the cottonwood tree with my firstborn asleep on my belly just so as I could think about it all, and whether it was a lie or a truth and get sure in my heart about it one way or the other and it was then I remembered the way Jeremiah could get all fevered, like that first time we were with one another as husband and wife are together and his face was hot and full of something at the time I thought was God's love and light but now I know that if God could fill him up like that, then the Devil could too, because of some unwholeness in his heart that perhaps grew when he left us here in bountiful country and we left him for dead even though he was maybe not. Not Dead. Which at that time was enough to hear in itself for its own hurting, that my ghost love was no ghost waiting for me in the after but instead lived on in this world, under this sun, somewhere without me. Then on top of that I had to hear he had gone and committed a mortal sin like to ruin my then plans for our Celestial heaven, ruin it as two wet fingers pinching a wick.

But in the end what I was to learn about myself is that this murder that Jeremiah had stained his soul with was not the part that hurt the most because what I also had come to learn was that it was in fact a crime of the heart, they said, something I did not believe as easily as I came to believe he even kilt someone with his own hands. But they said it was a woman, not so much older than me, seventeen with no name I know, who he had been with, and been with before, and then she said no, she said no like some poor fool whose never lost anything before and then he took what she wouldn't give then after he killed her with his hands they said, in a gruesome enough way to make anyone sick, like the image itself was rotten meat stink, but it broke my heart still, and so I experienced the second of what I thought then to be the two most grief-stricken moments of my life, the first being when I thought my Jeremiah was dead in the desert, and the second being when I actually ached for this girl and the way I hated her and the way I wished it had been me who was in the position of refusing, in the position of the dying. If he was going to kill some woman with his own two hands, I wanted it had been me. My neck with his hands around, my eyes getting all squoozed out and tearing, and even though it didn't take me long under that cottonwood tree to know that I was glad to be alive, and not dead, even if living hurt, it still was there, a jealousy of that girl and her not-giving ways.

She must have kissed Jeremiah and maybe they got to be with one another in a way we hadn't before she died, holding hands and resting their heads on each other and sharing candy in their mouths like I would have done with Jeremiah had it been written as want to happen in this world but it was not and now I am grateful as I have not been sent to a place where punishment is for all time.

But right then I wondered if she did things he liked, or if she was pretty, or if she seduced my poor Jeremiah and in killing her he sought to kill out the Devilish desire that had so taken him from me and this made more sense than anything else.

Yet that world don't reward no blood atonement, and I didn't think somehow that God would see us together in Celestial heaven now that Jeremiah had broken our covenant, and I had too, but not by my choice, and so it seemed our eternal seal might be cracking and even as I began to shake about it, I thought perhaps it was good, my sitting there and figuring it out before anything else got muddled by the Devil himself. The whole past with Jeremiah might have seemed then like the Lord's cruel trick on my as-yet-young heart had I not remembered that my Mama always said it's not that God always make it easy, and that He don't always work how you think He will and it's true that now I see there was a bigger plan to my earth time and now I understand its relation to the Celestial life I was born to live, but at that time I couldn't help but hating the way that terrible other woman had come and been murdered and in all that managed to steal my hope of some other love. My first true love I thought.

And I did wonder if that filthy girl had been with child, or had a child by Jeremiah, and if this child was somewhere, a sinewy echo of my own babe right under my hands. So I hated this girl all afternoon by that famous tree, exhausting myself until I was just breathing in and out. I let my chest fall and rise like it was the air working my body and not the other way, like I was Adam being breathered into for the first time and then I saw by His grace that even as the jealousy ate up some small dark part of my heart, making me fear an unwholeness like had been in Jeremiah, there prevailed a sense of peace as I lay under the cottonwood with my firstborn's nothing headweight on my lap and there were the leaves rustling ever so light and some mourning dove off on its time, and I felt the earth below me as I had when Jeremiah had been with me. And I felt as if he had returned and kilt me now and let my body fall completely from this earth, heavy and light at the same time, and it came to pass that in this bodily peace, I saw the way in which I was not kilt, and how my child's lovely head was not of Jeremiah but of his better father and as I let myself sink into tree and earth I whispered to my child:

> Deliver me, o Lord, from the Devil man, preserve me from this stink, deliver me out of great waters, from the hands of strange children.

And my own child let his eyes fly open like wing flaps and looked at me clear as day, and he let his lips part a little and reached his toy hand up toward my face as if he himself was going to deliver the Lord's benediction I had asked for, but instead he tugged on some loose strand of my red hair and pulled it toward his mouth.

And that's when I began to cry and I sat falling into that tree and cried for all that had gone some other way than we had prayed it and God must have seen this, too, for his change was ever coming.

*And then I opened my eyes and I was here. Red air, hot sky, a people I knew to be his.*

*And I was back again whispering to the Prophet.*

*I was listening to them discover my death, whispering it, getting it wrong in details. Not knowing how I'd bled.*

*Not knowing I've been with them all this time. Waiting for them to know me.*

*I watched them try to catch the blame like a wet live fish, how it flopped through their hands.*

*The Prophet's fallacy larger now, the embarrassment of God's misstep felt by all.*

*And there she was. Redheaded childmother for the women to hate.*

*But the men had their sights on him.*

*On you, my friend.*

*On you, Old Prophet.*

*I saw you Prophet on your knees. Asking, asking, squeezing your hands together as if to hold water. You were by the window of your great house with its burnt black corner and the night was coming through the glass like winter and the moon did not shine as you asked and I, in my death, laughed.*

*And you startled.*

*You could finally hear me.*

# *Annalue*

And when the word Jeremiah woke my morning, when Emma came running in the house with her face all hot and crying, pressing herself into me making no sense so that I thought Jeremiah who had already been dead, and then alive, was dead again and this time irretrievably so but as she began to slow her words so that I could hear one of them against another she told me that people were saying that he had strangled someone, a girl, up in the city, four nights before. He had his way with her and strangled her and he did it in front of people, and Emma was saying those liars, those Devils, those booze-licking heathens, they are trying to trick us and I was trying to tell her to breathe, but then she started saying how she had her own head inside a dead sow for that boy and if she didn't know him no one did and she was like to go up to that Devil-sunk city and tell that dead girl all about it.

I got a cup of cold metal water then and dripped it back over her bastard hair and told her to shush and remember she was married under the covenant of God and his Prophet, our Prophet, to a man she was not crying over so she best do it quietly or not at all. Then I held the child-mother to my chest and tried to muffle her voice so that the many ears that live in our Mama's house would not hear while she said how first and foremost it warn't true, warn't true at all and second how none of this would have happened if she and Jeremiah hadn't a got caught, or if her Pa or Josiah would have let it go and let them just be the children they were, and children of God they were, she said, but most of all if Josiah hadn't made Jeremiah leave for a world that wasn't his and making the Prophet say he was dead, and that if this murder had in fact happened, she said, it was all the fault of Josiah for Jeremiah had had to die and then be reborn so who's to say the Devil didn't intervene then and rebirth a bad version of her love out there in the world. Josiah is at fault, she said, and maybe even I don't know that Josiah isn't the Devil's right hand. And it was then I had to stop her with a light slap and hold her chin like a spool of thread I was getting ready to wind and tell her that she better bury those words that she just let fall out of her mouth or get ready to bury the both of us and her child, too. You make a grave inside you, I told her, and you make it big enough to fit all you just said and you close it up tight with dirt and wood and the stone-heaviest thing you got in you willful little Emma, or else we are all going to be in a lot of trouble, and then I held her while she worked herself greatly into her own silence.

I spoke to her then of small things we loved as children so as to calm her mind away from murder, fictitious or not. I spoke of a book we had had once about the King of France, and his beautiful wife, and their beautiful palace. I reminded her how we would take turns playing Louis and Marie, us both wanting to be Marie and how once we even put flour in our hair to imitate their white wigs, and pretended our mama's oatmeal cookies were their fine cakes, and that our bedroom was filled with gold furniture, but how we would always make another ending for ourselves when we played the game so that rather than be beheaded we would meet our real selves, and come to God and give lots of money to the poor. In this way we baptized poor Louis and Marie.

And if she was listening to these things she already knew, I did not know, but she started to breathe regular and finally bit her lip and said she'd go check on her child and perhaps walk for a while but would be back later and she gave me a little kiss and walked away like one not quite in her body.

I did not even have the chance to tell her of the child new to our house not even two days before, that slept in my Mama's bed as she sat weeping one room over.

I walked down later that day with the baby to see if I could see her at Josiah's but the door was closed in such a way and me with this unstoried baby I dared not knock.

I walked back down the road with the swaddling to our house so small against the evening sky, and my Mama was sitting on the porch, rocking on the swing like time itself. Her voice was even as I came up the stairs as she told me trouble was coming. Not brought by God but by his men. Then she reached out and offered to hold the babe while I peeled carrots for dinner.

Emma came back the next afternoon steady as stone which did not surprise me as often she changed her mood and her belief into their exact opposite so quickly that it was not unusual for God and the Devil to be in one mere sentence for her. She came back and was finally looking in at the found baby sleeping and saying how it must a been a miracle given to me by God, didn't I think so, when Mama came in the house from leaving her two smallest boys at Jenna's and gossiping down the road and she looked at Emma, who looked away, before she said Don't let no foolish tears run over this, Emma, you already walkin one thin line. And Mama came to her daughters then and I saw her hands were shaking and for the first time she lowered her voice and she did something like confide in us like we were women folk just as her and in fact we were. Mothers.

Tressa somehow blaming you Emma, she thinks you tainted the family name forever by seducing a son, and getting him exiled into the wilderness to become a slaughtering Lamanite and then she said, what will you do next, having seduced the father? And you better believe Josiah ain't none too happy either and the Prophet is having to come over and tell them that Jeremiah had this evil in him from the beginning, and used it to so corrupt little Emma into disobeying the laws of God, and the Prophet, having had his holy dream of Jeremiah dead in the desert says he now misread it as one who was invoking hell rather than dead and inhabiting it and he, the Prophet, should have gone at that instant to find and murder Josiah's son out in the desert.

God, the Prophet said, does not always speak in words.

Emma began to tell Mama how untrue this one was, and Mama clamped a hand over the child-mother's mouth like her lips were a fly Mama was aiming to catch.

This is good, child, Mama said ever so slow then, and then again, This is Good. You are to wait here until someone come here and tell us that the Prophet has calmed them with His Words and revealed to them the unalterable destiny and prophecy of their son Jeremiah which has culminated in his murdering of a sinner, if in fact he even murdered anyone at all.

Emma was shaking with her own silence then and so with the baby still napping on my bed and my arms free I was holding her upright when Pa came in and looked at us gathered and clucked his tongue, It's the women getting in all the trouble, he said, Don't see why the boys have to leave. Then Mama gave him a look and he said Well, now you hiding babies, so don't be surprised when we have no home if He deems fit. And then quick as a dust storm he left but by his words we knew the baby could stay, that he had talked to Josiah about it and as long as he had this one powerful ally, all he had to do was wait for a calmer time to tell the Prophet we found a lost gentile baby and were keeping it.

Then Mama said, Emma, go get a flour sack from the cellar, it's time to make.

I asked her what she had in mind and she said our Emma here is going to make a Penny Cake for that Prophet so as to show him her appreciation for making her own home open to her again, so that she can go back and get her own son from the sadly clipped wings of that Tressa, and live in peace with her husband and Lizbeth and even that orphan wife. And she said this like it was fact, but really the only thing she knew was that something was coming and how she hoped it was this. Forgiveness. We going to make, she said again. Which even as differently as things went, I still think was a good idea on Mama's part, as she was by far the best baker in Redfield.

And she started to roll up her sleeves and wipe the wood table clean ready and I knew then that I had never seen my Mama so shaken even as she readied to bake a cake, her hands were atremble and her eyes downcast so that I wanted to put my hand on her arm and steady her but knew that that was like to earn me a slap first and foremost and that I best keep quiet or she was like to make me beg the Prophet to let me be his wife after all in gratitude for what he done for Emma, but then as Emma came bumping a sack up the stairs she yelled Don't Drag, Carry Girl, and her voice broke just a little so that she had to lay her rag on the table and as I stepped toward her, she turned to me and whispered something I won't ever forget.

*We never used to be scared.* She said this and then began to look around the table as if she'd misplaced something and was sitting staring like this when Emma appeared, sack against her leg, bending her over to one side looking up at Mama and about to say What, when instead I shook my head at her and said I'd get the sugar though sugar sounded like the worst thing in the world right then, something about all this, displacement and anger and a murder, gruesome as it was, his hands upon her throat bruising up her skin, and blood somewhere, there must have been, somewhere she must have been bleeding and then Manti's sunken head, bandaged for his grave and his sallow face like an aged glass doll now under the red silt and there we were, measuring out white sugar so as to make a cake to celebrate us not being punished for her death, or for his, as if Jeremiah was a true scapegoat sent out into the desert and the fact that we remained alive amongst the unfound blood was sweet.

But still the three of us quiet baked the cake, while we waited for someone to come, while the baby napped, and it took us longer than usual; I think now because we did not want to be done and still feel as if we were waiting. It was too many hands for one cake but we took turns. I watched the most as Emma and Mama beat in eggs, and pinched in salt and I wondered if either one of them would say anything if I leaned over and spit into that hay-colored batter, or if they would just stir in my perfidious saliva with silent accomplice against a force equally as silent or perhaps it *was* the sonority of the thing we felt to be quaking, reverberating in the air what we could not see, could not know, until some arced moment when it would finally show its apparition to our eyes.

*So I whispered:*

*Oh Prophet.*

*Carry, carry Deseret.*

*Cup your old hands over it; let it buzz softly in your time worn palms.*
*Bumping its felt head against your handchurch.*
    *Let the honey body simmer until it has relieved you of your tired and*
*ugly power.*

*He looked for me but couldn't see me. He wanted to ask if God is finally*
*speaking in words and not images and why this voice so young and so . . . but*
*he dared not.*

*Carry it to Emma. Let it fly up into her cherry mouth. She started this, tell*
*them, so she can end it. She is strong tell them, has known the Devil, will*
*lead us well, tell them. I will make sure they will believe.*
    *And then you go quietly into the desert.*

*It is that, or add your red to the land. Darken the stain with your own life.*
*My blood is on your hands, you know now. I am the murdered girl.*

*Point, and shoot.*

# Annalue

We were baking and waiting. And then that baby cried awaking and had made such a mess of herself that as the batter went into the oven she went into the sink for a bath. And we kept our voices low but giggled at her tininess until a real and at once proverbial shadow came in across the doorway light, the darkening that just three nights before I had craved in reprieve from a bewitched full moon.

On the threshold, enjoying the effect made by his presence, was that Prophet I knew better than I ever hoped to know and whose smell made my skin itch still. We all stopped.

The first one to move was my Mama and she picked up that naked newborn in such a way, her hands straight under its unbaptized back so that I thought she might offer, in fact, this prodigal child instead of that Penny Cake as penance for the uncertain crime or crimes that did not really involve Emma, but could not be extricated from her when no culprit lay in punishable reach.

But Mama said nothing, as the air still quaked. But she took that child and wrapped it in a clean dish towel and took a step back, as if to perhaps hide its presence from that Prophet, or as if, I thought, Emma, was small again and could be swaddled. As if my Mama could protect us, her one trouble girl and her near-exile son and even me and my borrowed life, protect us from this man as she walked backward with this unknown child toward the cellar stairs so that my breath caught in my throat and I dared to wish that rather than the Prophet know her, that my mother would take her down, down those fruit-fly smelling stairs where one could feel metallic water seeping into one's skin and bury that baby. Dig her a crib out of the summer soil, lay her down, sing to that babe, and then, crumble the cool pieces, like sweet cake topping, over the child. A blanket of dirt no one would have to cry over. And now I am grateful she did not, but that is what I thought, and knew myself to be thinking, when that shadow crested into our already forlorn light and my Mama backed away with the only body in the room she could carry.

The Prophet took a step in and nodded at my Mama. Sister, he said. And he looked tired, his lean shoulders were hunched forward, his face older than his fifty years, ragged and even, I thought, shriveling.

Emma, the Prophet said, and I'll never forgive myself for the lightness I felt then. But Emma did not look up, her chin aquiver and oh how I wanted to take her, my baby sister, and disappear away somewhere with her.

Emma, he said again, and she looked up then at him, her lips so red and wet that her childhood was still a palpable thing within her, and she said, Why we're making you a cake Prophet Ellis.

The trembling in the air now feels as if it was what it was: not enough. But at the time, it felt like it was all we could do, we as a group: sister, mother, daughter, not one of us willing to take one of the butter cutting knives and commit some murder, just like the kind we were presently trying to distance ourselves from. The trembling felt not like an earthquake, no shaking of the ground or glass, but a shaking of the air between us that you could feel both in and on your skin, though the Prophet perceived nothing that he admitted. Early summer wavered in a bird's voice outside the window as He just stared at my temptuous little baby sister and extended a finger out to her, curling it like he already had it under her chin and was caressing her jugular.

Emma left the tableside to come and stand before him.

Then he turned to my Mama, and said All is Well, Sister Downs.

And as my own saliva droughted up from mouth he said, God has Spoken: it seems the Devil invaded here briefly in the form of a boy we thought our own, but it is our good fortune that I hath exiled him from our people's land before he did worst; I acted before he could do to one of our sweet sisters what he has done elsewhere. And I have told Josiah and his brethren this: Emma, who was chosen to endure the most difficult of tests that God may have, came out unscathed from her consortiums with one of Satan's earthly forms, showing her true Nephithetic faith.

The Prophet wiped his brow. His voice hoarsed down almost to a whisper.

Emma is a Savior Angel and they are to hail her as such.

And then the Prophet, who had been in me, and had scorned me, did something I never thought him to do, he knelt his grown form in front of my baby sister and he began to cry.

It started as a choking sound so that I thought I may be mishearing because the baby behind me had been making sounds, but now it was the Prophet of God under serious scrutiny that knelt before my baby sister and began to weep into his hands.

We have, he said, and looked up.

We have been saved. He palmed Emma's cheeks.

We are saved, he said. I did not kill that Devil, though God asked me too, and I see that now, that's what he wanted, like Abraham, out on that Egypt highway. I did not kill him, and I will be forever punished with the blood of that young girl.

And a desert hawk screamed, now, outside the window and we all started but for the Prophet who didn't seem to hear it.

Instead he shifted on his knees and slowly unbuttoned his white collared shirt, each button a year without breath.

Then he slipped it off in our still kitchen to show us things we did not have eyes for.

I saw only briefly some of the self-inflicted lashings of a godly man before I heard my mother gasp and turned to her and the child.

The still wet child of nowhere was bout to fall out of my mother's gaping hands and so I reached to take her just as my mother fell to faint, me catching her with my body, helping her to the floor where she slumped while Emma reached a shaking hand toward the Prophet.

She reached toward the man kneeling before her, and time stopped.

Time stopped. And I lost my baby sister.

I lost her and could see I was losing her as she began to trace a map of His open wounds with her finger and the voice of God must have winced but I do not know because I did not take my eyes from her face. Her pale freckles were still and entranced as the Prophet began to moan, to cry, to be salvated, and Emma also began to sound and I heard the two of them making tiny exasperated sighs of some tired pain, the sounds I imagined that they imagined to be the sounds of souls suffering and I saw her reach a stuttering hand to the balled forehead of our leader and I knew that she was lost.

He had given her a silver fish for bait, and she, little sister, had swallowed it immediately and wholly.

I knew she was lost.

And I was already walking out the door when that man whose weight I had been under told Emma, sweet, sugar-crusted fingers Emma who was baking a Penny Cake that he would take her. Take her. Teach her. Take her.

And as I left with the swaddled child, I heard her saying, I heard her saying I made a cake, I made a cake and I imagined a hot batter poured over the two, the un-risen sweet mud concentrated over them like some unholy blanket and I took this baby out into blooming day where the rising moon was again beginning to unbed itself as chipped on one side but still almost full and I was all the way to the edge of the field when I heard those clod steps behind me.

I found it.

Levi stood behind me, hands in pockets, sick with his own grin.

Whose is it? I swallowed.

None of your business, he said. Might as well be Jesus, he said then, stepping toward me.

You don't know, and I began to sidle away.

Still, I found it, I want to see it.

No, Levi, leave it.

Boy or girl? And he stepped forward. He'd left us to this child for three days, hiding, and now he wanted to know it.

I looked at the small ungendered face, like a small pale nut of new fruit. He could not see it was a girl. Could not know it was a girl. Could not know the way the word *girl* hurt in a world like ours.

Bastard is what it is, Levi said then, leaping at me so as to grab the child like she was some toy he wanted but I stepped back and he missed and I began to run through those cottonwoods, as fast I could, which is not very fast owing to my limp, but Levi didn't follow and only his laughter chased me through the underbrush, the ducksound always just behind me.

I ran until I felt my chest bones the way you suddenly do when you are on some verge and I was holding this runt child, whose mother I did not know, and whose father I wouldn't water, and suddenly I didn't know what reason I had to save her because in the northern lands of my uncertain mind, I had not yet planned to care for her forever.

In fact, I had that first night in the kitchen planned to do just as I imagined Mama doing. I had imagined giving it some kind of soft bed of death where it would not have to run through the night carrying its likeness just to protect it from that thing she didn't have a name for, that other trembling sonority that didn't haunt, but buzzed with light in the back of a head, the way that the softness of the skin of something that would live would pulse with the inevitability of its time for this world.

V

*I whispered again to Emma: If you turn your mind-dirt over to where it's dark, where you don't often go and it smells cool and mineral, then maybe now you are ready to listen.*

*This is what your Prophet does whenever he tries to dream God but I'm talking so loud he hears me instead.*

# Mercy Ann

We are working on root words and origins in English class so as to give us a "one-up," as Mrs. Kendricks likes to say, and so we each get a letter and we have to go home and look up the origin of ten new words that begin with that letter and then write a sentence that will help us learn it. I get "B." Stan pulls down the dictionary with the best etymology, and then wonders with a giggle what the etymology of etymology is, but he doesn't bother looking.

B. As in belittle, betroth, betray, beloved, behoove.

As in *Banish,* from vulgar Latin, cognate, bannire: bandit. As in, we must banish any bandit from the community to keep our people pure and worthy.

As in *Beasts.* From Latin bestia. The word for wild creatures until it was ousted in the 16th century by *animal,* from the Christian Apocalypse story. As in, the four horsemen. As if the original animal is actually a man connected to an animal, a two-bodied figure. *Animal,* as in, that which is alive, living, from "anima" breath, soul, current of air. As in, the animal breathed hard as it tried to outrun the Beast.

As in *Belittle*: A new word, coined by Thomas Jefferson. To make someone feel small: As in whenever you remind me I never learned multiplication tables, you belittle me. As in, when you ask me how I'm adjusting to the real world, it belittles my other world. As in, when you tell me that it's okay, I'll catch up someday, I feel belittled. It's an act of belittlement when you tell me, too, that it's nice I'm trying so hard, or that at least I can read.

As in *Betroth*: Be- as in transit, Troth- as in truth. When my mother became my father's betrothed, she promised to be true to him and the laws of plural marriage and so cannot come back for me. Never mind that I would never have done that to her. Never mind that when Estelle tries to make me feel better by saying, you just got to remember that that life is all she's ever known, I want to yell, But she knew me! She would have me and Ziona and Bess and wouldn't that be something. But *beget*, as in, Old English, begietan, *to get by effort*, has no root meaning *to keep true*.

As in *Betray:* Be- as in thoroughly, Trair- as in hand over. My father's third wife, Adaleen, betrayed us when she *handed us* all over to the authorities. She didn't miss a single one of us in her palm. She ran away in the night, picked up by a nurse she met in town a year before when she'd had to go the doctors because of a hemorrhage that wouldn't stop. The nurse stopped the bleeding and then plugged her with an IV needle and as she did she said that no man had a right to marry her at fourteen. Not in this great country, no siree. Adaleen tells me this story. She tells me she wanted to go to school, she tells me on the phone when she calls that first time. She tells me how she never wanted to be married, how she fought my father kicking and screaming that first night. She wanted us all to go to school and not have always just to obey and to have babies. She wanted some breathing room. She wanted the best for us all. For me. And I hang up on her.

As in *Belie:* From Old English beleogan: deceive by lying. When Estelle asks me if I'm okay after Adaleen's call, I tell her I'm fine and I hope my face belies my feelings. I never lied back home. Now, I lie all the time. When kids ask me if I was promised to some old man, I say of course not and try to think about whether Brother Jens is old. He wasn't old there, only in his forties, but he would be here. There he's a husband, because he has a house and two other wives but here he would be a teacher or a gym coach or some other adult, on the other side of a line from us kids. There, it was ordained. Here, it wouldn't be *appropriate*.

As in *Believe:* Old Germanic, literally to hold dear, love. As in I believe my mother would have stayed if she held us dear. If she loved us. She would have held us because she knows that while she can go back, we can't. Not by our laws but by state laws. We are wards, *believed* to be in danger from our parents. We are held dearly away from them. I *believe* I never would have left her. And if I had children, I would hold on to them, too.

As in, you have to believe me, Mercy Ann, Adaleen says. As in, I do.

As in *Behold*: from be- thoroughly, halden- to hold. Behold, the document in my hand is the one you sign for me, saying I will be yours, and not my mother's anymore. Understand it thoroughly, so you can't *hold* it against me later, when I am getting Fs in school and have started hanging out with someone besides you and Stan. *For behold, at that day shall he rage in the hearts of the children of men.*

As in *Blood*, from old English blod, as in to swell, gush, burst. As in, when they took my blood to verify my parentage, it gushed into the glass vial but when they took it again to see if I had been vaccinated as a baby, they couldn't even get the vein right. As in, *the blood of the saints shall cry from the ground against them.* As in, trying to get a word out of you today is like trying to get blood out of a stone. As in, they're out for blood. As in, when the phone rang again not one minute after I hung up on Adaleen, my blood boiled.

As in *Behave.* Be + have, from Germanic sich behabben, to *have* oneself in a particular way. As in, when my mother told me to behave myself when she said goodbye, she was really telling me to have myself, because she wouldn't anymore.

As in *Brethren.* From the Book of Mormon, plural for brother, meaning brotherhood even among sisters. As in Adaleen is my mother too, a betrayer who believed the brethren were beasts and who betrothed and belied my father and still I pick up the phone that second time because she is all I have left.

As in *Burn.* From Old English, birnan, to be on fire and boernan, consume by fire. As in, the whole of it is on fire, and so will burn to the ground. As in, to leave the community is to ensure your soul will be consumed by fire, to burn, but to leave your child. There's no law for that. Not when outsiders are involved.

As in, I'll burn this. As in, I'll burn this in the bathroom with a match and flush the ashes down the toilet and rewrite the assignment with words like backgammon and breathless. I'll meet with Adaleen maybe just once, but not yet. Not until I finish this school year I'm barely hanging on to.

Not until I look up something for Stan:

*Etymology.* As in -ology, the study of, and -etymos: truth. As in, the true sense. As in, etymology can help us understand a word's many histories.

As if, in studying every letter of every word, the truth would just surrender itself, hands up, and tell you what it means.

And not until I look something up for myself:

Polygamy. 1) From Greek poly–many + gamos–marriage. *Betroth.* 2) Zoology: Having more than one mate. As in, when someone is polygamous, they have more than one mate. As in, they have children. As in, even if you, Adaleen, bled out your first and only baby, it doesn't mean your sisterwives didn't have children. *Beget.* 3) Botany: the condition of bearing some male and some female flowers on the same plant. As in, children on your same plant, some male, and some female. *Brethren.* 4) Prophet: It is through our laws that men become gods, and women become heavenly mothers. *Behave.* 5) Mother: The only path to eternity, to be adhered to no matter, with children who are living so as to be with their mothers, forever, in the world they knew entirely but did not know to love or not love. *Blood.* 5) Estelle: It's just not how people are meant to live. *Beasts.* 6) Stan: Well, to each his own.

*Animals.* 7) Adaleen: It's a sick world, and as soon as you get used to being away from it, you'll thank me. *Beholden.*

8) Me: My mothers, my sisters, my lamb, my bed, my room, my house, my road, my friends, my Pa, the spoon in my mouth, the dust in my nose, the water in my hair, the earth at my feet.

*Banished.*

*Annalue*

The next night after she became some Angel of hearsay, Emma came into our bedroom, now just mine, when I was awake lying down and watching the little face, seeing if its hard beginning had left any kind of sign, and I saw my sister's shape move like one on stage. I asked her if she was not all right.

Yes, she said. And then she began to talk quietly, quickly, saying well at first she just couldn't believe it and was just going along with it but then she'd had such dreams the night before that now she really did see how it was all as meant to be. Her Celestial love for Jeremiah had been a mistake, a misinterpretation of God's will, still God's light and love but in the wrong direction, and that she had always felt herself to be different, matchstick hair and all, and didn't I think it all made sense now, now that the Prophet had declared her, no not just the Prophet but God himself speaking through the Prophet, to be made of the same material as God himself, female as she was, something of her was light and power and hadn't she always prayed the hardest, believed the most, even when I spoke my doubt and even when the Devil catcalled her and sucked her neck she was still there, in God's light because she was *of* it, didn't I see, and I listened to her with a stone in my throat, and I turned on my side, my back to her cadence, my face to the baby, and I saw the world for the first time in two stories.

There was the Prophet, there was the story of God and his will and his words and his wrath and his light, with revelations and testimony and resolving all doubt and all was God or Satan. And then there was the second world of I and the baby, the world of Alice Parley Smith, Emma's lust and Levi's restlessness and my disgrace and Jeremiah's murder and murdering, there was language as empty as an oil drum, there was a long road where a girl had sinned and a boy had disappeared and a man had lied and yet only spoke more words on top, the layering words of His world, words that made Angels out of sisters and wives out of children and that had now taken Emma for its own.

When she rose and came around to the fruit crate and asked me if I wanted her to bless the child, I spoke like choking water around the stone and said not yet. She said she really thought she should, lest it die in the night and I told her "it" was a she and she wasn't like to die in the night, and that blessings should be done in light not in dark to which she acquiesced and then she fell silent and I was left to wonder for this child and I. Us two of that second world, and whether we could really hold on if things got slipperier, hollower.

And the end was so nigh, you could feel it in the air.

And in the next days, Emma was gone, walking the world now like it was the top notes of a hymn. And Mama sat me down to tell me that in fact what the Prophet hadn't said, or maybe he did but she'd never know it, fainted out cold as next day meat, was that Josiah would not be taking Emma back, on the count of Lizbeth whose heart too had been strangled or shot up by her son's hands. That raising up Emma was the Prophet's last way to save face against Josiah, who would not obey this man any longer.

She said that Emma now was like one with a fever, dazed and walking, and went to Him, and lived with him as not just a wife but as some kind of heavenly mother/angel/darling prophet the likes of which this place has never seen and isn't one never too old to have seen it all.

She was gone, and all was amiss, and the end was so nigh but it was not over yet.

And still it was not over when I learned to whom this baby belonged, would hear from my Mama who heard it from Lizbeth who heard it from Josiah that Cadence had seen Manti's mother, Beth, had seen her big-bellied and now she was not. And now this baby. And what man had gone to her? What man visited her? It was not hard to guess.

So I began to understand her perfect little hands to be the product of that same pain I had had inside me. Later I would begin to remember that pain as not coming from without, from Him, but from within, from her. As if it was childbirth that left me limping home that long ago August day, my thighs slimy. And even though it wasn't until a year after that she was found, she would still be mine. My gift. And even if she was also His, I had given her a name that would not be known to Him. And it was I who would see when she grew the first white grain of her first tooth, and I who would finally know how to read all her motions and hear her sounds, and I who would know that she had not just a cry for hunger, sleep, and pain, but also one that was more desperate. One that told me we would leave.

But not before the eastern sky blackened once more.

*Emma*

I was hungry less and less. While I fed my child still from my own breast, I was at home less and less, living now in the home of the Prophet where he would kiss my hand and take me to his bed but only if I desired and if I did, it was not a base sentiment of the inadequate body, but a desire to know God closer and to hear him better myself and perhaps I did and perhaps I didn't in the short time I lived with Him before He was called to His own becoming.

Josiah spoke no longer to me, and while his face carried what looked like anger, I knew it myself to be fear. He was afeared of his young prophet wife so out of grace I did not go near him. I did not deem speak to Lizbeth but Tressa was suddenly kind and quiet, and I spoke to her when I could summon the words for the mundane. Cadence edged around me like I was a lamp whose light she did not want to come under and this was her, always, with her white hair and scaredy-cat ways and I thought when I saw her that when I knew more about the ways in which God was up in me, I would lay my hands on her head and tell her not to be afraid and make her cry and come to God, really, because while she said that she believed and she wore that arrowhead as a token of her conversion I could see that she did not bend down to His Mercy, and even still the black point of the old thing left a red mark in her pale chest plain as day.

And when I saw Annalue, sweet sister of mine, and spoke to her in the days after these things, she tried to put her hand upon my head, to soothe me as if my faith was a fever and so I would not speak anymore but move her hand and say Leave me Sister. While I was sad she could not see what I could so plainly now about my life and my fate before the eyes of God, I knew that someday I would cure her earthbound limp and then she would see.

She would know and she would thank me, and would no longer tear up when I talked to her again of His grace the Prophet, and of his wisdom, and she would listen, and kneel at my skirt, and I would raise her up again and even that originless child would be blessed and we would be sisters again as we once were.

Her limp, his shame, her stutter, his doubt, her spite, his crushed head, the babe: I would heal them all. I would extinguish the illness that smoldered here and burned the edges of our community so that outward and upward we could grow. We would not be a wayward people out in the desert any longer with no bounty for our sowing, but a prosperous people who carried indelible signs of favor in His eyes.

Then Annalue would know, would see. I would lay my hands on Annalue's leg, I would feel the death in its flesh and I would call back the bones and blood and skin from purgatory where the yoke of the Devil could still reach that poor tissue and into the Celestial of a working limb, a body that contained humanness in its essence, humanness without the divine, but pure in soul, which is what my sister was.

I would fix her and she would walk, stand even, and together we would run into the field where God could see and she would kneel, her leg able to bend beneath her for the first time, and I would kneel and she would cry and hold me and say thank you, thank you dear Emma and then she would take my poor child, my poor poor baby born not unto a woman whose life was bound only to motherhood, but to things above the earth we walk, and she would care for it, care well so that I could go.

Go and do my unending work of God, which would begin—I knew, I dreamt, I heard whispered in the estival hum of the air—when I saw some great sign, some great mercurial darkness that filled the sky and was for me and for me alone to surrender myself unto,

so that my hands would unfold and

touch
bless
come apart
the bones gone red
with the culmination of prayer.

# *Annalue*

I dreamt once that I could walk straight and it's not an easy thing to tell you that I only dreamt this once, and not more. Having a limp is an inconvenience in most ways, and feeling that coldness in one's own body is something one gets used to till it really does start to creep upward, and the sky goes black, and you wake sweating, free, and able to run, quickly, toward that blue and formidable escarpment that you know suddenly to be the edge of your heart, and the end of your ability to know even where in the body just one bone might fit.

## *Levi*

For days the summer air was still and hung like a sheet on a line that would not dry. No breeze to blow it. Two murders like that callin out to each other 'cross distance like owls in the night. One here, one there. One horse, one Jeremiah. One boy, one girl. Two sinners dead but the crimes echoin in the air, atonin nothin. Emma gone to some high place, and there never was nothin more wrong than that and so I didn't even bother hidin anymore and Pa and I were waitin together now for Josiah to climb up His steps, knock Him down, and then let God know he'd be the one listenin from here on out.

I waited to show Pa I was man after all, be there to help him, to help Josiah, to wait till we were needed. Maybe soon as the wind kicked up just a little bit.

# Emma

I was waiting always then for some great sign, some great billowing darkness that would fill the sky and be for me alone to surrender myself unto.

I waited and whispered Nephi's words to the summer sky like they are written in my blood *I shall show unto you that the tender mercies of the Lord are over all those whom he hath chosen, because of their faith, to make them mighty even unto the power of deliverance.*

My milk dried up and I knew my body to be wringing itself out of mother heaviness, preparing for the great task ahead, and I told Josiah: I will not come here any longer at all and he finally spoke to me again to say But your child, and I motioned to Tressa and Mary behind her in the corner. Mary, arms folded, glaring, like I had taken something from her person, when it was she who so long ago took from me with her half broken mouth that could still speak truth. I saw Josiah grow angry and I know it's because he thought it would be himself the Prophet would choose to be under his wing but I did not say that, holy as I had become, but rather told him *Sing, oh heavens and be joyful, oh earth, for the feet of those who are on this land, for they shall be smitten no more; for the Lord will have mercy on the afflicted* and he waxed of natural covenants and two sons now spurned and false prophecies but his blasphemous storm was not the one I had been awaiting so I stood like a stone eye in the eddy center of it and felt not even the dust kicked up and heard not the unholy words but only sound, as if I was under a soft and timeless current.

I walked down the road, back to the one who understood me.

The one, the Prophet, who knows what it is like to have one ear listening. To have a belly of dreams stemmed with an umbilical cord to the Celestial, fed without eating in the night by a voice that speaks only in images. Overturned tin pail. Coyote pups. Listing fence. Bloody legs of childbirth. Blue dresses.

Light. Light. Light.

The one who grew steadily quieter, who I could see grew tired, old. His long face withering. He was old, and I was young. I could see that as I grew stronger, he weakened. He waited for me to speak, and then one early day he gave me a honeybee sleepy with the morning cold and rolled its bumping body into my hands and told me to cup it carefully.

This, he said. Everything is this. And I knew then what he meant and I could see that he was preparing to depart and that I would continue to grow stronger and more in spirit, if less in body, waiting for the time when I would become the voice itself, the language and the pail, the legs, the fence, the dress and speak with my hands

open before me

walking all the way, even through flames, to the time when

*the spirit and the body shall be reunited again in perfect form.*

# Annalue

Waiting, it seemed, more so than our usual state of waiting always for the end to come to save us, to show as the chosen ones, the state we lived in always heightened to a high note that held like a breath, a heavy storm cloud of sound ready to drop any moment. And then suddenly, after all of that waiting:

smoke smell and a bell ringing and voices shouting.

It was a good fire this time, not one put out so quick. I left the baby sleeping with Mama in ear reach and limped down the road to see what was happening, to check to make sure the house was empty as they said it was. Empty of Emma, who'd been at our house but then had left to wander.

And as I came down the road I saw her. I called her name, but she kept walking toward the fire.

I called her name again before I knew myself to be in another dream where one can scream but no sound is made.

I saw her walk towards the fire like she wasn't going to stop. But no, I thought, she will turn. She will hear me.

I saw her walk towards the fire and imagined her elsewhere. She was often elsewhere, often not there, where she walked now: foolyouth shining like work on her cheeks, red hair afire with light, moving with the cadence of an old heart.

Oh, Emma. I walked faster. My limp a curse always and now. I knew she would turn around. *Emma.*

But it became hard to say *when* she was going to turn around.

Everything was like that then, hard to say, even the taste in the air. Hard to say, to remember. Even the names of the horses in the background were hard to place. Or you could say the names but not which horse they belonged to, and it seemed odd that it had ever been clear.

Bridger, Appleseed, Mary Legs, Star of Celestial.

All words without bodies as the earth underfoot eroded ever so quiet and smoke smudged out the day.

She was too far ahead of me.

And even as she was right close, I knew she would, she would. Turn away from the fire.

*Emma.*

The sight of the day, the place, was becoming more granular.

I knew she would. I had always known it, I thought. I knew her. A convert. She would convert away before even the heat reached her.

I saw her and I watched her and her white dress through the smoke like a dab of paint, hem stiff to the ground until the sky turned the color of stale blood and then I could not, not any longer.

So I watched the road.

*And so here we are, after all this time.*

*I stopped screaming and I opened my eyes and I was here. So I started all over and I waited and whispered and presided ghostly until I knew what I was waiting for, what I had been waiting for since I circled back to the beginning of this story and it was this:*

*I saw her, Manti's mother, black hair maddened, face smudged, dark blue nightgown torn, lost husband/lost Manti/lost baby, light a match just where her son had lit his.*

*I saw the mad woman fan the little flames up under the porch of the Prophet's house.*
    *I saw Josiah see the smoke and run down the road. I saw him, in his son's likeness. Josiah.*

*I saw the flames rise higher. Heard children, everyone, everyone coming out of the house. Someone yelling, Again.*

*I saw her. Emma. I watched her.*
    *I watched Josiah watch his youngest wife walk slowly towards the flames. I watched him wonder if God was somehow inside her small body. He sucked in his bottom lip.*
    *I watched the age on his face, and the sun of a thousand different days all the same, but all different than this one, rise their heat up to the surface of him.*
    *I watched him watch for the Prophet.*

*I heard him as he wondered how to stop God's Voice, the Voice within the* man, whether he would have to kill the man, the Prophet, and whether it would stop if He was dead. He wondered if he didn't have to kill the man, too, if he could just cut out the Voice. Find the part of the throat or stomach or chest which spoke, and he wasn't sure which it was, where it was. I saw him touch his own body looking for where voice was, his hand on his chest, then his throat, then his mouth.

I watched him watch her also, black hair wild, the remnants of childbirth a paunch, walking up the steps to the Prophet's house.

His hand stayed on his mouth.

She stayed in the doorway watching her work, her flames, her son's real funeral. Then she took a step in.

Emma kept walking.

I watched him watch things burn. Fabric burn. Sky and shoe, melt.

I watched him get close to the source of the flames, breathe in smoke, then buckle over himself, straining face to stomach, choking his own throat, pressing his arms and hands into the parts of himself he couldn't see, couldn't know, pressing and trying to smother the voice that might be within him, also.

I saw the other, the voice, the Prophet walk out of the back of the house and into a crack in the mesa. A split, a wound for him to infect.

I heard nothing. No sound as Emma kept walking. Up the porch steps.

I saw Emma commit herself to flames on one side of the porch and then I heard Annalue calling her sister's name and again I heard the sirens on the patio.

Emma. Emma. Emma.

I whispered, shouted, screamed.

Burn it all.

*And my voice was the smoke, the sky, and the water sitting useless in the creek.*

*And then I saw her crippled sister stand frozen and the wild-haired woman, Manti's mother, Beth, try to do one thing right. To turn and see the girl, a mother herself we know but remember a girl. To run back out of the house, blue nightgown billowing, howling, to grab Emma by the arm and pull her out of the fire and down the steps and extinguish her smoking and black-ened dress with the weight of her own body.*

*She did this and then she sat back as others surrounded them.*

*Then she saw right through that gathering crowd, and for the second time looked right at me.*

*She looked right at me, her dark hair nest, her cheek smudged black, her gown smoking. She looked at me and raised her arm to point back at the burning house.*

*Ashes falling like snow.*

*I nodded back at her, my shape singing with her gaze.*

# *Annalue*

Within minutes the Prophet's house burned to good, and with it the blue hot center of my shame.

Everything was all smolder now, ember and ash. But no one could say it was all over as grass was still burning to the west, catching a barn and one other house. And Emma was silent in her pain, one arm, one leg burned well, the flames licking her face on one pink cheek, her hair half gone, silent she lay as Sister Beth rolled upon her, as someone came with a pail of water, as I turned to scream to limp to go to find Pa. No one could say it was over even as Pa pulled up his truck and we got out and wrapped her smoking body in a quilt and pushed my moaning mother away and still Emma did not make a sound and I knew it was bad, my sister's pain, and I was in the colder parts of my own flesh relieved that it was not only half-bad. Half-bad my Pa could pretend she didn't need their medicine but as it was he did not think on it but swooped her up and drove fast out of town, leaving a red dust swarm, fast to their clinic where they sent them both by ambulance to the city. She, still his child.

No one would say it was over even as our Prophet vanished out of sight. Some say he had walked into the desert while the fire still burned, and our people wandered about with open hands, and even then there was a reluctance to end any of our story. For there was Josiah and there was a tired and dogged hope. We can rebuild in three days, he said, natural leader with twice-dead son and a burnt-up child wife. But even he was tired.

It was hard to say.

*The fire sits on the horizon that day, like some hot and brief second sun, spreading into dry brush, a second house, then a barn. It is the brightness in the back of my skull, the pain that makes your eyes see nothing.*

*The smoke muddies the desert sky into night. People run, buckets of water splashing on their shoes, a pump turned on to wet the road. But no one shouts. All work in silence. No one asks where the Prophet is. What had happened to the girl. The crazy woman is back at home with her daughter, they say.*

*And I wish I could say to Jeremiah: I never knew. Even when you told me, I never knew.*
   *A man with two hearts, a place with two suns.*
   *To tell him: I understand now.*

*But it was always too late. Forgiveness was buried long ago in layers of sediment, hardened by time and sealed too deep to be disturbed by water or blood.*
   *But let it all not be for nothing.*
   Ashes. Ashes.
   We all fall down.

# *Cadence*

The fire smoke wrote into the sky everything that would happen next, which was not what I expected but warn't in any way worse. They did come back, the black cars, the state, the men and women in suits, they come for a week straight. Flagged by murder maybe, or the warning sign of a half-burned mother child, and this time when they come they did not have questions but answers.

My new child was two days old when they come, my brain and body only for him and his gaping gumless mouth. In other words: in no place to leave Josiah. Nor Lizbeth who brought me warm milk to drink as he drank mine, nor even Tressa who quietly showed me a dented tin of udder balm for my raw and wringed parts, nor the bed that kept me and my tiny swaddled safer than I had ever been.

And it seems that finally the Lord see me living here now and done with my sinning ways and He decided to finally change my luck because they did not take Josiah. They had no questions for him, no answers for us.

Not that they left empty-handed. First Crazy Beth and her daughter one day were seen by the Prophet's bewildered son Daniel to come out of their house with one small potato sack of their belongings and get into one of them black cars and the first thing he did, fatherless since the Prophet ghosted off, was come rushing into our house and even upstairs I could hear the ruckus. Josiah, he yelled, Where's Josiah and I could hear Lizbeth hushing him, but not what she said. And he got no quieter as he told it: Beth and her girl, gone, gone into a car and what we going to do?

I heard the back door open with creak and close with bang and then Josiah's strong voice smooth like polished wood telling him to calm down. I heard Daniel knock a chair or something scoot across the floor and my boy stirred at my chest and I lifted his mouth to me so he could suckle back to sleep and I could listen. Daniel was still shouting, saying something about a posse, about the need to stop them, about atonement and blood and even whores, which reminded me of my stepfather, that word that I didn't know anyone used around here. Josiah's voice continued on slow and deep like old furniture always there to sit down in, telling him that there was nothing to be done. Nothing to be done, now.

Daniel slammed the front screen door on his way out and I sat up in my little mother throne and was secretly glad she had got out—spare us her trouble, spare the baby she left with Annalue, and off maybe to somewhere where someone would comb her hair, wash that little girl's face. I wished her better luck out there than I'd had.

The black cars came back two more times that week and the next week too, and it started to feel like they would come forever and people were getting itchy for a Prophet, a sermon, something Josiah was trying to give but without any guarantee from God. At least not yet. We thought they'd do something more, the cars, and when I was not tired, I was worried. But then came the last day, when they must a got what they wanted, or who they wanted, because they didn't come back.

# *Annalue*

It was hard to say when things were over for Redfield. No plague came down like in the Book. There was no locusts, no blood on the doors. Just one fire, one missing Prophet and then the dogs came, feeding on garbage, and it just eventually became clear that things had gone all rotten and even as we thought it, the orchards all turned sour and the sick sweet smell of softening and bruising apples hung about everywhere.

But it's not hard to say when things were over for me. That's easy to say. It was the day that the black government cars came back that final time. I was limping the road with the baby girl, bouncing her and telling her the sky so as to quit her tired fussing and get her to a place of sleep. It had rained and when the cars came toward the house for the fifth time in a week, they were a ruddy brown with mud. They drove slow so as not to splash, so as to watch, and as they watched me I did not turn away. I did not run. A woman and a man watched me through a windshield, their shapes fragmented by the newly born sunshine on the glass so that I could only see half of the man's face, half of the woman's face and as they came to me and I stepped back off the road, the woman signed to the man and they stopped and she rolled her window down and looked up at me and on her mother face I saw worry and saw that she thought I was a child and I was not, had not been for over a year now since that August day but she did not know this so in grace I looked away. She asked me, is that your child? And coughed as she said it. I looked at her lips shiny pink and quietly said Yes, I said Yes and even as I said it I knew it again to be true, especially to her an outsider, and my eyes wetted then without my consent, it all so clear to me—both my child and my love for her and also what was on her face, what we were to her. And she nodded and opened her mouth like to say more but did not and the man said something behind her and she nodded and they drove on towards Josiah's, towards the blackened chimney of the Prophet's house standing sentinel, and I watched after them and hummed in the baby's ear and thought to myself: My, baby My, baby and something that felt like tiny sparrows of relief swooped up and into me as I watched the car slow to a stop down the road and as their lights went off and the door opened I knew it was nigh time to finally give now forever this child and all her perfect limbs a name, time to get some place where no one, no Prophet would take her away from me.

And this was my end and my beginning.

And now I can only remember.

And if I remember it when I am awake, as a place, not a world, but just a piece of earth, then I remember only sand. Pink sand that would stain your hands, your feet, whose ocher mark is still smeared somewhere on the skin of my heart. Sand that turned to stones and then the low mesas that rose up like two hands lightly cupped around our town, keeping us in it. All of us gathered there so close that it was not just our whole world but our whole earth, and the only sign of it not being the whole and only earth was the road. The road ran straight through town like a pious bloodline, red dust for twenty miles to the west and then it turned to pavement and then, only forty miles later, was a town bigger than ours, and beyond that, though I could never have imagined it at the time, was a city bigger than that. And this road didn't stop as it went through our earth, it cut right through and went to the east, toward another desert or wilderness, and if you could follow it you'd eventually get somewhere. And so even as we knew there was more world and that this world was part of there and here, this other world was made farther away by the road which was so long and straight so as to disappear on either end. And you could watch it and you could see a car coming from a long while away but not very often, sometimes days apart, and so the points where the road disappeared in each direction were stretched longer in space by the length of time that one would have to wait for a car to come and these two kind of distances, miles and days, together uninhabitable, meant that the rest of the world was not for us. It was dry, and hellish, and full of sagebrush and rattlesnakes and had no water for our plants or our beasts or our mouths. And we had irrigation and a crick and green fields but still wildness would creep in with sandstorms and sunburns and cold cold nights and yelping coyotes just to let us know it was there, and that we belonged where we were. A lonely people.

If I remember the place when I am asleep, it is not just the whole earth but also the whole world again. The world as it was for years and that is this: My hand over Emma's smaller one, teaching her to milk, squeezing the hot gray teat through her fingers to show her the pressure, the pulling motion, her cry that I am crushing her fingers, the cow stamping away flies, and the milk finally sounding in the pail.

That's all it is.

# *Epilogue:* Emma

The spirit and the body shall be reunited again in perfect form. *My hands are open, my skin apart from itself, but this earthly body matters little and pain matters little though it makes me sharper as I wait. I am home finally again and I wait for the times that are already here, only needing to spill over the edges of their days to start us all anew, and as I wait I listen and I can hear the quiet coming of God, a drop in a bucket counting out the moments, and the hushed footsteps of my Mama bringing broth, and sparrows chirping and ravens grating their throats with sound and the echoing absence of One, and my whole body is twisted upon itself to become an ear. An ear that listens always and—in the night, in the wind, I do hear something. Not an image.*

*More like a voice. A voice like mine, light and high. She sings to me. That same song. And I listen and I think of you my sister, and I speak softly back into the inky glass of night's window. To you, my sister, and I tell you that I know you can't hear me.*

*Though I want you to, I do. And even though now it is only the one thing, the feathery song caressing my ear body, that strange girl's voice, it will someday be another. More prophecy than just that old song vibrating in my ears, in the back of my throat, humming now, out my mouth in a whisper:*
Ashes, ashes,
We all fall down!

# *Acknowledgments*

It's hard to know where to begin. This book started as a story, and then four stories in 2009. So many people have helped it along its journey. Thanks to Joe Wenderoth, Yiyun Li, Lauren Kate Morphew, Rachel Thomas, and Christina Thompson for being early cheerleaders of the project: you are the reason this book exists. Thank you to the Tanner Humanities Center for a fellowship which gave me a year to dedicate to this project, and especially Bob Goldberg for his enthusiasm and dedication. Thank you to the University of Utah Taft-Nicholson Center for time to work on this in one of the most spectacular spots on earth. Thank you to Scott Black, Lance Olsen, and Christine Jones for their thoughtful commentary on a draft of this book, and above all their encouragement. Thanks to my colleagues and students at University of Louisiana at Lafayette, especially Jessica Alexander, Skip Fox, John McNally, Henk Rossouw, Dayana Stetco, Charles Richard, Shelley Ingram, and Hannah Chapple. Thanks to Joe Worthen for his careful read at a crucial stage. Thanks to my editor Kate Gale, for knowing this book twice over. Deep gratitude is owed to the entire Red Hen team, for their meticulous editing, dedication, and enthusiasm for this book. Thanks to Julia Borcherts for her help getting the word out, always. Thank you to Rikki Ducornet for her almost magical insights in the final draft of this work. Deep gratitude is owed to Melanie Rae Thon, who read this book and my work and me with such care and energy and investment: my wish for everyone is to have a teacher like her. My agent, Madison Smartt Bell, was instrumental in helping this book reach its full potential, and believing in it at times even more than I did: thank you.

Thank you to my grandmother, Virginia Lambourne Gibbons, for telling me stories of our own polygamist roots.

My people: as always you are ever supportive, loving, and interested. Thank you, Mom and Dad, and thank you to my brother Noah. Thank you Lynne, Hillary, Dave, Anne, and Lynne Whitesides. Thank you to all my besties—you know who you are.

Thank you to Ninah and Emile, *my* two hearts.

And nothing would be possible without marc, who has lived with these characters for a decade, read multiple drafts, and never let me give up. Thank you.

Lastly, thank you to the survivors and investigators of polygamist communities. This book and its setting are completely a work of my imagination but there are real people whose lives are profoundly impacted by polygamy and systemic abuse. I tried never to forget that when I was writing this book.

## Biographical Note

Sadie Hoagland has a PhD in fiction from the University of Utah and an MA in creative writing/fiction from UC Davis. She is the author of *American Grief in Four Stages*, a short story collection published by West Virginia University Press that earned a Kirkus star. Her work has also appeared in the *Alice Blue Review, The Black Herald, Mikrokosmos Journal, South Dakota Review, Sakura Review, Grist Journal, Oyez Review, Passages North, Five Points, The Fabulist, South Carolina Review*, and elsewhere. She is a former editor of *Quarterly West* and currently teaches fiction at the University of Louisiana at Lafayette.